Cabinet Jack

Ellie Jordan, Ghost Trapper,

Book Sixteen

by

J. L. Bryan

Published January 2022

JLBryanbooks.com

Acknowledgments

Thanks to my wife Christina for her support and my son Johnny for always doing his homework and his chores.

I appreciate everyone who helped with this book, including beta reader Robert Duperre (check out his books!). Thanks also to copy editor Lori Whitwam and proofreaders Thelia Kelly, Andrea van der Westhuizen, and Barb Ferrante. Thanks to my cover artist Claudia from PhatPuppy Art, and her daughter Catie, who does the lettering on the covers.

Thanks also to the book bloggers who have supported the series, including Heather from Bewitched Bookworms; Michelle from Much Loved Books; Shirley from Creative Deeds; Kelly from Reading the Paranormal; Lili from Lili Lost in a Book; Heidi from Rainy Day Ramblings; Kelsey from Kelsey's Cluttered Bookshelf; and Ali from My Guilty Obsession.

Most of all, thanks to the readers who have supported this series! There are more paranormal mysteries to come.

Also by J. L. Bryan:

The Ellie Jordan, Ghost Trapper series

Ellie Jordan, Ghost Trapper
Cold Shadows
The Crawling Darkness
Terminal
House of Whispers
Maze of Souls
Lullaby
The Keeper
The Tower
The Monster Museum
Fire Devil
The Necromancer's Library
The Trailwalker
Midnight Movie
The Lodge
Cabinet Jack
Fallen Wishes

Urban Fantasy/Horror

The Unseen
Inferno Park

Time Travel/Dystopian

Nomad

For Johnny

You can read it when you're older

Chapter One

Stacey and I took Highway 21 out of Savannah, past the busy industrial center of Port Wentworth and into neighboring Effingham County, which was almost completely rural. Or had been, the last time I'd gone that way.

"Wow, when did this area blow up?" I asked Stacey as we passed through the suburban town of Rincon, where new apartment buildings, strip malls, and big-box retailers had sprouted along the central four-lane road. "I remember when this was basically just a gas station and a stoplight. And that was like five or six years ago." I checked my map app. "Twenty more miles to Timbermill."

"The meetup spot sounds fun." Stacey looked at her phone. "Turntables Cafe, in something called the Old Mill District. Are we investigating a haunted coffee shop? Because that would be pretty ideal for those long late-night observations."

"No, we're just meeting the client there. Now *this* looks more familiar." As we left the once tiny but now sprawling town, dense pine woods sprang up on either side of the road. Soon we passed fields of plump reddish-gold wheat, puffy white cotton, and towering rolls of hay.

No interstate ran out this way, so the highway was the fastest route. There wasn't much traffic, either, since we'd left our coastal home city of Savannah for the rural inland.

We eventually turned off onto a single-lane road, marked with ten-foot signs advertising new neighborhoods. One read MILLBURY ESTATES – NEW HOUSES FROM THE LOW $500s. YOU COULD BE HOME BY NOW! A watercolor painting of a house with a flower-filled garden implied the subdivision would be an idyllic realm of soft pastels.

"Thank goodness it's the *low* five hundreds or I'd have to get a second job," I said. "Maybe I'll buy a house the next time I have a half million lying around."

"Maybe your future husband will help," Stacey said, which made me snort laughter. I was glad nobody but Stacey was there to hear the snort, but I still would have preferred fewer witnesses. "That neighborhood does look nice, though."

"For that much, it better be more than nice." I eyed the neighborhood under construction. Three-story houses with picture windows overlooked sprawling lawns. An Olympic-sized community swimming pool sparkled at the end of the street. People who wanted to work in downtown Savannah but still have spacious homes could live here, without having to splurge and spend more than a low half-million or so.

As we reached downtown Timbermill, a cheerful sign with more pastels read *Welcome to Historic Timbermill – A Friendly Traditional and Modern Family Community.*

"That's a mouthful of a slogan," Stacey said.

"Sounds like it was workshopped by a marketing department for maximum buzzwords."

"But, hey, cute town."

Stacey had a point. This was no sprawl of strip malls, but an idyllic old-fashioned town laid out in squares, with aged brick buildings facing a town green with a freshly painted white bandstand. An apple-red train caboose was parked on the green, next to a small historical marker.

Some of the stores looked like they'd been empty for years, maybe decades. Others, though, had been refreshed with vibrant exterior paint and new signs. Every place seemed to have a fun, happy name to match the fun, happy paint colors. The exterior of Aspire Yoga was a cool celestial blue. Slappin' Tails Dog Grooming was a cheerful banana yellow. Barbershop Gelato inhabited a storefront with a candy-cane barber pole, possibly original to the building. Red Caboose Hair and Nails was located, appropriately enough, across the street from the historic caboose.

"Look at that," Stacey said. "'Coming Soon: SweetCore Cider House'? How do they have a cidery? Is this town some kind of hipster colony?"

I parked in front of Turntables Cafe. A graphic of a giant vinyl record dominated the plate-glass window, advertising *Records, Cookies, and Caffeine.* The coffee shop was on the bottom floor of a two-story brick building with shops below and empty-looking windows above.

"The guy we're meeting is David Brown," I said. "I get the sense he wants discretion, so let's get our coffees to go so we can talk outside, away from people."

The coffee shop interior looked like it wanted to be a jazz lounge. Framed black and white posters of musicians from the 1940s and 1950s adorned deep purple walls. The seating was soft and sunken. An electric keyboard and microphone stood in one corner, though nobody was using them.

Vintage vinyl records were displayed for sale on antique, hand-carved shelves built into the wall, conveniently located where customers could browse while awaiting their coffee or tea.

There was no line. A few customers sat at the round, glossy-black tables painted to resemble records. A gang of sweaty, cheerful-looking yoga moms sipped smoothies at the largest table.

A guy in his late thirties or early forties sat alone at the tiny back-corner table, as far from everyone else as possible. He had an extra-large coffee and a tired, unshaven look. He wore a rumpled brown suit, his tie loosened, the top button of his shirt undone.

Stacey nudged me. "You think that's our Dave?" she whispered.

He was already looking up at us, the two new arrivals in the sparsely populated space.

"Welcome to Turntables," said the lone staffer, a balding, pudgy white guy in his mid-sixties. He wore a coffee-colored apron—probably a smart idea—and stood under a chalkboard where the menu had been written in assorted colors. "What can I brew for you?"

"Um, good question." Stacey approached the counter and read the selection. "I'll have the Muddy Waters Mocha. Ellie, what do you want?"

"Just plain black coffee." I texted *Are you here?* to our prospective client.

The guy's phone chimed, and he tapped something back.

Yes, I'm the one not wearing yoga pants appeared on my phone.

"One Muddy Waters, one Nancy Sinatra," the retirement-age barista said, with a joviality that implied he'd probably made up the names himself. "Can I interest you ladies in a fresh-baked cookie? The Peanut Buddy Hollies are my personal favorite. Or a Marvin Gaye Muffin? I heard it through the grapevine that they're loaded with top-shelf raisins."

While Stacey turned down the sales pitch, I gave her my empty portable coffee cup and walked over to meet our possible new client.

"Hi, Mr. Brown," I said, approaching his tiny black record-shaped table while he rose to greet me.

"Dave," he said. "You're Ellie? The lead investigator?"

"Yes, sir. And over there, getting our coffee, is my tech manager Stacey."

"You're both...a bit younger than I expected."

"That can happen. I can assure you I have many years of experience, unfortunately."

"Oh, yeah, I didn't mean anything by it. Sorry, I'm pretty drained lately. Want to have a seat? Or maybe step outside?" He glanced at the table of suburban yogis like he didn't want them overhearing us.

"That park across the street looks nice," I said.

"It's great." He looked relieved as he got to his feet.

We met up with Stacey at the exit door. I grabbed my coffee, introduced them, then noticed she carried cookies in a white paper bag.

"I got some Johnny Cashews," Stacey said, looking guilty.

"Lucky pick. Those are actually good," Dave said. "Avoid the muffins."

We crossed the street to the park, then climbed the steps to the deserted bandstand and sat on the built-in benches for a little shade. The hot, humid June day made us feel like crabs getting boiled.

"You say you have a lot of experience." Dave sat across from us. "What's your background?"

"I was trained by Calvin Eckhart, a former Savannah homicide detective. He was a private investigator by the time I worked with him. Savannah has a lot of ghosts, and there was nobody to deal with them, so he became that person. Then he trained Stacey and me to be that person. Er, those people."

"And where is Mr. Eckhart now?"

"In Florida, semi-retired. But he's available to consult and assist if needed. And we have access to other specialists. It really depends on the case."

He nodded along. "That's fascinating. And how many times have you succeeded?"

"Success is...kind of a spectrum, sometimes," I said.

"You mean you can't always resolve the problem?"

"Our track record is as good as you'll find in the local area," I said. "Due to our lack of any local competition."

Dave laughed a little, but it was forced. "This is

great."

As it turned out, Dave liked to ask questions, far more than the average soul. He asked about our techniques and past investigations and listened attentively. After a while, though, I felt like he was using his questions to maintain distance, to keep us away from him and his problems. We needed him to stop asking and start talking if we were going to make any progress.

The town around us wasn't exactly bustling, but it was active. Someone, maybe the local chamber of commerce, had been making an effort to revitalize and rejuvenate the little town, attracting new businesses, builders, and homebuyers, and it seemed to be working.

"Are you from Timbermill originally?" I asked Dave, by way of turning the conversation toward our particular case.

"Not remotely," Dave said. "We moved here from Kansas City. Nicole—my wife—thinks there are opportunities in the area."

"What kind of opportunities?"

"She—I mean, *we*—are realtors. Well, I will be once I pass the exam. I'm not supposed to use these until I do." He drew a business card from his wallet, showing a smiling, better-kept version of himself, with a recent haircut and shave, wearing a blue blazer and tie. Smiling next to him was a woman with short, professional dark hair and pale blue eyes, wearing a matching blue blazer. *Brown Realty of Savannah*. "She worked with her family for years in Kansas City. Pagonis Realty. So she's the one who knows what she's doing, obviously." He put the card away instead of giving it to me.

"Are you new to real estate?" I asked.

"Just what the world needed, right? More people selling each other houses."

"What did you do before?"

He sighed and looked over at the compact, red-brick city hall by the weedy, overgrown railroad tracks that bisected the town. "I was a newspaper reporter. My last position was city features editor for the *Kansas City Citizen*, founded in 1891, shut down for good last fall. Bankrupt."

"Oh, I'm sorry to hear that," I said.

Dave shook his head. "I know it's the twenty-first century and nobody reads the paper anymore, but it was still kind of a shock. I grew up reading the *Citizen*, starting with the comics over my breakfast cereal as a kid. It was the lifeblood of information for the city, always had been. A major institution. It seemed unsinkable, like the *Titanic*. Their downtown building is an historic landmark. It was once the tallest building in the city. I heard they're redeveloping it into condos now."

"Did that lead to y'all moving here?" I asked.

"Sure. Well, Nicole had the idea already, but it was just something she was toying with. We vacationed in Savannah once, back when Lonnie and Penny were still little, and the younger two weren't even a thought yet."

"You have four kids?" I slid out my pocket notebook.

"Yep. Nicole kept reading books on Savannah, saying it was such a beautiful place and it was growing, would grow more as people switch to working remotely and can live in whatever nice-looking place they might want. Savannah has the downtown squares, the parks and gardens, the beach, the warm climate, all of it. But we were rooted pretty hard in Kansas City, and adding more kids didn't make it easier to experiment with our lives. Then the paper shut down." He winced. "We should have seen it coming, but we trusted all the assurances from above. Newspaper people ought to know better than to trust the word of the people in charge, but some of us did."

"And you're having problems in your new home?"

"Right." He glanced at some teenage boys skateboarding down an alley. "It's a nice little town, though, isn't it? Nicole was right about it rebounding."

"So, are you staying in an apartment or a house?" I asked, yet again trying to understand why he'd called us.

"Both, in a way," he said. "We bought an old boardinghouse across town. A house flipper started the process of restoring it—electrical, plumbing—back in 2007, but they lost it in the 2008 crash. It's in no worse shape than the house we bought in Kansas City when we got married. We fixed up that old wreck and even got it registered as an historic home. Selling it off gave us the new start we needed down here, for our new house and Nicole's new real estate business. I mean, *our* new business. Newspapers aren't exactly staffing up these days, no matter where you live, so I have to leave writing behind and move on to things that will actually pay the bills."

"Have you experienced anything unusual while restoring the house?" I asked the question in a casual tone, as if it weren't the whole reason we were here.

"I...have, yes." Dave sighed and slumped on the bandstand bench, like admitting that much was a kind of defeat for him. "I started coming down to work on it months ago. Long weekends, working alone, getting it ready. It's not like I had a job to keep me busy anymore. Once the sale of the old house closed, Nicole and the kids were left in the lurch for a couple of months, staying with grandparents and aunts and uncles while finishing out the school year. Good thing Nicole has a such a big family. But the kids hated that, and they aren't too thrilled about the new place, either. Hating things is their favorite hobby now."

"Are any of them having strange experiences?"

"It's hard to know what's normal with four kids who've been uprooted and moved," he said. "I can't even say this was the right move. But it was a plan, Nicole's plan, and it was the only one on the shelf."

"I'm sure it's difficult. But anything you might call paranormal or supernatural, specifically?"

"Right. I realize I'm being a difficult interview subject. I've faced those before. Sorry." He took a deep breath. "There's something in the house. I'm starting to believe that. Before, when it was just me, I'd try to convince myself it was all in my mind. That's easy to believe when you're alone. But then the kids…" He shook his head. "It's partly my fault. I should have painted over it sooner. I never really paid much attention to it, up there in the attic, but the little ones saw it and took it seriously."

"What did they see?" I asked.

"I can show you." He flipped through his phone's image gallery, then showed us the screen. "This graffiti was up in the attic bedroom."

Stacey and I leaned forward. The snapshot on his phone showed a room lined with wooden cabinets and shelves.

A sloppy rendering of a door, basically just an uneven rectangle with a big scribbled ball for a doorknob, had been spray-painted on the wall.

From behind the painted door leaned out a stick figure with a big smile and angry-slash eyebrows, holding a simple triangle of a blade in its three-fingered hand.

Below that, in the same paint, were the words *Close your doors and cabinets tight or Jack will come out and get you tonight.*

Chapter Two

"I wish I hadn't bought this," Dave said. For a moment I thought he meant the house into which he'd moved his family, but then he sloshed around the coffee in his to-go cup. "It'll just kick up my anxiety."

"How old are your kids?" I asked.

"Andromeda—Andra—is the youngest. Eight. Jason's ten. Those are the two who have the biggest issues with the new house. Penny's thirteen, Lonnie's fifteen. They were born a week apart. Well, a week and two years."

"Have the older ones reported any problems?"

"Not really. Lonnie's made some local friends already, and he's always out of the house, playing soccer and skateboarding with those boys. It's hard to tell what's going on with Penny lately because she doesn't talk to us much anymore. She used to be more outgoing, and always helped with watching the younger kids, but now she treats it like another chore she hates. The younger kids are the ones having the most difficulty. Andra, the youngest, was originally excited about the move, before we got here."

"What's happening with the younger kids?"

"Jason and Andra are obsessed with this idea that they have to run around at bedtime, every night, making sure every cabinet and door in the house is closed. I thought it was a game the first time, but they're serious about it. The boardinghouse had a lot of built-in cabinets, too…it's really hard to overstate how many little doors are in that house…so it's exhausting and easy to lose your temper about it sometimes. They say Jack—from the graffiti—will come out if anything's left open."

"Have they ever reported seeing Jack themselves?" I asked. "Aside from the graffiti?"

"Jason has some drawings. Andra says Sunny and Rainy warn her before Jack comes, and then she hides or comes running to our bedroom. But if everything's closed up, she sleeps fine and doesn't come to our room in the middle of the night, so we've been sort of going along with it."

"Who are Sunny and Rainy?"

"Andra's current imaginary friends."

"Did she have them before moving here?"

"Sure. There was Banana Sam and Ruffles the Flying Dog. Sunny and Rainy kind of replaced them after the move. I think they're supposed to reflect Andra's moods."

"What do Sunny and Rainy look like?" I was already concerned about these imaginary friends. I'd encountered ghosts before, even ghostly children, who were trying to lure living children into danger under the guise of friendship.

"My impression is that the imaginary friends are children," Dave said. "It's hard to say, though. Was Banana Sam a kid or a talking banana? Andra managed to avoid making that clear for two entire years before we moved here and she dropped him. You might say she split from Banana Sam when we left Kansas City."

"Does Jason also see the imaginary children?"

"He hasn't said anything about them, but his drawings have grown a little unsettling. He's a talented artist, always has been. Very quiet, a loner, couldn't be more different from his older brother. Some of his latest drawings show a man coming out from behind a door, like the original graffiti, but Jason's are more detailed than the stick figure. More realistic." Dave hesitated, then added, "Scarier."

"Do you have pictures of his drawings?" I asked.

He shook his head. "I can show you if you end up coming to the house."

"What have you personally experienced? You mentioned the period when you worked there alone for a few months."

"Right. Sometimes, usually at night, I felt like someone was in the house with me. More than once, I thought I saw someone walk past an open door. Or the cabinets would be open at random."

"The kitchen cabinets?"

"Almost every room has multiple cabinets with little hand-carved doors. Amazing custom work, one of the main things Nicole liked about the house, in addition to the work already done by the house-flippers. Before we moved, she'd spend an hour at a time looking through the pictures of the house on the real estate listing. And it is impressive. There's truly a place for everything. But combine that with two kids who won't go to sleep until all the cabinets are closed…" He shook his head. "Nicole wants to put them in therapy. We're looking into it."

"But you think what they're experiencing is real."

"I think it could be. And I'm usually the skeptical reporter type. But if there's anyone in denial about the strangeness of that house, well, it's not me." He tossed his to-go cup into a public trashcan. "So, what do you think?"

"Until we look for ourselves, I don't know much. We can do a preliminary investigation of your home, and if you want us to continue from there, we'll set up an observation with our equipment." I'd already explained this in some detail earlier, when he'd been peppering us with questions. "It's just a matter of making an appointment."

"What about the kids?" he asked.

"That's up to you. It can be convenient to have the whole family gone for a night of observation, but we can also work around them."

"We don't have any family to stay with nearby. And we'd have to rent multiple hotel rooms. They don't look kindly at six people in a standard two-bed room."

"If the entities are interacting with your family members, then staying home might enable Stacey and me to document and study that. But you'll have to explain to your kids why we're there."

"And your wife," Stacey said.

Dave nodded at her, smiling wearily. "Getting Nicole to go along with it could be the tricky part. Well, I appreciate yout coming out to speak with me.

Maybe we'll be in touch."

"Feel free to text or email me if you have any questions," I said.

"Or call," Stacey added, and I shrugged and nodded.

"Thanks. I'll do that." Dave started to walk away across the yellow grass of the park, which was wilting under the relentless summer sun. He stopped and turned back to us. "What causes things like this to happen, anyway?"

"Usually something tragic," I said. "What we usually find at the root of a haunting is a deep, unhealed emotional wound. Or several of them."

He nodded slowly. "Makes sense." He walked off and climbed into a blue Ford Explorer, in the XLT size one would need for a family of six, though he was alone at the moment.

"Do you think he'll hire us?" Stacey asked as we returned to the van.

"He clearly believes there's a problem."

"Sounds like there's major reluctant-spouse issues, though."

"Either way, let's take the rest of the day off." I backed out of our parking space and pointed the van homeward. "We deserve it."

"Uh-huh. I'm sure that has nothing to do with your date with Michael tonight."

"We're just going to the beach for a sunset swim. It's not really a date. What do you think I should wear?"

"You could get crazy and wear a swimsuit," Stacey suggested.

"That's a little too crazy. I'm not sure I own one."

"You brought one to Satilla Island. Not that we ever got to go swimming."

"That was before I knew about the sharks. And I thought that if we did swim, it would be alone in a secluded cove somewhere on the island, or if we were truly lucky, the pool of a hotel that hadn't yet opened to the public. And that experience made me realize something."

"Which is?"

"My swimsuit is kinda ugly and worn out."

"Are you...suggesting we go shopping?" Stacey asked. "Are we about to stage a swimsuit shopping montage?"

"No—"

"I'll take video while you pop in and out of the dressing room in different swimsuits. Then later I'll splice it together over some classic 80s music so you can have your own montage."

"That's not how this is going to happen."

"One time in school I made a montage of classic montages for an editing project. A meta-montage."

"I'll just find something on the discount rack at Coat Barn."

"I thought this was for a date. Sounds like you're shopping for a trip to Waffle House."

"What do you mean? Coat Barn has some great values. Lots of remainders from other clothing stores that went out of business."

"And you can see why they went out of business based on what they sold," Stacey said. "Please stop trying to suck all possible joy from this occasion. We're obviously going to Half Moon Outfitters, and we'll get you a bikini that will drop Michael's jaw all the way down to those pectorals that you'll be looking at anyway. Remember, his eyes are up here, Ellie."

"No bikinis," I said. "I have too many scars. I'm thinking more of a head-to-toe wetsuit."

"Very funny. You have to show off those kickboxing legs, at least."

"I guess running from evil dead monsters all the time keeps them in okay shape." I self-consciously touched my leg, clad in my black Coat Barn pantsuit since we'd just been meeting a potential client. Coat Barn really does have great values. Maybe not great style, though. "I didn't have a huge budget in mind."

"A good store isn't about high prices, it's about having a carefully curated selection," Stacey said. "Some of which might, you know, happen to be pricey. But you'll be fine, I promise."

We drove into downtown Savannah and managed to park on East Broughton Street, in a nifty, artsy little area, not far from the boarded-up Corinthian Theater where I'd once confronted the ghost of a magician, or from the Lathrop Grand Hotel, where we'd grappled with a powerful haunting full of suffering Civil War soldiers and a nineteenth-century society of Spiritualists, mediums, and fortune-tellers. The area had also been the haunt of movie star Adaire Fontaine in her early career on Savannah's small local theater scene before she'd moved on to New York and California.

Now the antiquated brick buildings were crowded with colorful little bistros, day spas, and a kale-centric health food place, the kind of district downtown Timbermill aspired to be. Half Moon fit right in, a shop with supplies for camping, hiking, and kayaking.

I didn't need anything for those activities, but they had some swimwear and other beachgoing supplies.

"I like this one, but it could be hard to swim in." I pointed to a rainbow-shaped dress-style garment hanging on a rack.

"Yeah, that's what they call a changing poncho," Stacey said. "You're supposed to change clothes in it, not swim in it."

"Too bad." I ignored the skimpy bikinis and focused on the one-pieces on display. "Hmm."

"Don't see anything you like?" Stacey asked.

I looked around the store and started toward one display. "That looks perfect."

"That's…not a swimsuit, either, Ellie."

"Obviously." I picked up a long, curved tool and read the description on the package. "The Frogmore shrimp cleaner. Peels, deveins, and butterflies shrimp all at once."

"That's not going to fit any better than a bikini."

"It's a present for Michael. If I give him this, he won't even care what I'm wearing."

"Should we try another store?"

"Maybe this tankini thing…" I checked out a top that looked promising, but the back was nothing but thin straps. "That'll show the devil dog bite on my upper back."

"I'm thinking a rashguard will work for you." Stacey pulled a short-sleeved, lilac-colored swimming shirt off the rack, one that would conceal everything but my arms and neck. "At least you won't get sunburn."

"You're not going to push me toward a regular swimsuit?"

"Wear what makes you comfortable. Like you said, he'll be staring at his shrimp tool all night, anyway."

"Let's hope not. Does that swimming shirt come in black?"

"So you can look like a depressed goth at the beach?" Stacey asked. "Should we find you a black-lace parasol, too?"

"Ideally, yes."

Once I was done shopping, Stacey spent some time looking over the kayaking gear, which was possibly half to three-quarters of her motivation for bringing me to that shop in the first place. We finally left after she picked out a new paddle.

"Want to eat at Namaste?" I nodded up the street. "I could go for a tikka masala, or something spicy."

"So would you say you're pretty serious?"

"No, I'm flexible. Let's go look at the menu, though." I stashed my recent purchases inside the van.

"I meant about Michael."

"He's not really into Indian food."

"It's technically Nepalese fusion."

"Yeah, I can read the sign, Stacey." I started up the sidewalk.

"How long have you two been together?"

"Since the boggart case in his apartment building. So what?"

"Just, you know. Do you see it getting more serious?"

"The last thing I need is more serious issues in my life. Or wait. Is this really about you and Jacob? Are y'all getting engaged or something?"

"What?" Stacey nearly jumped out of her shoes. "Jacob and I are a totally different thing."

"How so?"

"We're super-casual." She pulled open the glass front door to Namaste.

We stepped into the restaurant, a small nook of a place lit by lanterns suspended from the high ceiling, their glow warmly reflected by the polished tables. The rich, sharp aromas full of garlic and cumin made my mouth water.

"I might have the dal makhani," I told Stacey once we had our table.

"What's that?" She skimmed her menu.

"Black lentils and beans."

"What were we talking about before?" she asked.

"That old boardinghouse in Timbermill," I said, fully aware I was changing the subject away from my personal life. "I don't know much about that town. I don't think it was really a suburb until recently. Just an isolated country place caught up in the new sprawl. But it'll have ten Starbucks before you know it."

"I mean about you and Michael and whether you're —"

"Did you tell Wyatt that you and Jacob are super-casual?" I asked, cutting off her attempted conversational U-turn with an abrupt lane change. Stacey had hit it off particularly well with Wyatt Lanigan, creator of the popular social media app LookyLoon, who traveled on a luxurious private airship among his homes and offices around the world. He'd also recently broken up with his fiancée rather dramatically.

Stacey blushed. "Wyatt was just a client."

"So, you've deleted him from your Look Closer list?"

"Well, no. I mean, the way he buys houses, he's bound to end up with another haunted one sooner or later. Could we talk about something else?"

"Yes. Food." I tapped the menu, and Stacey quickly looked at hers.

"Should we get some momo?" she asked. "I'm in a definite dumpling mood."

"Sounds good to me." I smiled at our approaching server and ordered the savory, pan-fried appetizers. My stomach growled in anticipation.

Chapter Three

At home, I spent some of the afternoon straightening up my little studio apartment, which didn't take long since I don't own a lot of stuff in the first place. Later, I felt restless and blew off some steam at a kickboxing class. My black cat, Bandit, snored on my bed all day, unaware of my coming and going, or indifferent to it. Probably both.

Finally, I dressed in the modest swimwear, which covered the scars on my back and stomach; I was like an alley cat who'd been in too many fights, but my attackers had been supernatural.

I had a few scars on my calves and ankles, too, but those didn't bother me so much. Scars at the extremities seemed less personal than those around the core. Those on the inside, of course, were the easiest to hide.

I drew back my hair and spent too much time on my makeup, considering the whole plan was to go swimming around sunset. The outdoor heat was broiling, the steamy humidity oppressive. The trees filling Savannah's parks and squares no doubt enjoyed the sunlight and moisture, but I wasn't a tree, so I looked forward to a cool dip in the ocean.

Michael arrived right on time, as usual, like he'd calculated the drive to my apartment building down to the minute. That was the part of his mind that enjoyed restoring old clockwork. I wondered if he had any Swiss in him.

"You look great," he said when I opened the door. He looked great himself, tall and broad-shouldered, brown hair cropped close for the summer, green eyes drinking me in. "Ready to leave all this behind and run off with me?"

"How could I ever leave all this?" I closed the door on my small apartment and antisocial cat. Then I handed him the present I'd wrapped in paper featuring Rudolph, Yukon Cornelius, and Hermey the dentist elf. "Sorry, I didn't have any non-Christmas wrapping paper."

"Oh! Is it my…is this our…has it been—"

"It's just something that made me think of you."

"Right. Okay." He unwrapped it and read the label. His jaw dropped. "Peels, deveins, and butterflies shrimp all at once. This is, very possibly, the greatest present I've ever received."

"That's what I expected you to say."

He rewarded me with an extra kiss.

"How are you?" I asked. "Put out any fires lately?"

"Not in weeks. Pulled out a few car-crash victims, though."

"That's rough. Anything you want to talk about?" We walked out to his truck, a red 1949 pickup that looked like a relic from a museum. It worked fine, though, painstakingly revived by Michael, who had a talent for bringing old and dead things back to life. Not in a necromancer-type way, though.

"We did pick up a guy in a painfully revealing kilt passed out behind Molly MacPherson's. He wasn't actually Scottish. Had a Chicago accent." He opened the truck door for me.

"Alcohol poisoning?" I asked.

He closed the door and walked around to the driver's side. "Bee allergy. A bee had flown up his kilt."

"I think I see where this is going."

"Too bad the bee didn't. The moral of the story is respect local wildlife."

"It sounds like the wildlife is at fault here."

"Sure, take the annoying kilt guy's side." Michael drove us away from my decrepit brick apartment building.

Soon we crossed over the marshy, grass-lined Wilmington River onto the Islands Expressway, a patchwork of bridges, causeways, and small islands leading to the lovely, if touristy, oceanfront on Tybee Island.

The salty marsh smell used to soothe me, evoking happy childhood beach memories, but now I thought of our recent case on isolated Satilla Island, the nightmarish ghosts stalking its crumbling Gilded Age estate.

Soft, scratchy blues, a digitized version of T-Bone Walker playing "Stormy Monday," played over the speakers. The music was probably as old as the truck itself.

"Are you sure you're not like a hundred-year-old

man in disguise?" I asked.

"What do you mean?"

"This truck. The clocks, the mechanical restoration. The blues. You like all kinds of old things."

"Not all kinds. Just things that have a little something special that ought to be preserved. That extra touch of ingenuity."

"So, you're picky?"

"Of course. Believe it or not, a lot of stuff in the old junk shops is just old junk."

"I think they prefer 'antique stores.'"

"That's a stretch for a lot of those places. So you have to recognize something of value when you see it. Even if you don't fully understand it." His gaze seemed to linger on me an extra moment before he looked back at the road.

"Is it me you don't understand?" I asked. "Just because I hang out in the gray zone between life and death and talk to evil spirits? What's weird about that?"

"I work in that zone, too," he said. "Fire, EMS, street cops, we see death every day. You're not so far from me."

"Yeah, but you face death from this side, like a normal person. I'm like way over there..." I pointed to the darkening horizon ahead, full of marshes on the way to the ocean. "The old ferryman said it could damage my soul over time. I've had other signs of that, too."

"Do you ever think about changing to a different line of work?"

"What would I do? Become a regular private investigator, taking pictures of cheating spouses for divorce lawyers?" I imagined this for a moment too long. "Gross. I'd rather deal with the affairs of the dead than the living."

"You could do all kinds of other things."

"But then who would do my work? There's not exactly a line of people behind me waiting to charge into that breach."

"That doesn't mean it has to be your job."

"It kind of does. But we don't have to talk about it now. What would you do, if you weren't a firefighter?"

He shrugged. "Coast Guard, maybe?"

"Interesting choice. Would you be fighting smugglers and pirates?"

"Yeah, I'd be rounding up all the Jimmy Buffet song characters."

"It's past time somebody dealt with them." I sighed, hoping we could keep the mood light for the rest of the evening.

The lights of Tybee Island were already on, little storefronts along the main road trying to lure tourists with promises of fried shrimp, ice cream, and island-themed trinkets.

Michael avoided the pricey, and probably full, public parking. Instead, he drove up a narrow residential back street and parked on a sandy, grassy patch in front of a small brick bungalow flanked by palm trees. He assured me he knew the house's owner. It looked like nobody was home. There are benefits to being a local.

We walked past the turquoise Chapel by the Sea, then across the busy main street of the island, and finally down a quiet side street of large rental cottages toward the ocean.

A boardwalk took us out to a sparsely populated

stretch of beach, considering it was June. This was the Mid Beach area, quiet compared to the South Beach area in the distance, where beachside bars and hotels pulsed with music and colorful lights. In the opposite direction lay North Beach, marked by Tybee's iconic black and white lighthouse, where the population tended more toward retirees and year-round residents and their sedate cafes.

Mid Beach, though, was a long stretch with no amenities to draw people from either end of the island, convenient only to the nearby cottages. Being the least crowded made it just the place for a quiet evening swim with your significant other.

"This looks nice," I said, my words not really encompassing the serene vastness of the ocean, the fresh primordial taste of the ocean air, or the rich royal purple of the sky ahead, lit by the last fiery red glow of the sun sinking behind us.

"Yeah, it's cool," Michael agreed, his words also falling short of expressing the visual majesty. "There's a good spot over there."

He quickly set up a beach tent, open toward the ocean but blocking the sandy wind from all other directions. We placed our towels and his cooler inside.

"How about a long walk on the beach?" he suggested.

"Like in some personal ad?" I looked up and down and picked out several couples spaced out along the shoreline, walking hand in hand in the surf while the sun set, each having their private romantic moments.

"Or a commercial for arthritis medicine," Michael said.

"I'd rather swim first, before it gets too dark. There

aren't any lifeguards around here."

"I'm certified to save your life a dozen different ways."

"Well, I'm not. Best I can do is remove your ghost if you hang around haunting your apartment afterward."

"What if I haunted your apartment instead?" he asked.

"You wouldn't. You'd haunt your truck."

"Good idea. Haunt something mobile—car, boat, airplane. Then you're not stuck in one place forever."

"Yeah, you wouldn't want that." I waded out into the water. It was like a warm, salty bath, instantly soothing little aches and pains I'd barely noticed I'd been carrying, though it didn't do much to cool me off. Neither did the sight of Michael in his swimming trunks, leaving bare the muscles of his chest and stomach for my visual enjoyment. *His eyes are up here*, my memory of Stacey reminded me.

We swam for a while, then floated for a while, the night arriving from the ocean like a vast black ship coming in to port.

"She's already packing up," Michael said, after a long moment of quiet. He didn't have to tell me he meant his sister Melissa, bound for college in North Carolina. "Classes start in the middle of August. That seems early, doesn't it? I kind of imagined her moving after Labor Day for some reason."

"She'll be fine," I said.

"She's definitely ready for a lifestyle change. An upgrade."

"You've been great with her." Michael had been her primary caregiver for several years, since their mother had died. Their father had left long before that. "Does it feel like your kid's all grown up? Empty nest syndrome? Do you need to start a new hobby or join a bridge club?"

He laughed. "No. It's more like I can finally relax for the first time since…well, anyway. It's not like I was on the high road to responsibility when all of that happened."

"And now you don't have to be responsible for anyone?" I asked.

"Melissa's more responsible than me. And tough. She's ready. And she'll stay in touch, at least when she needs somebody to help her move. Which I'll be doing for the first time in just a few weeks."

"You should be proud of yourself."

"Oh, I know. Melissa gave me a 'World's Greatest Dad' mug a couple years ago. But it had Darth Vader on it, so there were mixed signals."

"I'm sure she appreciates you."

"That's a stretch." He sighed. "I was always planning to get out of town when she moved away. Go live somewhere new, leave all the bad memories behind. Out west, maybe."

"I remember you saying that," I said quietly, keeping my eyes closed even though it was getting very dark. "Not recently, though."

"It always seemed so far away until now. The future that would never really arrive. I always wanted to get out of that apartment because I resented it, I guess. It was the place we had to move after we lost the house to Mom's medical bills. Me and my sister, sharing the attic of an old, rundown house divided into little apartments."

"And haunted by a boggart, until I came along."

"Right. It's been nice because I can trade maintenance and repair work for part of our rent."

"But you want to leave it?"

"That's what I thought. What I've thought since the day we moved in. But...now that weird attic apartment is the place where we landed, and where we righted ourselves. There are some good memories there."

He went quiet, and I opened my eyes to see him gazing at me. The sun was gone, but there was a bright moon and a hundred thousand or so stars instead.

"Like your spaghetti," I said. "And your cuckoo clock repair table."

"It's not just clocks. I like all mechanical automatons. The older the better."

"Would you say you're cuckoo for them?"

"Oh, yeah. Like they were chocolate cereal."

"Let's go for that walk," I said. "We can go down to the pier."

"That's a very touristy choice."

"Maybe it'll feel like we're on vacation." I walked toward the shore, feeling the soft, muddy sand squish pleasantly between my toes.

"Want to eat first? I brought lunch." He caught up with me quickly.

"Lunch at nine p.m.?"

"Sorry, I meant breakfast. I'm trying to adapt to your nocturnal lifestyle."

"What did you bring?"

"Leftovers from my actual lunch." He reached the tent and opened the cooler. "Barbecued chicken, potato salad, baked beans."

"Oh, good, I was worried it would be something

messy."

"We can always rinse off in the ocean."

"Looks like we'll have to, because I'm not seeing a very adequate napkin supply here," I said.

"What? I brought one for each of us."

The barbecued chicken and beans were cold, of course, which is not normally how I'd eat either dish, but it wasn't bad on a hot night. The chicken had a thick, sweet, somewhat congealed sauce. I was hungry from the swim, though, so it was all perfect to me.

"Did you cook this?" I asked. "It's so good."

"Of course. Melissa's never really gotten the hang of cooking. Or cleaning. Or laundry."

"Maybe dorm life will teach her about that."

"Unless her roommate's an even bigger slob. Hey, not my problem anymore." Michael walked with me to the retreating edge of the water. The tide had been high, but was now on its way out, exposing wet, hard-packed sand and sharp shells below.

I rinsed the sugary goop of cold barbecue sauce and baked-bean juice from my fingers, scrubbing salty water into the webbing between them.

Michael broke down the tent and set it next to my mesh beach bag on top of his cooler, which had built-in wheels and a telescoping handle. It didn't roll well through the fluffy loose sand up near the dunes and the cottages, so we walked on the hard-packed wet sand by the water instead, looking out at the stars, like a loving elderly couple in an arthritis drug commercial.

The cottages gave way to rowdy bars around the boulevard-sized fishing pier that extended out into the ocean. The pier's little bait shop and hamburger stand were closed for the night, but it was still a nice spot to walk out among the night sky and the dark ocean, as so many tourists were currently doing.

We ambled up the pier. During the day there would have been gray-haired fishermen, their long lines drooping into the water, and sunburned kids running everywhere. At these later hours, it was more like young-adult revelers wandering away from the bars for a place to smooch.

"It's strange," Michael said as we reached the end of the pier, where the ocean lapped softly against the barnacle-covered supports below. "It seemed like it would take forever for Melissa to go off and become independent. But looking back, it kind of went by in an eyeblink."

"Yeah." I remembered a beach visit here with my parents when I was a kid, before I grew sullen and rebellious, unwilling to spend any more time with them than necessary, before they died in that fire and our time together ended much sooner than I'd expected. "I bet," I said aloud, keeping my memories to myself.

"What do you think, when you think about the future?" he asked.

"Well, I don't think the flying cars will ever happen, but that's probably for the best. People who don't use their left and right turn signals probably wouldn't use their up and down ones, either."

"Come on, Ellie. Your future. Five years from now? Ten?"

I shivered, looking out at the horizon, too dark and distant to see. Somewhere the black sky merged with the black water, the galaxies of stars with their own reflections. "I'm not even sure about next week, Michael. All I know is I have to do what I do, and it's dangerous. So I can't have anybody depending on me." This was about as close as I wanted to skate to any talk of marriage or children that night. I've seen horrific things rise from the grave, but they didn't scare me as much as the idea of being responsible for small, clueless, recently born people. "And you're probably glad to be free of that for now, too."

"I am," Michael said, turning to look at the invisible horizon along with me. "For now."

The tide continued to draw back, and eventually we returned home.

Chapter Four

Dave the Potential Client called a few days later.

I was sitting at the long, tool-scratched table in the workshop, catching up on basic administrative work. I have a desk with a couple of cubicle walls for that, but for some reason seem to prefer the workshop table. There were bills and taxes to pay, and other expenses like our meager paychecks, which I'd been writing since our boss Calvin had focused on his family in Florida. He still kept an apartment upstairs, above the office, for his increasingly rare returns to town, but I was managing things on my own lately.

Stacey was in the equipment closet with a tablet, adding a few pieces of new gear to the inventory record. We'd picked up a couple of new cameras and motion detectors for our recent case on Satilla Island, where a vast amount was needed to monitor the sprawling Gilded Age estate, but most of that had been leased for the investigation. We were back down to shoestrings again, but we were used to it.

"How are things at your house, Dave?" I asked when he called. "Any more disturbances?"

"I think Nicole may have seen something," he replied, his voice low like he was worried about being overheard. "I'm not sure what, but she's decided she's willing to meet with you after all. And that was not on track to happen three days ago."

"Does she want to meet us at the coffee shop, too?"

"You may as well come to the house. We're trying not to upset the kids with this. But we do want them to know something's being done. The younger ones are out of their minds over this stuff. I think it's affecting everyone to some degree."

"We could stop by tomorrow," I said.

"I'm sorry, would you hold on a moment?" The phone went silent, like he'd put us on mute. Maybe he was discussing it with his wife. "All right," he said when he came back. "Would the afternoon work for you? Lonnie is usually out with his soccer gang by then, so that's one less kid running around. We'll have Penny watch the younger ones."

"Sounds good." I understood their desire to try to protect their kids against hearing about the haunting and the possible paranormal investigation, but the kids are usually the first to sense a supernatural problem. And Dave had already told us his youngest kids were experiencing the greatest problems. I didn't argue about it, though; if they hired us, we'd end up hearing the kids' version of things sooner or later.

The next day, Stacey and I drove back to Timbermill, but this time we continued past the newly built suburbs and the refurbished downtown, crossing the overgrown railroad tracks. A sign by the tracks read "Future Home of the Timbermill Bike and Pedestrian Greenway!" and featured a watercolor painting of white paths flanked by flower gardens.

Down the tracks, a chain-link gate hung with warning signs blocked off a small wooden trestle bridge that crossed over the creek, where the water looked sluggish and black, not shiny and baby blue like in the greenway painting.

"They'll have to fix that bridge, or replace it," Stacey said. "It looks ready to collapse."

The ruins of the old mill, three stories of cracked stone walls and hollow window holes, occupied an intersection of the railroad tracks and the wide creek. My phone's map software indicated that the creek eventually joined the Ogeechee River, which ultimately reached the Atlantic just south of Savannah. Perhaps timber had once been floated here to be cut at the mill.

Beside the mill stood a two-story brick building, also long abandoned. The front door area and a few of the lower windows were sealed with graffiti-tagged rotten plywood, but other windows were open portals to the darkness within. The faded letters peeling off the front read *Wandering Creek Wood Products*. Smaller words elaborated the products that had once been available. *Housewares - Furniture - Cabinets - Coffins - Etc. Finest Quality!* A similar but smaller building had been the *Timbermill Tool Company.*

"Look at that graffiti." I stopped the van to take a snapshot of a spraypainted stick figure climbing out of a squarish door, armed with a pointy blade. "It's like what Dave found in his attic."

Stacey leaned over me to read the words aloud.

"'Close your doors up tight or Jack will come for you tonight.' Well, that's a fine message for welcoming people to town."

We drove past the stone-walled town cemetery, where the trees grew tall and wide, providing deep shade for the dead.

Past the cemetery stood a row of completely empty shops. A yellowed sign behind a dust-caked window offered radio and television repair. Beside it, Jude's Diner hadn't fared much better, its door padlocked and its booths abandoned.

The gas station had shuttered decades earlier, too, as indicated by the lone, rusted-out pump on the raised concrete island and the promise of FULL SERVICE on the sign. The petroleum racket in the area was now monopolized by the El Cheapo Gas we'd passed on the highway several miles back.

On the next block stood houses of two and three stories with intricate, layered woodwork around their doors and windows. Lacy gingerbreading or rows of hourglass-shaped spandrels hung over every porch and balcony. It had been a well-to-do neighborhood in its prime, the rich Victorian-style facades and window trim embellishing the fronts of otherwise plain big-box houses. Some of the houses looked abandoned, their lots overgrown. They faced a small central neighborhood green, which looked recently mowed.

"This area could use a few of those yoga studios and smoothie shops," Stacey said.

"Here's the client's address." I parked on the street in front of a wrought-iron mailbox.

The old boardinghouse was enormous, with first and second-story front porches that ran the width of the house. While the entire neighborhood featured impressive woodwork, this one looked like it had received extra attention and artistry. The balusters and rails were carved to resemble trees with sprawling branches and ripe fruit. Leafy wooden grapevines spiraled up around one of the upper porch's corner posts, looking almost lifelike despite their brown wood-stain color. More of the delicate, flowering tree-limb carvings formed an upper trim across the tops of the upper and lower porches.

"It's so pretty," Stacey said as we hopped out of the van. "Now I see why they're willing to live on the creepy side of the tracks."

The front gate was open, admitting us to a cobbled path through a small front yard with recently planted squares of emerald green grass. A yard sign featured a picture of Nicole in her blazer, advertising her realty services—I recognized her from the card Dave had shown me. Presumably, Dave would be added to the sign when he passed his exam.

"It's kinda treehouse-esque," Stacey said, tracing her fingers along a thick, spiraling newel at the base of the front porch steps, part of the organic tree-branch design. She touched the budding flowers and fruits of the supporting balusters. "Someone put a lot of work into this."

We ascended the wide, welcoming front steps, made of wood that looked antique but remained as solid as brick. The tree-branch upper trim created an arboreal arch over the steps, seeming to invite us into the enchanted forest of the front porch, offering cool shadows where we could escape the scorching sun.

I rang the doorbell.

Rapid footsteps sounded inside. A curtain fluttered in a nearby window, and then the door was wrenched open from the inside by an elementary-age girl who gasped with the effort.

"Hi!" she said, regarding us through the screen door with a gap-tooted smile. She'd used makeup to draw a curly mustache under her nose, and she wore a chaotic ensemble of cowboy hat, bedsheet cape, and fuzzy bear-faced slippers. "What are you selling?" she asked cheerfully, like she couldn't wait to hear our amazing offer.

"Andra! Don't open the door…" Nicole emerged from deeper within the house, dressed in the same royal blue blazer and white blouse from her signs and business cards. She wore small sapphire earrings and a matching necklace, all of which seemed selected to go with her bright blue eyes.

"Somebody's hee-ere!" the small girl called Andra sang to her mother.

Nicole seemed taken aback by the sight of us, but instantly snapped a professional smile onto her face. "Hi there," she said, approaching the screen door. "It's so nice to meet you. Would you mind holding on just one more moment?"

"Of course not," I replied.

She nudged the door most of the way shut, but it didn't close, and we heard them through the screen.

"Put that bedsheet back in the laundry basket," Nicole's voice admonished, fading as they retreated from the front door. "That's not one of the old ones you're allowed to play with. Where's Penny?"

"She's in her room."

"She's supposed to be watching you and Jason."

"I *know*. Duh!"

"Don't say 'duh.' It's rude and crude."

"But Penny says it all the time."

"Fold that sheet properly, Andra."

"But folding sheets is *hard*."

"That's why you practice."

Stacey paced up and down the wide porch, which cried out for rocking chairs or a swing but only had a few mismatched lawn chairs.

A vehicle approached along the otherwise deserted square of narrow, unlined roads that surrounded the neighborhood's common green. It was Dave's mega-family-sized Ford Explorer, which he parked in the driveway behind Nicole's fairly new silver Subaru station wagon.

"Hey, did we get here at the same time?" Dave climbed out, carrying grocery bags with the logo of Garden Gnome Grocery, another store over in the trendy part of town.

"Just about," I replied. "Can we give you a hand with those?"

"Oh, no, no," he said, though he had about half a dozen bulging bags. "Just trying to support local businesses. I didn't have time to drive to Food Lion in Springfield, anyway."

I pulled the screen door open to let him into his house, just as Nicole was returning after disposing of her daughter. Nicole and Dave nearly collided in the doorway, like ill-fated trains entering opposite ends of the same tunnel. He dropped a bag, and she reached out to catch it.

The bag slipped past her, though, and struck the threshold of their house with a smash of breaking glass.

Red juice soaked the cloth grocery bag, making it look like the smiling gnome on the front had just been gored through the chest. The acidic tang of tomato rose from the mess.

"Great." Nicole shook her head and looked at us. "Would you mind waiting here…again? I'm so sorry."

"No problem," I said. "We're happy to help—"

"We can handle this ourselves," Nicole said, smiling again, but it was a little sharper and less friendly, like she was trying to mask a tremendous amount of strain. "I just need a minute."

"Sure." I backed away and joined Stacey in quietly studying the woodwork.

Once they'd straightened things up, Nicole stepped out with her wide, photo-ready professional smile again. It looked a little fake, but probably less than the one big one I was putting up to try to cover any awkwardness.

"This is my wife, Nicole," Dave said, closing the front door as he joined us outside. "These are the paranormal investigators."

"I'm sorry, things are a little chaotic today. Everybody's on edge." Nicole took a deep breath. "Dave says maybe you can help with some of our weirder problems."

"I hope so," I said. "We often find the causes aren't even paranormal in nature. Usually we're just eliminating the possibility of a ghost more than anything."

"A ghost, I could handle," Nicole said. "We had a ghost at Pendleton Avenue, our last house in Kansas City, by Maple Park. We called her Constance. I don't even know where the name came from. She didn't bother us often. Mostly she'd turn off the lights in the main stairwell, or turn them on. And sometimes she'd pull the duster out of the kitchen pantry and leave it somewhere in the house."

"A ghost who dusts?" Stacey asked. "That's convenient. No wonder you kept her."

"Oh, Constance didn't dust," Nicole said. "She just left it as a sign that she felt a room needed dusting."

"Sounds kind of passive aggressive," I said.

"It absolutely was," Nicole said.

"Too bad," Stacey said. "It would be great to have a ghost duster."

I cringed inwardly. Dave laughed. Nicole cringed outwardly. I thought Nicole and I bonded a little, cringing there together.

"Anyway," I said. "Have you experienced any trouble in the house, Nicole?"

"Not much that you could put your finger on." Nicole jumped as a curtain twitched inside the window beside her.

Andra stood at the gap in the curtains, spying on us. A boy watched over her head, moving her cowboy hat aside for a better view. He had big, dark eyes like Dave and midnight black hair like Nicole. He pulled the curtains tight when everyone turned to look at them.

"I'll keep them busy." Dave opened the door to reveal the two kids standing at the window inside. "Who wants to play Monopoly?"

This was met with reluctant groans, but he herded the younger ones into a parlor on the left side of the foyer and closed the door.

Nicole led us into the foyer, which was all wood, from the hardwood floors to the paneling inset with a labyrinth of shelves and nooks all the way up to the ceiling. Most of the shelves were empty, but a few displayed framed pictures of the family at different phases of their history as they'd expanded from a smiling couple at their wedding, to adding a baby, to finally becoming a family of six with two boys and two girls.

"Is all the woodwork original to the house?" I asked, remembering Dave mentioning how much Nicole liked it.

"Oh, yes. They don't make them like this anymore." Nicole stopped to run her fingers over the flowery motif carved along the borders of the shelves and across the front of each shelf. She smiled as if intoxicated by the rich detail, knowing she'd scored a visual gem of a house. "It's in good repair, too. It's so well-made that we've barely had to do a thing to fix up the old woodwork except dust and polish it. And dust and polish it some more. That's a never-ending job."

Ahead of us, the grand front staircase wrapped around the far end of the room. With its wide steps, monumental posts, and intricately decorated posts and balusters, it was almost too big for the house, but certainly would have accommodated a lot of foot traffic during the boardinghouse years. Ornate shelves, cabinets, and small closets were built underneath the stairs, leaving no potential storage space unused.

"It really looks amazing," Stacey said.

"Would you like some Greek mountain tea?" Nicole asked. "I was just about to make myself some. It's full of antioxidants."

"Sounds great, thank you," I replied.

We followed her through a side door into the dining

room. I'd seen a lot of antique houses around town, but this was unique.

While the foyer had felt cramped by the enormous staircase, the dining room was long and spacious. The artful carpentry continued here, in the form of a buffet with large cabinet doors and countless little drawers, next to a pair of glass-fronted china cabinets that could have held a restaurant's worth of dishware. The Brown family's china occupied only a smidgen of the available space. Their dining table with eighteen chairs, too, left a lot of empty room.

"The built-ins just keep coming," Nicole said, definitely sounding like a real estate agent now, as if automatically trying to sell her house to us, like selling was a comfortable mode for her. "This town was known for its woodworking. Local carpenters had their pick of material right from the source. This whole neighborhood is like hidden gold, yet it's been sitting here abandoned like a car on blocks for years. I know we can sell them to the right kind of buyer, the ones who see the intrinsic value of these antique homes."

"Just in time to catch the sprawl from Savannah, too," I said.

"Which has some of the fastest-growing suburbs in the entire United States, according to the census." Nicole slid apart a pair of pocket doors into the kitchen, floored with hardwood tiles. Shelves, cupboards, and a heavy mantelpiece above the kitchen's brick fireplace virtually encircled the room with more woodwork.

A narrow open door in the back corner of the kitchen stood open. Beyond it, stairs twisted down out of sight. Blistering music roared up from below, an angry male vocalist screaming himself hoarse over ultra-fast electric guitars and thundering drums, until Nicole closed the door to block it off.

"Sorry. I don't care much for the cellar, personally, but Lonnie doesn't seem to mind it, and it's the perfect spot for all his weights and muscle magazines."

"Lonnie's your fifteen-year-old?" I checked my notepad as I took one of the six chairs jammed in around the kitchen table.

"Yes. Solon, technically. All of our kids have ancient Greek names, sort of in honor of my family." She set the teapot to boil and placed herbal teabags in coffee mugs. "Solon, Penelope, Jason, Andromeda. It was partly Dave's idea, but my grandfather certainly approved."

"Has Lonnie reported any unusual experiences at the house?" I asked.

"Lonnie hasn't reported much of anything except being angry that we moved here too late for his new school's soccer tryouts." Nicole set out the mugs of tea, which smelled like flowers and citrus, and sat down with us. My mug advertised the Kemper Museum of Contemporary Art in Kansas City. "He qualified for varsity back home even though he'll only be a sophomore. Now he has to play at the YMCA, which he feels isn't good enough. He barely talks to us lately, just runs off to practice with the local soccer boys he's found. I'm glad he's making friends, though they seem a little rough. I don't want to judge, though. We're the new ones in town." She took a deep breath and sipped her herbal tea. She was twitchy, unsettled, with dark bags under her eyes as she looked us over. "And now there's all of this."

"Your husband seemed to think you were

skeptical," I said.

"Well, how can you really help us?" she asked.
"Dave made it sound like one of the ghost shows on
TV. You put cameras all around our house and then
watch all night, waiting for things to jump out? How
will that help? It sounds so, I'm sorry, but it sounds so
intrusive. And things are so chaotic already."

I nodded, understanding now that she'd been less
skeptical about the existence of ghosts, and more
skeptical about the hiring of paranormal investigators
to deal with them.

"If we learn why the ghost is here, we might be
able to make it move on," I said. "But we have to
understand its identity and motives."

"The kids call it Jack," Nicole said. "They got the
idea from the attic graffiti. They say we have to close
every cabinet and drawer in the house to keep him
away. And, well, you've seen the house." She indicated
the dozens of little doors and drawers around us. "So
that's turning into an exhausting bedtime ritual. 'Close
your doors and cabinets tight or Jack will come out and
get you tonight.' It's like a threat invented by a parent
for a kid who kept leaving a door open."

"Yeah, if you don't mind giving the kid
nightmares," Stacey said.

"It wouldn't be the first time parents were willing to
do that in exchange for obedience," Nicole said. "I
don't think that's what is happening here, though. There
is something strange in this house."

"What have you seen?" I asked.

She glanced at the doors in and out of the kitchen,
then lowered her voice. "There's the master bedroom
armoire. I haven't said anything to Dave about it,

because we sleep in there, and...I've been sort of in denial until he started talking about bringing you out here."

"That's completely understandable. What happened with the armoire?"

"Well, it's beautiful, like everything else here. But it has this mirrored front door, and more than once I thought I saw the reflection of someone else in the room with me, coming up behind me. I usually think it's Dave at first, but it turns out I'm alone."

"What does the figure in the mirror look like?"

"I've never really gotten a good look at him, straight on. It's always at an angle, out of the corner of my eye. Then he's gone."

"But you think it's a male figure?"

"I suppose, since I'm always thinking it's my husband."

"Do you have any other sensations when you see it? Sounds? Smells, even?"

"I get the chills. And actually, now that you ask, there's a smell like wood shavings, or sawdust. It's not always unpleasant when I see it. It's almost like a little thrill." She laughed. "I definitely need more sleep."

"So you don't feel the figure in the mirror is threatening?"

"More like unnerving, or startling. Part of me doesn't even believe it's real."

"Do you mind if we have a look at this armoire?" I asked.

"Of course. It's upstairs." She took her mug of tea as we returned to the staircase to check out the ghost problem in her room.

Chapter Five

The staircase took us to a windowless upstairs room walled in almost completely by doors, except for a hallway that led deeper into the house.

"Like I said, everything was cut up during the boardinghouse era. Some of these little rooms don't even have windows. Just look at this one." Nicole opened a door to a dark little cave that would barely have fit a single bed. It was currently used to store moving boxes. "They carved it out of the original master bedroom."

"Even this one has nice storage, though." Stacey pointed at the rows of shelves and small cabinets along two walls. "That's handy when you barely have enough space to turn around in."

"Our room is this way." Nicole opened the door beside it and took us through a short, narrow throat of a passageway to the master bedroom.

The compact, L-shaped room was built around the

glass double doors to the upstairs porch, capturing the porch access. The Browns' queen-sized bed took up a lot of the space.

"Is this the mirror?" I stepped toward the armoire, which was taller than me and had a full-length mirror built into its main door. The armoire was crafted from dark, heavy wood, adorned with little scalloped flourishes at every drawer pull and corner like a giant jewelry box. It was the centerpiece of a furniture-scape that ran all the way along the wall, full of drawers and small ornate doors, almost like a consolation for the room shrinking so much from its original size.

"That's the one." Nicole adjusted the throw pillows on her bed as if trying to make the room look perfect for us outsiders. The room was already spotless and neat, down to the framed family pictures on the dresser. One showed Nicole with a multi-generational group of women who resembled her, possibly sisters, cousins, and aunts, like in the *H.M.S. Pinafore* song. All wore matching blue blazers. They stood under a wall sign that read PAGONIS REALTY, the logo a stylized blue peacock.

I gazed into the armoire mirror. No shadowy phantoms came leaping out; the glass faithfully reflected the room around us. Maybe I'd have better luck if I looked into the mirror while alone, perhaps late at night, repeating the words *Bloody Mary*. Or maybe *Cabinet-Door Jack*.

"Did this armoire come with the house?" I asked.

"It *is* the house. I mean, it's all built in, like downstairs. It seems like an extreme commitment to a design scheme, locking everything into place, but fortunately it looks nice. And it has some useful features." Nicole unfolded a small writing table from one end of the dresser, revealing a row of pigeonholes full of envelopes and folded paperwork.

"Have you experienced anything else unusual?" I asked.

"Besides what I already said, I just feel a lot of uneasiness. Like someone's watching me. I sometimes felt that in our old house, too. Especially when it was messy. Constance, our old ghost back home, liked everything neat and clean. And so do I, of course, but you have to be realistic with four kids. I don't think Constance understood that."

"Where have the younger kids reported seeing things? Like this Jack character?"

"I'm not clear whether they've even seen him, exactly, or they're just scared of him because of that graffiti," Nicole said.

"What about your younger daughter's imaginary friends?" I asked. "Where does she see them?"

"They're wherever she is, usually the playroom," Nicole said. "You don't think Sunny and Rainy could be real, do you? Andra always makes up friends. She puts on little shows with her stuffed animals and dolls, too."

"I don't know anything for sure yet, but I did have a case where the imaginary friends were actually ghosts of dead children, and they wanted the living child to become their playmate forever. By dying in the house."

"Could that happen to Andra?" Nicole looked ill.

"That's not a common scenario, but you can see why I worry," I said. "If you decide to go ahead with the investigation, it might be helpful if I spoke to Andra."

"As long as you can do it without making her more frightened," Nicole replied.

"I'll be careful. I have a degree in psychology." I hoped this tidbit helped put her at ease, but to be honest, I've never been that great with kids.

"She may try to rope you into watching one of her shows. She hung an old sheet in the playroom as a theater curtain."

"Sounds cute!" Stacey said.

"Whatever gets her talking." I nodded.

"She's the one kid who still talks to us," Nicole said. "Jason's always been quiet, even as a baby, but now he's even more so. And the changes in his art are disturbing."

"We'd probably want to speak to him, too, or at least look at the drawings."

"I can show you those right now." Nicole stepped back out into the windowless room of doors around the staircase. Another door brought us into an elementary-age boy's room, the small bed neatly made, everything in order except for a card table by the window, where pens and markers, mostly black, purple, and blue, were scattered over several sheets of drawings.

More hand-drawn pictures hung on the walls, some of them lovingly framed. Superheroes and animals were heavily featured in these works, as well as an attempt at a cityscape that was better than anything I could have done.

"Did he draw all of these?" Stacey asked, leaning to study a squirrel etched in pencil on a ragged-edged spiral notebook page.

"Yes, Jason's always been a busy little artist. We had to hide the crayons when he was a toddler because he'd graffiti the walls. But lately..." She flipped over a sheet of paper on the card table and grimaced before turning it toward us. "A lot of this."

The drawing showed an irregular door with a sloping, diagonal top, about halfway open. Jackets and coats hung inside, with a row of shoes on a shelf along the bottom and assorted hats and caps on a shelf above. A particular central arrangement of hat, coat, and shoes suggested a man standing inside the closet, with scribbled shadows where his face would have been.

"It looks like the coat closet under the stairs," Nicole said. "This one's not so bad, but then there's things like..." She slid it aside to reveal another drawing full of dark, slashing pencil strokes.

Here, a man slid out from a square cabinet door, levitating, lying stiff on his back like a corpse floating headfirst out of an open morgue locker, only no metal rolling tray held him up. He held some kind of hatchet or sharp tool in one hand. He wore a flat cap like an old-timey workman. His face was just scribbles, except for a wide, toothy smile.

"Is that Jack?" I asked.

"I think so," Nicole whispered.

Another drawing showed a face peering out from behind a rectangular cabinet door that was three-quarters closed. One eye was visible, large and light-colored. A lock of white hair was visible over the eye, but perhaps meant to be blond or gray; it was hard to know when it was sketched in black ink.

"What does Jason say about these drawings?" I asked.

"He says they're things he sees. He's vague and won't really talk about it. But he's obsessed with closing the doors. You can help him and Andra check the cabinets at night, that will get them on your good side."

"And he says Jack is the one who comes out at night?" I looked at the sideways figure, irrationally sliding out of a small cabinet where a person couldn't possibly have fit inside.

"Andra does most of the talking," Nicole said. "But Jason's right there with her, on the same wavelength, as if closing doors to keep the boogeyman out is just something all people ought to do each night before brushing their teeth and getting into bed. The first time it felt like a game. But it's been every night for weeks now. It's the consistency that scares me, the fact that they didn't just move on to something else after a day or two. I told them Jack isn't real and can't hurt them, but I might as well have tried to tell them the moon was made of ice cream."

"So, they're both scared of Jack? What else have they said about him?" I asked.

"Andra says Sunny and Rainy help her look out for him."

"How does she describe those imaginary friends?"

"I think they're supposed to be other children," Nicole said. "Andra's a little short on playmates, unfortunately. Jason prefers to keep to himself. Penny used to play with her, but she's getting into that moody, rebellious teen stage now and mopes around uselessly —"

Someone gasped, or maybe hissed.

Stacey and I looked at each other, then at Nicole.

"What was that?" I asked.

"It wasn't me. I heard it, though." Nicole stepped

out of the bedroom and looked among the rooms of doors. "Who's there?"

A thump sounded in Jason's closet, which was barely ajar, showing an inch of darkness inside.

Stacey and I looked at each other, confirming we'd both heard it.

I stepped over to the boy's closet door and took the knob, wishing I had my flashlight so I could spear any nasty dark entities with white light, but I hadn't strapped on all the bulky gear for our first meeting with this hesitant potential client.

I swung open the closet door.

Inside, a yellow hooded slicker swayed on a hanger, as did a flannel jacket beside it, as if something had jostled them. It was possible the clothes had moved because of the door displacing air as I swung it open, but I hadn't pulled the door with all that much force.

I slid the jackets and sweaters aside. The closet was deeper than it was wide. A cavity extended beyond the clothes rack, its ceiling sloping low toward the back, as if we were underneath a stairway, maybe to the attic. Assorted shoes were scattered on and around a low shelf at the back—boots for winter, black shoes with fake buckles for formal occasions, Spider-Man flip-flops for everyday casual wear.

"I didn't see anybody out there. What's, uh, going on in here?" Nicole asked, having returned to the room's doorway behind us.

"We heard something in the closet. But it looks like nothing's there." I backed away and closed the door tight, like the younger kids would have wanted. "I didn't mean to get nosy."

"It's easy to hear things in this house," Nicole said.

"Especially at night. Though half the time it's just Penny rummaging around. She sleeps half the day then stays up at night, staring at one screen or another—"

"Seriously, mother? Telling everyone my personal life?" The girl who'd spoken stood outside the door. She looked like a preteen mirror image of Nicole, not much shorter than her mother, though her black hair was much longer, falling in rumpled cascades over her shoulders. She had the same bright blue eyes and similar fatigued bags under them. She wore a very out-of-season sweatshirt hoodie and a pair of shorts. "Are these the wackos Dad called?"

"That's rude and crude, Penelope," Nicole said. "You were supposed to be watching your brother and sister."

"Well, Jason wanted to draw, and Andra wanted to go work on her magic show with her schizo voices inside her head. So I took a nap." Penny looked us over, clenching her small jaw. "What exactly are these people going to do?"

"We'll talk about it later."

"More like you'll yell at me about it later."

"Penny, your room!"

"Like I even want to be out here." The girl trudged off down the hall, and a door slammed.

"Just to be clear, that's the moody one?" Stacey asked.

Nicole gave a short, tired laugh. "We used to call Penny extra-extroverted. She was like Andra with her energy, only less of a whirlwind and more of a freight train, relentlessly on track. At her old school, she was in student government, spirit squad, and some other things, but she insists she won't join *any* activities at her new school. I'm hoping she'll change her mind once the year begins in August. She was really upset about moving away from her friends. It'll be some time before we're forgiven for that. And for now, we've lost our best babysitter." She shook her head. "I guess you should meet the younger ones, but I wouldn't start out by mentioning Jack and the cabinets."

"Of course. We'll go gently."

We returned to the front parlor downstairs, which the family had made into a living room. A TV hung over the fireplace. Board games, kid-made decorations, photo albums, and other family memorabilia occupied the bookshelves. The extensive bookcases and wainscoting gleamed with a fresh coat of white, reflecting sunlight from the porch windows, creating a brighter atmosphere than most of the rooms had.

Dave and eight-year-old Andra occupied a minimalist IKEA-style couch, leaning over a Monopoly board on a square coffee table. Ten-year-old Jason sat in a matching armchair, shaking the dice, preparing to roll. The furniture didn't really match the room, but it was too neutral and simple to truly clash with anything.

"Andra," Nicole said, "our guests were asking about your magic show."

Andra gasped and jumped to her feet, visibly panicked. "But I haven't scheduled a show today!"

"You could schedule one," Nicole suggested.

"I'm not ready! Everyone wait here!" Andra raced past us and opened a door at the back of the room. She hesitated at the sight of the narrow, dark hallway beyond. "Dad, can you walk me through?"

"Of course." Dave stood up to join her. "Jason, I'll be right back so we can keep playing."

"I don't really care." Jason set the dice down without rolling. "I'm hungry."

"Andra's a little scared of the hallway," Nicole told us, in a low voice.

"No, I'm not!" Andra argued, but stuck close to her father as they stepped away into the hall, deeper into the old house.

Chapter Six

Stacey and I followed Nicole and Jason into the kitchen through that dark, unwelcoming back hall, which was clearly carved from portions of three original rooms, with abrupt transitions in the hardwood floor pattern and the crown molding. A couple of side rooms had claimed the windows, leaving the hallway dark.

The back hall crossed somewhere behind the front stairs, by my calculation, and dead-ended near two facing doors. One was closed with a DO NOT ENTER!!! sign written in red crayon thumbtacked to it, presumably the playroom door where Andra was hurriedly preparing her show.

We passed through the other one into the kitchen.

Stacey and I sat at the kitchen table and finished our tea while Nicole made Jason a peanut butter sandwich. He ate it solemnly and silently while staring at us with his huge brown eyes, as if we were aliens who'd just landed.

"Your mom says you like to draw," Stacey said. "That's really neat."

He looked at her, chewing slowly.

"I went to art school, you know," she continued. "I did more painting than actual drawing. But I mostly studied photography and film. Do you like to paint, too?"

He blinked.

"What kinds of things do you like to draw?" Stacey asked.

He shrugged. "Usually pictures," he finally said, very quietly.

"Pictures, huh? That's great."

He kept eating his sandwich, staring at her.

I could see the playroom door from where I sat at the table. It opened slowly, and then we heard the girl's voice.

"You go announce us, Sunny," Andra whispered from the space behind the open door, that last-minute go-to spot for desperate hide-and-seekers. After a few seconds, she whispered again, "Okay, I'll do it if you're too scared."

"I think there's an announcement coming," Nicole said.

"Ladies and everyone! Now presenting…Grizalda, the Magic Witch! Hooray! Yay!" Andra leaped out through the playroom door, dressed in a cone-shaped paper hat with HAPPY BIRTHDAY in glittering silver letters, as well as a snarling Incredible Hulk mask and a long, drooping black shirt that had to be her father's, the loose sleeves bunched around her wrists. She waved a rainbow-spiral toy broom like a magician's wand.

"A witch!" Stacey gasped.

Andra lifted the green mask to show her face. "It's just me!" she said in a loud whisper.

"Oh, okay," Stacey whispered loudly back to her.

Andra lowered the mask again. "But really I'm Grizalda! This way to the stage!" She raised her broom with a flourish, spun around, and marched back into the playroom.

Stacey and I followed her, along with Nicole. Jason took the rest of his sandwich and walked off in the other direction.

"Wow, this really is a room for plays," Stacey said as we stepped through the door. The overhead light was off. Folding chairs and beanbags faced a curtain of two old bedsheets that hid the back half of the room, illuminated by flashlights placed on end tables like spotlights. A card table draped in an unzipped sleeping bag stood in front of the curtain.

Andra dashed behind the curtain while we took our seats.

"Now comes the magic show!" Andra announced, popping out through the curtain with the short toy broom in one hand and a beach bucket decorated with cartoon crabs in the other.

Stacey clapped, so I did, too.

Andra set the bucket on the covered table and raised her mask. "You're supposed to clap at the end, not the start," she told us.

"Oh, sorry," Stacey replied.

"It's okay." Andra pulled her mask back down. "Now, you will be amazed!" She pulled a plush rabbit toy from under the table and waved it around. "As you

can see, this is a perfectly normal rabbit. His name is
Carrots. And there's nothing up my sleeve right now. So
watch!" She placed the rabbit out of sight inside the
bucket, but kept her hand in there with it while she
waved her little broom. "Presto, change-o!"

"I wonder what's going to happen," Stacey
whispered.

Behind us, Nicole was looking at her phone, hand
wrapped around the screen to dampen the glow it cast
in the dim room.

"Wall-la!" Andra removed her hand from the
bucket, her oversized sleeve bulging suspiciously. She
turned the beach bucket toward us to show it was
empty. "Oh, no, Carrots disappeared! Where-oh-where
did he go?"

Stacey and I made a show of looking shocked while
Andra made a show of searching the room's numerous
shelves and low cabinets for the missing rabbit, her
bulging sleeve pressed against her stomach the whole
time.

Finally, Andra reached the bulging sleeve into a
cabinet, shook it around, and pulled it back out holding
the little rabbit again.

"I found him!" Andra announced. "He's fine,
everyone. He doesn't need to go to the vet. Carrots, are
you ready for your next trick?" She did a squeaky voice
and waved the stuffed rabbit so its head bobbed up and
down at a neck-breaking speed. "'Oh, yes, please! I
love tricks!' Okay, get ready, then!"

Andra placed the rabbit back in the cabinet and
closed the door.

"For my next trick," she said, "my lovely assistant
Sunny will make the rabbit disappear. Are you ready,

Sunny?" Andra looked at an empty space beside her, then nodded. "Okay! Abra-ca-da-braca!" She whacked the front of the cabinet with her broom.

When she opened the cabinet again, the rabbit was gone.

I leaned forward, expecting to see the toy rabbit jammed into a back corner. The cabinet held a stack of *Ranger Rick* magazines, but no sign of Carrots the rabbit. There was no suspicious bulge in her sleeve to explain it this time, either.

"Okay, Sunny, where did you hide him?" Andra searched the room again, giggling, opening and closing her way down the row of cabinets, as if she genuinely had no idea where it was. This mission took her behind the curtain. Out of sight, she exclaimed "Finally!" and then jumped back out waving the rabbit. "Here he is! Ta da!"

"Nice! I am genuinely impressed!" Stacey clapped. I joined in, too. The kid had fooled me.

"Anyway…" Andra tossed the rabbit onto the card table, but it tumbled off and landed on the floor. She made no move to retrieve it. "For my next trick, it's the mysterious levitating fish!" She dove under the table and rummaged around for a while. "Hold, please," she said after a minute, briefly poking up her head.

Behind us, Nicole's fingers clacked the screen of her phone.

"Wall-la!" Andra stood abruptly. A plastic red fish taken from a Let's Go Fishin' board game hung from her fingers. It was tied to her middle finger with dental floss, which was almost invisible in the low light, and swung in the space below her fingers as though floating in midair. "What holds up the fish? Magic!"

Stacey and I clapped. So did Nicole, glancing up momentarily from her phone. I wondered how many magic shows she'd sat through.

Andra performed a couple more tricks, such as the "amazing floating pencil" surreptitiously held up by one hidden finger.

"Now for something new! My lovely assistant Rainy will do the spooky sheet trick!" Andra waved her broom at one of the stage-curtain sheets, decorated with faded turtles. "Abraca-doozle!"

We watched the sheet. It may have shifted a little, but both of the curtain-sheets were constantly swaying anyway, the air around them moved by Andra scurrying around and the flow of air conditioning through the house.

"I said, abraca-doozle!" Andra waved her broom at the sheet again. She stood there for several long, uncomfortable seconds while nothing happened. Finally, she poked her head back between the curtains and whispered, "Rainy! Abraca-*doo*zle!" She fell silent again, then said, "But everybody's watching!" She stepped out of sight behind the curtain, whispering too low for us to hear.

At last, she announced again, still out of sight, "The spooky sheet trick!"

The sheet began to bulge toward us, pressed forward by something the exact size and shape of a child's head. Smaller bulges arose on either side of it, about the size of a child's hands. "Spooky sheet!" Andra intoned behind it. "Spooooky sheeeet!"

"That is getting kinda spooky," Stacey whispered, watching the child-shape with Andra's voice haunt us through the sheet, waving its arms slightly.

"Nothing's spoooookier than the spooooooky sheet." Andra stepped out around the far end of the other curtain. She waved her broom and paraded in front of the bedsheet-curtains, hamming it up as the trick went on.

With a cold sensation crawling up my back, I looked back at the child shape in the turtled-printed bedsheet, its head and arms plainly outlined. I heard Stacey swallow audibly beside me.

Then I remembered how Andra's brother Jason had silently slipped away before the show. Maybe there was another door into the room, behind the curtain, and he'd come in that way. Or maybe Dave was somehow behind it, portraying the spooky sheet monster. I wasn't going to be taken in by an elementary-age kid's magic show.

The sheet continued bulging toward us, drawing tight against the child-sized head and arms like a mummy's wrapping.

It crept closer, approaching Stacey and me. I was still getting the chills from the sight of the silent sheet-wrapped child reaching out its hands.

One hand moved toward me, and I pulled back in my seat to avoid it. I wondered if the kid could see through the sheet or was just pawing around blindly.

The sheet snapped loose from the clothespin securing it to the repurposed badminton net overhead, which served as the curtain rail. The sheet dropped all around the kid, who stumbled over the bottom edge of the sheet and tripped, falling directly toward me.

I reached out to catch him. My arms closed around the sheet, and I inadvertently hugged it close to me when I'd really only meant to steady him.

The sheet collapsed flat in my lap, empty inside, containing nothing I could feel. No Jason, no Dave. It was cold, like it had been stored inside a freezer.

The frosted sheet seemed to wrap around me. The icy material where the kid-sized arms had been embraced my shoulders. The sheet covered my face like I'd been declared dead.

"Off!" I shouted, jumping to my feet, shoving the sheet to the floor before it could smother or strangle me.

The sheet collapsed to a flat puddle. Nobody inside.

"Wow," Stacey said, rising slowly to stand beside me. "This is…more than I expected. Amazing trick, Andra. I'm a little freaked out by it."

I looked from her to Andra, who peeled off her green Hulk mask to stare at the empty fallen sheet.

Then Andra screamed "Daddy!" so suddenly and at such extreme volume that Stacey and I both jumped. "Daddy! Daddy!"

"What's wrong?" Nicole rose behind us, putting her phone away. "Andra, why are you yelling?"

"The dumb sheet fell off during the grand tamale!" Andra pointed at the turtle-print sheet at my feet.

"The grand…finale?" Nicole asked.

"Daddy!" Andra shouted again, just as Dave walked into the room.

"What's wrong, cupcake?" Dave asked.

"The sheet fell and ruined my tamale. My show was dumb."

"Oh, no, it wasn't!" Stacey hurried to say. "You made an audience member scream in surprise. That's the number one sign of a successful magic show."

"Really?" Andra smiled around the wide gap of her

missing front teeth. Her makeup mustache had smudged into a vague smear.

"Absolutely," Stacey assured her.

"You did fine, honey," Nicole said. "Now, I need to speak to these ladies for a minute. Why don't you go wash your face?"

"Wait!" Andra ran behind the remaining curtain, a sea-green bedsheet printed with cartoon mermaids.

I watched closely as Dave picked up the turtle sheet and clamped it back into place on the badminton net spanning the ceiling, presumably securing the clothespin with greater care. Nothing grabbed him from within the sheet's collapsed folds, and it hung flat on the line, generally behaving as a normal sheet should.

Once it was up, Andra burst out from between the curtains and bowed. We all rewarded her with applause.

"And a hand for my lovely assistants, Sunny and Rainy!" Andra gestured vaguely, pressuring us into a second round of applause for the invisible friends.

"They really did an amazing job," Stacey said, clapping.

I looked at Nicole, who didn't seem nearly as shocked as Stacey and myself. "Did you see that last trick?" I whispered to Nicole, while Andra rapid-fire chatted with her dad about the unacceptable curtain situation.

"Oh, sorry, no. Was it the floating pencil one?" Nicole asked.

"It was the spooky sheet trick."

Nicole shrugged and watched as Dave led Andra out of the room. "That's a new one on me. Usually she kind of wanders off after a few tricks. Dave told her that her shows need a big finale."

"Well, that was certainly one big tamale," Stacey said, looking at the innocuous-seeming sheet again.

"I think you should have us investigate this house," I told her. "I usually don't push it, but what we just saw was unsettling."

"But what will it cost?"

"We can work something out. I won't even charge for the first night. I don't normally pressure people at all, I promise. Some people live in haunted houses for years with no major problems. But I'm concerned that an entity may already be in contact with your children. Maybe multiple entities."

"You think there's something about those invisible friends, don't you?" Nicole asked.

"You really should have seen the spooky sheet trick."

She sighed. "Okay. Let's see what we can do."

We left the dim room. The makeshift stage curtains were still drawn, concealing anyone or anything that might have been lurking behind them.

Chapter Seven

Dave and Nicole invited us to start our investigation a couple of days later, once they'd had time to try to get their kids used to the idea.

Stacey and I drove over in the afternoon, giving ourselves several hours to set up before nightfall. Again we drove through the noticeable transition from the trendy, partly restored section of town to the mill ruins and empty industrial area. In both parts of town, I noticed the detailed trim around doorways and windows, sculpted by forgotten generations of skilled carpenters, much more aware of it than I normally would have been.

We slowed as we approached the little neighborhood. A few shouting teenage boys kicked a soccer ball around on the freshly mowed central green, shaded by the tall trees and empty houses around them. I recognized Lonnie from his pictures in the house, broad-shouldered and tanned, his hair shaved close except for one purple patch along the top.

The soccer hooligans stopped to watch us pull in at the boardinghouse. One whistled as Stacey got out, and another one punched the first one in the arm, hard, as if fueled by some mixture of embarrassment and malice.

Lonnie shook his head, then kicked the soccer ball to the far side of the green and took off after it. The other boys pursued him, colliding into each other like a pack of enthusiastic dogs chasing a tennis ball at the park, thankfully losing their brief interest in us.

Stacey and I carried a load of gear up the steps to the front porch. Dave met us at the door.

"Looks like you're setting up a whole movie studio." He grabbed a couple of tripods. "Where do these go?"

"We'll need to watch the locations where people have reported activity. Jason drew a picture of this closet, so we'll stick a camera in here." I opened the closet door under the front stairs and pushed aside coats and jackets. Stacey set up a thermal camera beyond the closet rod, then moved the coats back into place and closed the door.

"Where to next, boss?" she asked me.

"Nicole mentioned that she might have seen something in the master bedroom. It would be best if we could monitor that."

"Cameras in our bedroom?" Dave rubbed his chin.

"We'll position them carefully," I promised.

He frowned but led us up to the master bedroom. The armoire and the array of drawers and small sculpted doors that extended from either side of it looked like some kind of high-rise apartment building for fairies and gnomes.

"I was impressed with your daughter's magic trick," I said. "The one where she made the rabbit disappear from the cabinet."

"Yeah, sometimes it falls out of her sleeve."

"She said her invisible friend moves it for her."

"Right, the invisible friend. Do you think something in this house moves things from place to place? Maybe our resident ghost?"

"It seems possible. Is there a particular area associated with the invisible friends?"

"The playroom," he said. "There are little sub-rooms carved out of it that must have been for children. You can tell by the decorations."

"That sounds like our next stop."

"All set here." Stacey stepped back from the night vision camera she'd pointed at the mirrored armoire door. "I've got it so we can't see the bed in the mirror, Dave. It reflects the porch doors from this angle. You'll have total privacy."

"We'll see what Nicole thinks. She's got the kids pulling weeds in the back yard right now."

Stacey and I brought in another load of gear to set up in the playroom. Dave pulled one of Andra's curtains aside to show us the rest of the room.

The wall beyond the curtains was taken up by three doorways. At the center was a normal-sized door to a narrow walk-in closet lined with shelves and cabinets. The doors on either side of the closet were half-sized, with shelves above them. Adults would have to enter on hands and knees.

"Wow," Stacey said. "I want to say the little doors are cute, but they're giving me visions of tiny goblins instead."

"Andra certainly likes them," Dave said, kneeling by one door. "Especially this one."

He pulled it open, and we squatted to look inside.

The room inside was very small, like a closet, but had its own window. A built-in bunk bed and ladder made of creamy, pink-hued beech wood were adorned with a pattern of simple, cartoony carvings, including rabbits, flowers, and butterflies. A toy chest carved with similar bunnies and butterflies sat in the corner under the bunk. Everything had been recently dusted.

"Looks like a little kid's room." Stacey crawled inside to take pictures.

"Did you find the toy box in there?" I asked Dave.

"Andra did. She calls it her treasure chest."

After Stacey crawled out, I crawled in to check out the space for myself. There wasn't much I couldn't see from the outside.

I opened the toy box. Appropriately enough, it held a couple of hand-carved toys—a little train engine with a smiling clown face and six wooden wheels, a rabbit wearing a top hat.

When I stood up, I barely had room to turn around. I immediately felt confined, despite the large window, like I'd checked into a roach motel and wouldn't be checking back out. My heart thumped noticeably faster.

"It's a little small for me." I dropped to my knees and hurried out. "I would not want to be stuck in there during a fire."

"The other one's worse. We'll be removing these walls, eventually, opening this all into one room." Dave opened the other small door so we could squat down and look inside.

The other room was just as tiny, with a framed wall

mirror in lieu of a window, and a few shelves above a small cabinet door. Like the first, it had a built-in bunk and ladder that were still solid, but the detail work here featured balloons, lightning bolts, and sailboats instead of flowers and bunnies.

"What are you doing in Rainy's room?" Andra stood beyond the open curtain with crossed arms, her eyes narrow and accusing.

"Hey, kiddo, we're just showing them around," Dave said.

"So this is Rainy's room?" I asked Andra.

"Yes."

"What about that room?" I pointed to the other small door.

"That's Sunny's. She doesn't mind if you play in there. But Rainy minds sometimes."

"Okay, good to know. Are Sunny and Rainy nice?" I asked.

"Usually. But you have to follow the rules."

"What rules?"

Andra looked at her dad, who nodded at her. "It's okay," he said.

"You have to close everything so Jack can't come out," Andra said. As if to demonstrate, she closed a nearby cabinet door that was partly open, displaying a big yellow Lego box.

"What happens if Jack comes out?"

Andra's eyes flared wide. "It's bad." She walked over and closed the little hobbit door in front of us. "Jack pretends to like kids but really hates them."

"Where did you hear that?"

"Sunny and Rainy. Mostly Sunny. Rainy's quieter."

"What else have they told you about Jack?"

"To keep out of Jack's room. And we do!" Andra nodded vehemently. Then she picked up her rainbow broom and smiled impishly. "Ready for another show?"

"That's a lot to ask, Andra," Dave said. "They just saw one the other day."

"Actually, we were wondering if we could make a video of your next magic show," I said.

Andra gaped. "Yeah! And we can put it on YouTube."

"Or just show it to family and friends," Dave said.

"Then I can start my own channel!" Andra gasped. "And become a star!"

Dave shook his head. "Let's not get too crazy."

"You always say that! But sometimes I want to get too crazy."

"I'm aware," Dave said.

"Andra, which room did you say is Jack's room?" I asked.

"It's in the attic," Andra whispered. "Only Penny likes it up there."

"Good to know." I helped Stacey set up a couple of cameras, including a normal daytime video recorder to capture Andra's performance, and maybe a recurrence of the spooky sheet trick. We added an EMF meter and night vision camera to Sunny's room, but Andra didn't want us prying into Rainy's little hovel again. We went along with her wishes, since we didn't want to lose her cooperation.

"Don't come back for at least eleven minutes!" she told us, just before pulling the curtains shut, enclosing herself in the backstage area.

"You can do your show after dinner, before bedtime," Dave said.

Andra huffed and headed for the curtain. "Fiiiiiiine."

"Maybe we could have a look at that attic bedroom," I suggested to Dave.

He checked his phone. "Could it wait until after we get the kids to bed? I'd hate for them to get any more riled up about this stuff tonight than they already are. I already have to make them eat baked salmon for dinner, so I can't handle much more stress on top of that."

"Understandable," I said, smelling the strong, fishy odor slowly filling the house. "We'll break for supper, then, too. Maybe we'll go to one of those trendy places in town."

"The Chicken Salad Shack is pretty good, and not actually located in a shack." He walked us out the front door, where he yelled at Lonnie to break from soccer and eat dinner. The teenage boy barely glanced at him in response.

Stacey and I drove away from the desolate neighborhood. We left the dead part of town behind as we crossed over the tracks into the part that was gradually returning to life, like green growth emerging on a fallen tree.

Chapter Eight

The graphic on the front window of Chicken Salad Shack depicted a cartoon chicken eating a bowl of salad.

"Isn't that cannibalism?" Stacey whispered as we approached. "A chicken eating chicken salad?"

"It looks like a garden salad." I pointed at the lettuce leaves and tomato slices in the chicken's bowl. "The chicken probably ordered off the vegetarian menu."

"Chickens aren't as vegetarian as they look. Ever seen one attack a mouse?"

A bell on a ribbon chimed as we opened the door. The interior was cheerfully chickened up with kitschy chicken figurines and farm-related art, from a painting of a weathered chicken coop to a framed poster of Foghorn Leghorn.

The college-age girl on the stool behind the counter glanced up from her phone at the sound of the bell, but her gaze dropped back to it as we stepped inside. She apparently had a lot to do on her phone while we crossed through the small, chicken-themed space to the front counter, and she remained silently busy as Stacey and I looked over the menu on the wall. There was spicy jalapeno chicken salad, triple-fruity chicken salad, and teriyaki chicken salad, among other options.

"Do you have just a regular chicken salad?" Stacey asked.

"Southern style." The counter girl didn't look up.

"I'll have one of those."

"Regular or large?"

"Reg—"

"Saltine or Ritz?"

"Uh, saltine."

The girl took our orders and rang us up while barely glancing away from her phone. "Your order will be out soon" was what I thought she mumbled. She didn't make a move after punching our order into her machine.

While we stood around waiting, I looked at the designs of berries and leaves carved into the wall paneling. It reminded me of our clients' house. I traced some of it with my fingertip, then regretted it when my fingers came back dusty. I wiped them on my pants.

"Do you have any idea how old these wall panels are?" I asked the counter girl, who still made no visible move toward fulfilling our order.

She cast an annoyed look in my direction, then went back to her phone.

Finally, the door behind her, etched with similar designs as the paneling, swung open, unleashing a torrent of bright, brassy Spanish-language music into the room. A stooped, gray-haired man brought out two plates, each with a scoop of chicken salad atop a crisp green romaine leaf, and set them on the counter.

"Are those ours?" I stepped forward. I'd ordered the California style, which came with grapes, and one of them matched that description. Also, we were the only customers.

"Yes," he said. "Enjoy."

"Enrique, you're not supposed to talk to customers. That's my job," the girl said, never looking up from her phone. "Don't make me call Brad again."

The salad chef shook his head and returned silently to the kitchen, his upbeat music vanishing when the door closed behind him.

Despite her claim about her job duties, the counter girl didn't talk to us as we picked up the plates and walked outside.

We took one of the two outdoor tables and looked over the perky downtown.

"It's so colorful," Stacey said. "Like a tropical village."

"Yep. It's a happening place." It wasn't, really, but it wasn't completely deserted on this middle-of-the-week night. Scattered couples and small groups strolled the downtown. Several people arrived in yoga gear at one point, mats strapped over their shoulders, and piled into the studio.

After our chicken salad, which was high in quality but low in portion size, we stepped over to Turntables Cafe for fresh coffee to kickstart the long night ahead.

The balding, pudgy guy was there in his coffee-colored apron, wiping down the tables.

"We were just about to close," he said. "Actually

already closed, forgot to turn the sign off. But I haven't dumped the urn yet, if you want something."

"Just a couple of to-go coffees, if you have enough left," I said.

"I may." He began dispensing some dark, aromatic coffee into a tall paper cup. "Nancy Sinatra for you, Muddy Waters for her? Am I right?"

"Nancy's fine for me tonight," Stacey said. "I don't want to be any trouble."

"No trouble at all." He went to work.

"Are you the owner here?" I asked.

"Owner, operator, and chief custodian," he said, smiling. "Walt Lambert. Did y'all just move in recently?" He looked between Stacey and me. "Maybe one of the renovated lofts? Or the new neighborhoods?"

"We're just visiting somebody," I said. "Are you from Timbermill originally?"

"Oh, no. I was in risk management. Steelman Insurance of Macon. Twenty-two years. This cafe's my retirement business. I always liked the record store back home when I was teenager, though it's long gone now."

I glanced at the hundreds of records on sale, but I was more interested in the built-in shelves where they were displayed, heavily adorned around the edges with tiny carved embellishments that looked like wheat. "Are these original to the building?"

"They were here when I got here, I'll tell you that much." He chuckled. "I wanted a place with character and history, but cheap. My realtor said this town's growing fast, and I could get in on the ground floor. And like you said, the woodwork's got its charm."

"Do you know anything about the history of the building?" I asked.

He shrugged. "It was some kind of store. They've converted the upstairs rooms to lofts."

"Hey, there's some great stuff here." Stacey pulled an ABBA record off the shelf.

"That's my personal record collection I'm selling off," he told her. "Some of the rare ones have actually gained in value, like *The Who Sell Out*. I could sell that at a big profit if I wanted, which is ironic, if you ask me. The others, well, I'd just like to know somebody will listen to them from time to time after I'm gone. My daughter doesn't want them, doesn't have room in her little place up in New Jersey."

"Aw, I'll buy some records," Stacey said.

"Only if you promise you'll listen to them."

"I promise."

"My boyfriend likes classic blues records," I said. "Do you have anything like that?"

"I may have a sad old song or two." He shuffled out from behind the counter and took something from a low shelf. It had a frayed black and white cover. "Does he have this one? *Blues in D Natural*. It's a compilation." He looked at the back. "Robert Nighthawk, Elmore James, Earl Hooker. A fine set of fellows."

"It doesn't look familiar." I hesitated at the price tag. It was more than I'd expected to spend when we'd stepped inside the coffee shop. "Do you know anybody locally who can give us insight into the town's history? Maybe someone who grew up here?"

"Well, there's a fix-it man who's been out here a time or two. He's older than I am, and I almost feel bad making him work, but I'm not as handy as I should be, and this place needs a skilled hand at times. He's a genuine local. You don't meet many of them around town. Everybody seems to be a transplant from somewhere else, like me."

"Could you put me in touch with him?" I asked.

"I suppose. He's a strange duck, though. Eccentric." Bill took out his phone and scrolled through his contacts, squinting, until he found the phone number and gave it to me. "His name's Otis Traverton. He lives in an old place across town. Did you want to buy that record?"

"I think my boyfriend would like it, but the price is a little much for me right now," I said. "Can you think of anyone else who could tell us about local history?"

"There's Dorothy down at the hair salon. She'll talk your ear off any day. If you buy that record, your coffee's on the house."

"Okay, sold," I said.

"And I'll take these!" Stacey handed him five more records, including the ABBA and a David Bowie album with a faded, crumbling cover.

We made our purchases and stepped outside. The proprietor locked the door behind us and turned off the exterior lights. The sidewalk was dim now, lit by occasional streetlamps.

The town lay quiet, most of the little shops closed for the day. The occasional pedestrians had deserted the sidewalk and park.

"You can almost picture how this area was before they fixed it up," I said. "When it all looked like the other part of town, rundown and empty."

"A ghost town, only back from the dead," Stacey

said as she climbed into the van. "The whole place feels a little haunted."

We drove back to our clients' house, ready for a long night of watching the shadows for shapes and faces, and listening for voices in the dark.

Chapter Nine

Stacey and I parked on the street in front of the house so we wouldn't block the narrow driveway. Our van would be our nerve center, collecting signals from our cameras, microphones, and other sensors around the house while we watched and listened through the night.

I texted Dave to let him know we were there. The lights were still on all over the house, but I didn't want to knock on the door and interrupt any family activities. Texting seemed more considerate.

Andra's excited to do another show, he texted back. *Come on in.*

He met us at the door.

"The kids are just finishing up with the dishes." He led us on the circuitous route through the dining room to the kitchen. Lonnie, the teen boy, sullenly put away bowls while the two smaller kids handled the silverware.

Nicole smiled when she saw us, but it was definitely forced, like she'd rather not be dealing with us at all, but found herself stuck without other options. "Welcome back. How was your dinner?"

"It was great," I said.

"They're here!" Andra flung a few spoons haphazardly into the drawer and ran toward the far doorway. "I have to get ready."

"Not until the dishes are done!" Nicole said, and the girl froze.

"Mom, Andra slopped the spoons." Jason moved aside the misplaced spoons so he could put away a fork.

"Straighten the spoons, Andra."

Andra dragged herself back toward the silverware drawer as if heavy weights were tied to her legs and arms. "Fiiiine, but the show's going to open late now."

Dave ushered us through the door at the back of the kitchen and over to the playroom, leaving us there. "Enjoy the show," he said, shaking his head as he left.

While we waited, I drew aside the curtain and looked into each of the three doors again. The normal-sized one in the middle opened onto a walk-in closet whose shelves and cubbies were mostly empty, except for a few boxes of Halloween costumes, hand puppets, and other odds and ends for Andra's shows.

"Em-hem," Andra said, in imitation of a person clearing their throat. She stood at the curtain. "Sunny and Rainy told me you were backstage again."

"Sorry." I stepped past her and took my appropriate place in one of the rows of mismatched folding chairs.

"Andra, let me know when to start recording." Stacey swiveled the camera toward her. "Just say

'Ready...Action!'"

Andra nodded. She clicked on the flashlights that lit her stage, then turned off the overhead lights before ducking behind the curtains.

I watched the turtle-print bedsheet curtain sway on the line, wondering if the strange shape would return and come at me again tonight. Andra had identified that one as Rainy, the entity dwelling in the windowless closet adorned with patterns of lightning bolts and balloons.

The curtain twitched.

"Ready!" Andra shouted, poking just her face out. She was in her pointy silver HAPPY BIRTHDAY hat from earlier, but she'd left off the green Hulk mask, opting for a freshly painted mustache instead. "Action!"

Stacey gave a thumbs up and started recording, her eyes glued to her camera's screen.

"Ladies and everyone!" Andra bellowed, stepping out in a plastic tuxedo t-shirt and a red Doctor Strange cape. "Step right up and sit right down for the show!" She looked to the door, as if hoping some of her family members might arrive, but none did. "Okay, anyway, here's my first trick!"

Most of the tricks were basically repeats, including one where a stuffed panda bear mysteriously moved from one cabinet to the other. I still couldn't see how she pulled that off.

Noticeably absent was the one I'd actually hoped to record, the spooky sheet trick where one of the resident invisible friends had nearly made itself seen. The grand tamale this time was a card trick, where Andra's guess of my chosen card was incorrect, but I pretended she was right anyway.

"Okay, bedtime, Andra." Nicole showed up at the playroom door.

"First we check the cabinets!" Andra said.

"I know," Nicole said wearily. Ten-year-old Jason ran into the room to join his younger sister in checking over the cabinets and closets of the playroom, making sure everything was closed.

Stacey and I followed at a distance, observing the younger kids' nightly ritual as they moved through the house. I could see how this might get exhausting fast for the parents.

Andra and Jason were focused and thorough, not skipping any corner of any room. They even checked out the laundry room, where Nicole had to reach up to close the louvered cabinet door above the washing machine.

The door-closing party moved upstairs, checking every bathroom, bedroom, and linen closet.

In the master bedroom, Dave sat on the bed with a notebook and a number of bills. He wore reading glasses, which he removed as we entered, while hurriedly pushing the bills together in a stack.

"Cabinet check?" he asked with a big smile.

"Cabinet check." Nicole sighed.

The kids went down the armoire configuration along the wall, checking each drawer and door, fast as an Indy 500 pit crew. They also checked the doors to the upstairs porch.

"All clear?" Dave asked.

"All clear," Jason replied, without a hint of a smile, his dark eyes taking in everything.

"Onward!" Andra raised an imaginary sword and

charged back out into the upstairs hall.

Lonnie's loud, angry music poured out of the open door to his room, with a lead singer ranting about pain and death. We got an earful of it as we approached, as well as a powerful odor like a thousand dirty socks.

"Lonnie, cabinet check!" Andra announced as she walked into his room. "Your closet's open!"

"So deal with it." Lonnie sat on the edge of his bed in a tank top, lifting a dumbbell while he watched a soccer match on television. Posters of sweaty young soccer players from across Europe and Latin America adorned his walls, thumb-tacked to the antique woodwork.

Andra ran to shut Lonnie's closet door. Lonnie stood and smirked, then opened a few drawers and a small cabinet door near the ceiling that neither of his little siblings could reach.

"Lonnie, don't!" Jason hurried to close the drawers. "You'll let Jack out!"

"Oh, no, will I let Jack out?" Lonnie opened the closet door Andra had just closed, cupped his hands around his mouth, and yelled, "Jack! Come out, come out, wherever you are! Andromeda wants to be your friend!"

"Stop it!" Andra wailed, hurrying to close the door again.

"Why should I?" Lonnie re-opened more cabinets.

"Please, Lonnie!" Jason begged, closing them back.

"Pay me a dollar each. I know you still have birthday money, Jason."

"I'll go to my piggy bank." Jason walked out into the hall where we waited.

"Lonnie, don't extort money from your little

brother," Nicole said.

"What?" Lonnie feigned innocence, brushing his clump of purple hair back from his face. "It's the only way he'll learn."

"Learn to do what? Take advantage of people when they're afraid?" Nicole asked. "Andra, Jason, leave Lonnie alone now."

"It's your funeral, bud," Andra told Lonnie, closing the closet door a final time before leaving, then closing Lonnie's bedroom door behind her. "Keep Jack in there with you."

"Whatever," Lonnie grumbled through the door.

Andra and Jason moved on to Penny's room next, knocking on the door while we adults kept our distance.

"What?" Penny snapped from inside.

"Cabinet check!" Andra announced.

"Go away."

Andra pushed open the door.

"Are you deaf?" Penny sat on a single bed inside the room, looking at a tablet. She pulled her headphones down to her shoulders.

"We're just here to check—" Jason began.

"I know why you're here, you little creeps!" Penny snapped. "You can see everything's closed, so get away from my stuff."

Stacey grinned at the huge black and white poster over Penny's bed, featuring five hyper-attractive young men wearing cowboy hats, tight jeans, and not much else. They stared off in different directions as if deep in reverie, a moody vista of mountains and clouds behind them.

"Hey, you like Outlaw?" Stacey asked Penny,

stepping closer to the open door. "That's my favorite cowboy boy band, if I had to pick one."

Penny rolled her eyes. "Yes, obviously I like them."

"Who's your favorite? I like Delmar."

Penny sighed. "Who cares?"

"I thought you liked Branson, the tall one," Nicole said.

"Oh, he's cute, too." Stacey paused, then began to sing in a soft, sad whisper. *"Out on the range alone... feelin' a range of feelings..."*

"Yeah, everyone knows 'Range of Feelings,'" Penny said. "It was in a truck commercial. I'm not even that into Outlaw anymore. They're kinda old now."

"What do you listen to now?" Nicole asked.

"Who cares, mother? Would you brats get out?" Penny barked at her two younger siblings, who'd slipped into her room to check things despite Penny's clear keep-out instructions.

"Jason, Andra, respect your sister's space," Nicole said.

The younger ones left, closing the door behind them just as Penny screamed at them to close it.

Andra and Jason grew apprehensive as we neared the rear of the house.

"Who's going to check Jack's room?" Andra whispered.

"We'll do it," I volunteered. "Where do we go?"

Andra pointed down a short, windowless passage that was almost too narrow for an adult human. One could have almost walked right past without noticing it.

"There's no electricity up there yet," Nicole said. "No lights. Be careful."

"Thanks." I clicked on my flashlight.

I entered the passage. Like most of the upstairs warren, it had been carved out of larger, finer rooms into a miserly amount of space. It appeared to dead end after a few paces, like a pointless blind hallway. Only when I reached the very back did I see the small staircase, set deep out of sight from the casual passerby in the main hall.

The stairs led up to a door that seemed out of place, like the front door to a house, only mounted in the ceiling. It had a brass knob with a lock. At the center of the door was a glass circle where one could presumably look out before opening.

"Should we knock first?" Stacey whispered behind me, shining her light over my shoulder.

"I'd rather not," I said. "What if something answered?"

Stacey swallowed as I reached up and turned the knob, then swung open the door to the attic.

Chapter Ten

A long, rectangular trap door over a staircase was a perfectly rational feature, because when opened it created plenty of head room all the way up the stairs. Square trap doors offered more opportunities to crack your head on the way up or down.

Still, because it looked like a front door embedded in a ceiling, I couldn't help feeling like I was about to step into a different world, one set at a strange angle to our own. Not quite the Upside Down from *Stranger Things*, but maybe the Sideways Over.

I pushed the heavy door as wide as it would go, which was fortunately far enough that I didn't have to hold it open as I ascended the last few stairs. The hinges creaked, shedding dust and rust.

The attic bedroom was spacious compared to many of the rooms downstairs. It looked like it had been carved off from the main attic, taking about a third of the length of the house with it. One wall had been recently painted with a fresh coat of white, presumably covering the graffiti.

A strange wooden bed, easily queen-sized, occupied one corner. Its headboard was like a tree trunk, possibly carved directly from one, reaching to the ceiling with several branches snaking off. Some of the carved limbs curved down along the sides of the bed like thick roots, forming the bed posters and side rails that held up the wooden mattress platform. Others branched off sideways, flat at the top so they could be used as shelving.

A jigsaw pattern of small cabinets and shelves covered the wall that had severed the bedroom from the rest of the attic. This wasn't my first clue that much of the elaborate woodwork had been built after the house was subdivided into a boardinghouse. All the small rooms seemed to have some.

"Hey, some of those cabinets are open," Stacey whispered. "Time to do our jobs."

As we promised the kids, we got to work closing the room up tight, lest any evil spirits come crawling out later on.

Stacey pulled open a closet to find a few shabby, forgotten shirts and ties on hangers, a shelf holding a comb and some toothpicks, odds and ends left behind by travelers over the years. "This room is weird."

"Jack's room. I wonder why they call it that. Just because of the graffiti?" I looked among the root-like bedposts and the limb-like shelves and decorative branches that curved around and above it. I pulled open the drawers built into the lower part of the bedframe and found nothing but a couple of dead spiders.

"It looks like nobody's been here in years." Stacey

waved a hand at the grimy mirror over the dresser. It was too dirty to reflect anything other than a dim echo of our flashlights. "We're definitely returning later to set up gear, right?"

"Of course. In case Jack comes back." I opened one of the many shallow cabinets of different sizes along the wall. Empty, like most of those I'd checked. I closed it again. "Okay. Let's go tell the kids we've secured the attic so they can sleep."

We returned to the stairs...where a shadowy figure waited in the short, dim hall down at the bottom, just beyond the first step. It raised a finger and pointed at us.

"Close that one, too!" she instructed. It was Andra, followed soon after by her brother and mother.

"Don't order our guests around, Andra," Nicole said.

"I got it," I assured her, grunting a little as I lowered the heavy door back into place over our heads while we descended the steps.

"Was anything open?" Jason asked, his voice stuttering and hesitant, very different from his megaphone of a younger sister.

"A couple of little things, but we closed them," I said.

Andra looked back at Jason. He nodded, and the two of them returned to the main hall.

"We'll probably put a camera or two up there," I told Nicole.

"No problem," Nicole said. "Like I said, nobody's allowed up there, anyway. Fixing it up is not really a priority for us right now. You have to pick your battles with a house like this."

I nodded, wondering what kind of battles we might face in the nights ahead.

Stacey and I returned to the van for coffee and snacks. We checked that our monitors were receiving signals from the gear we'd set up, and generally stayed quietly out of the way while Nicole and Dave put their kids to bed.

The lights on the first floor went out. They left the front door unlocked and the porch light on for us.

The upstairs lights went out at a slower pace, until only the master remained, glowing behind the upstairs porch doors.

"No spooky sheet trick tonight, huh?" Stacey asked.

"Nope." I looked over the monitors showing the feeds from the playroom. "Let's hope her invisible friends won't be so invisible to the thermal camera."

"So what do you think is happening there, really?"

"I think the ghosts in the house have reached out to that little girl and developed some kind of relationship with her," I said. "They could be feeding on her energy, and they could have more malevolent intentions."

"The whole family already seems drained and tired. Andra's the only one with any energy left. I mean, I'm sure I'd be tired, too, if I had four kids. Or any kids. No, thank you."

"You don't want kids?" I asked. I wasn't wild on the idea myself, but I'd always imagined Stacey as more of the mom type.

Stacey laughed. "I'm kinda busy, Ellie."

"I mean in the future."

"Oh. Sure. Maybe. I think."

"You and Jacob haven't discussed—"

"No! Why are you being so…oh, my gosh. Did you have this talk with Michael?"

"What? No. Let's go set up in that attic bedroom." I climbed into the back of the van to collect more gear.

"Look at you, totally changing the subject," Stacey said.

"Grab a thermal and a motion detector. If it's the lair of the entity that's scaring the kids, we may as well give it the kitchen sink."

"So, are you guys talking about getting engaged? I see Michael as the type to want a lot of kids."

"We are not…let's keep it professional inside the house, all right?" I lugged a camera case and a duffle bag of gear up the porch steps. "I don't want the clients to think we're idiots."

"Yes, ma'am." Stacey closed the van door and followed after me with black cases of gear and a tripod tucked under her arm. We looked like roadies for a band, and not a very popular one, judging by the age and appearance of our van.

We tiptoed through the front door. Upstairs, we returned to the short, nearly blind hallway and the steep stairs to the attic-bedroom door.

I pushed the door open. "Feels a little cooler up here," I whispered.

"Yep, major red flag," Stacey said as we stepped up into the old bedroom. "Or would it be a blue flag? Since it's suspiciously cold?"

"Sure." I closed the rectangular trap door. "Let's do opposite corners to capture the greatest field." I carried the night vision camera with me to a spot where it could monitor the array of small doors and drawers next to the bedframe.

"Okey-doke." Stacey went to work across the room.

Our small movements setting up the gear were the only sounds up there. The gloomy space, lit only by our portable lights, was not exactly freezing, just abnormally cool by the standards of Deep South attics in the middle of summer. The thermometer built into my EMF meter confirmed this.

A floorboard across the room, nowhere near Stacey or me, gave a long, loud creak.

"Did you hear that?" Stacey whispered.

I swung my flashlight that way. Nothing was there but the rectangular door, lying closed flat on the floor like I'd left it—

No. *Almost* closed.

Eyes peered out from beneath the trap door, but vanished when my light touched them. The door dropped back into place with a thump.

I dashed over to open it again and shone my light down onto the stairs below.

"Okay, we get it!" Penny, the aloof teen girl, threw an arm over her eyes to protect them from the intense glow of my tactical flashlight, which might as well have been a searchlight on a police helicopter. "You're into blinding people for fun."

"Sorry." I pointed the light up into the slanted, cobwebbed rafters instead. "Did we wake you?"

"Like I'm asleep this early. It's only ten. What are *you* doing up here?" She climbed up the stairs and closed the door behind her.

"Did your parents explain why we're here?" I asked.

"Yeah, you think our house is haunted. Because of

Andra's imaginary friends." Penny trudged over to my
night vision camera, peered into the lens, and smiled
and waved enthusiastically as if taking a selfie video
for her LookyLoon account. Then she frowned,
instantly sullen again, and half-heartedly opened and
closed cabinets and drawers at random, idly
rummaging but seeming to find nothing of interest.

"Have you ever experienced anything strange
here?" I returned to my camera, adjusting it.

"Yeah. This room." She sat on the bare bedframe,
largely concealed by the bookshelves, and sighed.
"Look at it."

"Did you see something in here?"

"Yeah. I'm seeing it right now." She pointed at the
mirror over the dresser, the size of a picture window
but too grimy to show our reflections clearly. "There.
And there. And there." She pointed along the wall. "All
this closet space, going to waste, in this room that
should obviously be mine."

"Ooh, yeah, I get it," Stacey said. "You want this
room."

"Um, private staircase? A whole *floor* away from
the brats and the parents? But no. You saw where they
stuck me. I have, like, one window and zero space,
while all this goes to waste." She lay back on the solid
wooden platform of the bed, looked up at the ceiling,
and sighed. "I could be alone up here. Like Rapunzel
before all the princes started showing up and annoying
her." She ran her fingers along one of the thick, curved
branches that framed the bed like wooden tentacles.

"It's nice, but your parents don't seem to think it's
safe yet," I said.

"Yeah, and Dad's taking forever to getting around

to fixing it up."

"Plus, is there a bathroom up here?" Stacey asked.

"No, but I already have to share one with my eight-year-old sister anyway. So I'll walk a little. Who cares?" She sat up. "Do you *really* think you're going to find any ghosts in this house?"

"I'm just keeping an open mind for now," I said.

"What will you do if you find one?"

"We'll help it move on. Or remove it somehow, if it's causing problems."

"You've done that before?"

"We have."

"Oh." She stood up. "Well, I don't think you'll find anything up here. I think my whole family is just freaking out and needs to calm down. And give me this room. Maybe you can tell my parents it's safe for me to have it."

"If that's what we find, that's what we'll tell them. And I think we're just about done here." I opened the trap door, and Stacey walked over to join me beside it. "Good-bye, Penny."

The girl lingered behind, idly opening a drawer and peering inside.

"Have you ever found anything interesting, poking around the house like that?" Stacey asked.

"Just little things." She slid the drawer most of the way shut, but not all the way, then started toward the trap door. "Nothing important."

"We sort of promised your siblings we'd leave everything closed up tight," I said.

"Or what?" Penny snickered. "Jack will come out and get you tonight?" Leaving the drawer open, she walked past us and down the stairs to the second floor.

"Time to go cram myself into my stupid little room."

With a sigh, I walked over and closed the drawer, then passed my light over the room to make sure everything else was still closed.

By the time we left, there was no sign of Penny in the second-floor hall. When we passed the door to her room, it was closed with a slight glow leaking out beneath it, maybe a lamp or a tablet.

We returned up the hall to the room of doors, where the younger kids slept in rooms closer to their parents. The steps to the main attic were through a door near Jason's room, but nobody had reported any disturbances from up there. I was tempted to go have a look at the main attic anyway, but I figured we'd done enough clomping around for one night. I didn't want to spin the roulette wheel and find out which restless, unhappy kid would be our next prize.

Instead, we set up more gear downstairs, where presumably nobody would return until morning, then switched off the porch light, leaving the house in complete darkness.

Then we waited quietly to see whether any ghosts might come out of the woodwork.

Chapter Eleven

"Well, this is exciting," Stacey said a few hours later, yawning and stretching. "Looks like the ghosts have the first-night jitters. Come out, come out, little ghosts. Maybe we should have left a cabinet or two open."

"It hasn't made any difference in the master bedroom." I looked at the mirrored armoire door through the night vision camera. Nicole or Dave had left it slightly open, I assumed by accident, while getting ready for bed. In the mirrored front of the door, I could see part of our camera, as well as the curtains framing the doors to the second-story porch.

I'd kept a particularly close eye on the little rooms that Andra said belonged to her imaginary friends. More like sleeping closets than actual bedrooms, they looked like they'd been designed for small children, and I wanted to know more details, since it seemed like the spirits of those children were still hanging around and interacting with the children who now lived here.

I was just about to open the late-night lunch I'd brought for myself—tuna on not-that-stale sourdough, side of carrot sticks, with no salad dressing for dipping because I'd forgotten it—when Stacey caught something on a thermal camera.

"Look at the closet under the stairs," she said, pointing.

A patch of space near the back of the closet had turned colder than the area around it. We watched it grow to roughly the size and shape of a human torso. Another, smaller patch appeared near it, possibly a hand belonging to the torso, or perhaps a second, weaker entity.

"A draft that far from the outer wall of the house isn't likely," I said. "It's not exactly a cold night out, anyway. Maybe there's an air conditioning leak."

We watched. The cold spots didn't grow much larger or colder, but they kept their general shape as they moved through the closet, past the coats and jackets, toward the door, which was closed tight like every closet door in the house.

They stopped at the door and floated there, as if hesitant to pass through, or unable to do so.

"Looks like the kids are right," Stacey whispered. "Gotta keep those doors closed."

After about ten seconds, the cold spots reversed course, drifting away from the door and back into the depths of the closet.

"That's definitely not the air conditioner," I said. "Unless it has a reverse setting that turns it into a vacuum cleaner."

"And now they're going away," Stacey said, as the

cold spots reached the back of the closet and began to fade. Soon the closet returned to a uniform temperature matching the rest of the first floor. "Bye-bye, Coldy McSpots. I wonder where they're going to go chill next."

"It could be anywhere we can't see, which is most of the house."

"Should we go inside and nose around?"

"Let's keep it hands-off for tonight."

"Patience and watchfulness. Like Zen masters. Got it."

I nodded. Not interfering would give us a better sense of a typical night at the family's home. It also greatly reduced the odds of another unexpected kid encounter, which I was not in the mood to manage. The kids probably knew more about any restless spirits in the house than their parents, but I had to walk a delicate balance and not freak them out with direct but frightening questions like *Can you describe the scary man who haunts your house at night?*

As time went by, and more of nothing happened, I picked up my tablet for a little preliminary historical research.

The Timbermill Chamber of Commerce website focused on the trendy new downtown and local real estate for sale. A schedule of upcoming community events included a Fourth of July celebration in the town park, culminating in a laser show and lighted drone display in lieu of fireworks "out of consideration for our honored war veterans (and our pets!)." Very trendy.

The website's history tab was nothing if not upbeat.

Exciting opportunities

await your family and/or business in the "new" old town of Timbermill! Now Savannah's most sought-after suburb!

A Traditional-Modern Family Community

Timbermill offers modern living in a historic setting, and an easy commute to Savannah and other local destinations. A welcoming place full of Southern charm and the warmth of yesteryear, yet globally connected by new fiber-optic cables. Experience the best of both worlds here in Timbermill!

An Interesting History

Founded in 1911 by a group of investors, Timbermill was built among Georgia's ancient, untouched forests. Soon, fine lumber flowed out from the steam-powered sawmill and down the rail line to the port of Savannah. A woodworking factory and other industry sprang up around the mill.

Timbermill grew into a classic American family town, a happy and productive place full of fine homes and shops. Neighbors sang Christmas carols and hunted Easter eggs in the town park.

Sadly, the mill's closing in 1961 sent the lovely town into decline. The factories closed and the trains stopped coming. The population shrank as young people moved away.

A Bright Future

Now this historic jewel of a community has been polished up for the new century! Timbermill is growing like never before, with luxurious neighborhoods and a beautifully refurbished downtown. Will you join the Timbermill craze and become a part of this amazing town's bright future?

"Well, that was a little low on hard facts," I muttered.

"Don't worry, the house is a little low on paranormal activity," Stacey said. "Maybe the spooky sheet trick really was just a trick."

"Then that eight-year-old's an amazing magician."

"Maybe a stage-magic prodigy."

I returned to my tablet, looking up local newspaper archives. Timbermill, I discovered, once had its own paper, *The Timbermill Ledger*, but it had been defunct since 1970, and nobody had been helpful enough to digitize and upload the print run. Hopefully I could find it on microfilm at the library.

We had paid subscriptions to access the digital archives of larger area papers, so I searched the *Savannah Morning News* archives for mentions of the little town. I mostly found reports on timber and lumber production and advertisements for the town's housewares, tools, and furniture. Lathe-turned house trim like decorative spandrels, corbels, and gingerbreading were "guaranteed to lend your home an air of noble aristocracy."

One headline stood out: *Local Girl Missing in Timbermill*. The story had been far from front-page news in Savannah, buried in a back corner of the paper, an almost reluctant public service of relaying a story from the hinterlands. The story was from 1938, in the depths of the Great Depression.

> A 12-year-old girl, Solange Tondreau, resident of Timbermill's boardinghouse district, has been missing for nine days. Her mother, the widow Aurelie Tondreau,

operates the boardinghouse at
73 Park Circle for its owner,
the widow Ida Collins. The
lost child is described as
flaxen-haired like her mother,
last seen wearing a cotton
sleeping gown. Any sightings
should be reported to police.

I recognized 73 Park Circle right away as our
clients' address.

The article didn't include a photograph, so it
seemed pretty unlikely to have provided much help in
locating the missing kid.

I plugged Solange's name back into the search, but
no additional articles showed up. Searching her
mother's name didn't return any new information,
either. Whatever the outcome had been in the case, the
Savannah paper hadn't covered it. Hopefully I could
exhume that information from the *Ledger* microfilm, if
the library had it.

"Ellie!" Stacey whispered, pointing frantically at
one of the monitors. "Look!"

On the monitor showing Dave and Nicole's room,
one thing had clearly changed—the mirrored armoire
door was now wide open. We could see assorted
blouses and blazers hanging inside. Shoes lined the
armoire's inner floor.

"Did that just open?" I asked. "Can you replay it?"

"On it."

We watched the recorded video.

A minute earlier, all had been calm in the bedroom.
The green tones of our night vision camera showed the

armoire, with the curtains of the upper-porch doors reflected in its mirrored door.

I watched closely, holding my breath.

"Did that curtain move?" I whispered.

"I don't think so. Just watch," she whispered back.

The view didn't seem to change, until—

A pale shape appeared inside the glass, the palm of a hand pressing against the inside of the mirror.

I jumped back in my seat. "That's in the mirror, but not a reflection."

"Nope." Stacey's eyes were glued to the screen.

The armoire door swung open—silently, since we didn't have a microphone in that room—and the mirror on its front moved out of sight, replaced by the smooth, blank back side of the armoire door. The clothes hanging inside swayed and then settled down, like they'd been given a small push, or someone had just walked through them.

"Then what happened?" I turned to the live feed on the monitor, where the clothes had stopped swaying and the door remained halfway open.

"That's all we can see. Do you think Nicole and Dave are okay in there?"

"I…hope so." We couldn't see anything much beyond the armoire area, by design to protect their privacy, but it would have helped at the moment if we could see whether an entity might be moving into their room, menacing them as they slept.

I looked out the van window and up at the second-floor porch. The doors remained dark and still, curtains drawn, giving no hint of what might be happening inside. I lowered the driver-side window and listened carefully but didn't hear any sort of yelling or screaming to indicate immediate danger.

"Let's wait and see," I decided. "Barging into their room this late could make us very unpopular. They've survived plenty of nights here already. But we'll stay in high alert mode."

"I guess that means putting my shoes back on." Stacey sighed and reached for her sneakers.

"Which microphone is closest to their room?" I asked.

"Um...probably the one near the inner wall of the attic. It's not super close, though. We just didn't put much on the second floor."

"Turn up the volume on that one."

She did, until the speaker let out a low electronic hum. We still didn't hear any shouts or screams.

We did pick up one voice, though, soft and low. It was one of the kids, but definitely not Lonnie.

"I won't tell," the voice whispered, hard to hear through crackling static. "I promise."

"Who was that?" Stacey asked.

"I'm not sure." I motioned for her to stay quiet, waiting to see if more words arose from below. I noted the time: one-thirty in the morning.

We waited a few minutes, but we didn't hear the voice again.

"Did it record anything leading up to that?" I asked.

"I'll start a few minutes back." Stacey pulled up the audio recording.

We listened carefully.

The first thing the voice had said was simply "Hi." Then there was a long pause, then, "Yes." The voice murmured a few things we couldn't make out, between long pauses, as if we were hearing one side of a conversation. The next thing we heard clearly was, "I think they're looking for you." Finally, it repeated what we'd heard before. "I won't tell, I promise."

Chapter Twelve

"Okay, that gave me chills," Stacey said.

"I think it's definitely a kid. Jason, Andra, maybe Penny?"

Stacey shrugged. "Hard to tell. It's probably not Andra talking to her invisible friends from the magic show, since we already know about them."

"Let's set up more microphones tomorrow, in the main attic and in some of the little unused rooms on the second floor. We need to figure out who this is and what they're doing."

"Feels kinda like we're spying on these kids, though."

"Yep, that's basically the plan."

After a few more hours, it became apparent that the house had gone silent for the night, and soon the night sky lightened to purple. Stacey prepared clips of what we'd seen—the cold spot in the closet, the armoire opening, the shape of a hand inside the glass—to show the clients the next day.

I yawned as I climbed up front and started the van's engine.

We drove past the crumbling, empty mill and long-forgotten factories, over the weedy railroad tracks and through the trendy part of town, then on past the newly built subdivisions along the highway.

Back in Savannah, the town was just waking up, the gray morning light beginning to seep through the canopy of trees that would soon help defend pedestrians on the streets and sidewalks against the blistering summer sun.

Like a vampire, though, I would be holed up in my lair, blackout curtains drawn tight against the day.

My cat greeted me with a slow blink when I arrived. He lay like an indolent prince atop the carpet-covered cat condo I'd recently bought him. The green flakes all over his furry black face told me he'd found the catnip sprinkled inside. Like a mom juggling a demanding career and a small child, I'd resorted to buying gifts to try to make up for leaving him all the time.

I stretched out on my sagging couch and tried to relax with a book someone at kickboxing had recommended—*The Silver Pigs,* a murder mystery set in ancient Rome—but the case wouldn't leave my mind.

Eventually, I grabbed my tablet and pulled up the footage Stacey had marked to carve out for the clients. I again watched the cold spots arise in the downstairs closet, only to retreat from the closed door and withdraw.

Later, the armoire, already left open, had opened

wider.

I paused it at the moment when the mirrored door began to move, then I played it at ultra-low speed, studying the brief glimpse of the entity in the mirror.

The pale hand shape pressed against the inside of the glass. The hand was gauzy and pale, not a fully formed apparition. I could see through it to a blurred reflection of the porch-door curtains.

Something else appeared above the hand, just briefly, before the door's mirrored front swung out of sight to show the clothes swaying inside the closet. I backed up the video in slow motion.

A thin, white oval shape, almost like a white thumbprint, floated above the hand, superimposed over the porch curtain behind it. I paused the image. As I stared at it, I began to make out the suggestion of eyes, clear holes where the view of the curtain behind it was sharp instead of hazy. There were hints of a nose and mouth.

I thought of the scribbled faces of Jack in Jason's drawings.

So I put that aside and tried to think of less creepy things as I turned out my lamp, leaving my apartment pitch black.

I pulled the sheet up to my neck and closed my eyes.

In the darkness of my mind, I saw again the human shape in the sheet that had swelled toward me during Andra's magic show, reaching out to me, enshrouding me. I could almost feel how cold it had been.

My cat chose that moment to pounce on my feet in the dark, and I may have cried out a little.

It took a while to get to sleep.

I got up around noon, downed a couple shots of coffee, and walked about two miles through downtown Savannah to the city's main public library on Bull Street. I called Stacey as I walked through the park.

The library was a comforting sight, one of my favorite spots in the city. Its white marble facade resembled an austere Greek temple, but its doors opened onto a warm, welcoming interior full of sunlight and curved walls upheld by funky purple columns.

I soon occupied a seat in the microfilm room, searching through copies of the *Timbermill Ledger* from 1938, starting a couple of weeks before the missing-girl had run in the Savannah paper. Fortunately, issues of the *Ledger* did not run nearly as long as issues of the *Savannah Morning News*, so I could skim quickly.

Soon I found what I was looking for. The headline read *GIRL MISSING FOR THREE DAYS.* A black and white photo showed Solange, her long hair tied back with a ribbon. She looked cheerful, with sparkling eyes and a wide smile.

I read the article below the picture, skimming over the information I already knew.

>...a happy presence in the boisterous atmosphere of the boardinghouse, young Solange is sorely missed by her mother Aurelie, who has no idea where her daughter might have gone.

"Lots of men come through
that boardinghouse," reports
police chief Kilborne. "Plenty
of good working folks, but of
late there's been drifters and
degenerates coming in by rail.
We'll keep searching the
woods around town and see
what turns up."

The paper didn't mention any suspects. I also
noticed that the paper didn't quote the mother directly,
but reserved quotes for the police chief, as well as a
random millworker who lived in the boardinghouse and
called the missing girl "real pretty and friendly."

I flipped ahead, issue by issue, skimming for news
of the case.

There was nothing else—until I found Solange's
obituary, published about three weeks after she'd gone
missing.

Unfortunately, even this left me with more
questions than answers. The cause of death was not
given, nor was there any mention of how she'd gone
missing or where she'd been found.

I printed paper copies of what little I'd discovered,
then took a break and went outside to call Stacey.

"She died," I said when Stacey answered.

"Oh, no! Wait, who?"

"Solange. In 1938."

"The missing girl? What happened?"

"I'm still piecing that together. The local newspaper
was weirdly silent about it, considering they reported
her missing. I don't see how there's no follow-up piece,

especially if the girl was found dead. How'd you like to visit the Timbermill police department with me?"

"The town's big enough for a police department?"

"Let's hope the police were more interested in her case than the newspaper."

"I'm ready. Also, I've got those clips all shortened up, ready for the clients. Should I just send them?"

"Sure."

"What about the audio of the talking kid?"

I hesitated. "Let's keep that to ourselves until we have a better picture of what's going on." This felt like an ethical gray area, but those could happen.

I went back inside, hoping to dig up something more than what I'd found so far about the missing girl.

Chapter Thirteen

"So, did you dig up anything more?" Stacey asked as she climbed into the van.

"Nothing about the girl," I said.

"Weird that the papers would care more about her going missing than turning up dead."

"Very weird. I did find another obituary from several months earlier that could shed some light, or maybe make things more confusing."

"Was it Solange's father? Is that why the papers didn't mention him?"

"No, it was Ida Collins."

Stacey frowned. "Who?"

"She owned the boardinghouse, and her obit was much less skimpy. Apparently, her husband was one of the original managers at the old mill, and the house was built for them. When he passed away, she began taking on boarders. When she died, ownership of the house passed to her nephew, Charles Collins of Watkinsville,

Georgia."

"What did he do with the house?"

"The obituary didn't say. Maybe we can dig up the property title history while we're at town hall."

"Sounds super-fun," Stacey muttered.

We drove out along the rural highway to Timbermill, making good time since there wasn't much traffic to slow us down.

The town hall, containing its entire government, was a two-story brick building near the railroad tracks, on the still-inhabited side of things. The front door opened onto a narrow, musty lobby area without a human in sight.

Framed black and white pictures on the wall showed scenes from the town's glory days. Some showed the mill and factory under construction. One showed a big Christmas tree in the park, surrounded by people holding open hymnals and singing. Another showed kids in their Sunday best scrambling all over, while someone in a creepy bucktoothed Easter bunny costume with beady eyes presided over them from the bandstand.

"Looks like whoever wrote the town history for the website just cribbed their notes from these pictures," I said.

We followed the sign to the police department, which consisted of a few desks. The only officer there looked maybe three years older than me. He occupied a desk in the corner, watching a black and white video on a tablet, oblivious to our presence.

"Uh, hello?" I knocked on the open door.

The young cop looked up at us, startled, and jumped to his feet.

"Hey there." He looked between us briefly, like he was trying to figure out if he knew us. "What can I do for you?"

"We're in the middle of some historical research around town," I said, keeping it deliberately vague. "And we were hoping to look at an old missing-person case."

"Okay." He scratched his head. "Sorry, are y'all locals?" His accent was deep and slow; maybe he was from the South Carolina Lowcountry. "I'm just getting my bearings around here."

"Are you not local?"

"I just moved here from Cola City about six months ago," he said.

"Where's that?"

"It's a nickname for Columbia, South Carolina. Also called Soda City."

"What soda is made there?" Stacey asked.

"I don't think there is one." He scratched his head again.

"So how did you end up here?" I asked him.

"It seemed like a good opportunity. I mean, police chief, whoa! Am I right? Do you know how many twenty-eight-year-old dudes have that kind of job title? Chief Tyler Masterton. It's a pretty sweet set-up."

"What happened to the previous chief?"

He shrugged and made an "I don't know" kind of humming sound. "Mm-mmm. What are y'all researching, again?"

"A girl who went missing in 1938."

"Oh, snap! That's from before."

"Sorry, what does that mean?" I asked.

He leaned against the edge of his desk and popped

open a can of Mountain Dew Code Red, then slurped it contemplatively. I glanced around the cramped, dingy office. He'd hung his framed degree on the wall, a bachelor's in management from the University of South Carolina business school, next to a pennant featuring their mascot, a gamecock, which I think refers to cockfights. A matching rooster paperweight perched on his desk. This guy would have loved the Chicken Salad Shack. I might have even seen a Gamecocks flag among the chicken memorabilia there.

"Okay," he said, after killing half his Dew and letting out a sigh. "So, the town government of Timbermill was what they call 'dormant' for a long time. Since, like, eighty-eight, eighty-nine. I mean, we are talking the disco era here."

"I think that was the seventies," Stacey said.

"Who knows? Anyway, yeah, the population crashed hard and fast once the mill closed back in the day. I guess you could say Miller time was over, huh? It shrank so much they stopped bothering to elect anybody."

"There's been no municipal government for decades?" I asked.

"Yeah, but now this *new* town council came along —they're pretty much all real estate developer types— and they were like, 'Hey, yo, this town needs a police force and stuff.' And it turns out one of those guys was a USC Delta Sig Ep like me—he was class of '79. Crazy good luck, right? I actually knew his nephew, Wilmont. Wet Willie, we used to call him. Boom, now I'm running this town. But the bosses keep saying they want me to act like the sheriff from Mayberry, which is this old TV show, so I'm still hitting the books on that."

He tapped his tablet, and the *Andy Griffith* theme whistled out of it.

"I can see you're studying hard," I said. "We don't mean to slow you down. Do you know where we could find any files from 1938?"

"Yeah, that's gonna be a deep basement-er, with all the old files and junk. TBH, I have not spent much time down in that basement. We're going to need, like, a professional organizing company or something. Do they have those?"

"Do you mind if we have a look?" I asked.

"Uh." He scratched his chin. "Am I allowed to let you do that?"

"For sure. You're the chief."

"Right. I mean, hey, what are they going to do, arrest me?" He grinned and started toward a door near the back of the room.

The chief led us downstairs to a bleak basement, lit by only a few bulbs, with rusty, dripping pipes snaking overhead.

"There are...definitely files here," Stacey said, looking at the heaps of mildewed folders, very possibly the source of the smell from upstairs. Some files lay in drawers that had been pulled out from file cabinets and stacked haphazardly. More were crammed into the built-in shelves and cabinets along the walls, while others lay strewn across tables or piled on the floor, soaking up the dripping water.

"Like I said, I'm not proud of this basement, so let's keep the judgment minimal," the chief said. "I keep putting off dealing with it, with so much else going on. I guess you could say I keep gettin' my britches caught on my own pitchfork."

"Huh?" Stacey asked.

"It's a line from that *Andy Griffith* guy. Did it sound natural, like I dropped it in right?"

"Not really," Stacey said. "But close. You'll get there."

"Cool. So, like you can see, the basement's a wreck. Maybe give me six, seven, ten, twelve months to get it straightened out, you can come back and have a look."

"We're kind of in a hurry," I said. "We don't mind digging through it by ourselves, at all."

"You don't?" He gave me a suspicious look, as if my apparent enthusiasm for heaps of old paperwork was a sure sign of a criminal mind. "Do y'all live in town or what?"

"We're working for an investor who purchased one of Timbermill's historic homes and wants to learn about its past." I gave him one of our business cards, which do not actually mention ghosts or any other things that go bump in the night. "The investor is considering future real estate purchases around town."

"Private investigators? Wow. I did not expect that." He gaped at us like creatures in an alien zoo. "Okay. Well, I'll have to go upstairs and check your license, for, like, due diligence, I think? But as long as that checks out, you can have at it, if you really want to." He cast a dubious look at all the files. "Feel free to organize them a little as you go."

"Thanks, bro! Up top!" Stacey raised a hand to him, speaking his language like a native, and he grinned and slapped her a high five.

"You got it, detective," he said. "Hey, let me know if y'all want coffee or anything. My mom sent me a French press. I'm still trying to figure it out, but it might turn out okay."

"I may take you take up on that," I said.

"Sweet. I'll break out the bean grinder for sure." He headed upstairs.

I began rummaging through the nearest loose drawer of files. The drawers had been pulled from dusty wooden filing cabinets built into the wall, leaving a honeycomb of open, dark cavities there. A few drawers remained where they were supposed to be, but not many.

"Where do we even start?" Stacey grimaced as she opened the water-damaged top folder on a nearby stack, using her fingertips like tweezers in order to touch it as little as possible. "I wish I had my gloves."

"I wish I had my flashlight," I said.

"Should I run up to the van?"

"Grab some of Chief Tyler's coffee while you're up there."

"Do you want fries with that, ma'am?"

"If at all possible, yes."

While she climbed away up the sagging, creaky steps, I looked from one file to the next, trying to be methodical, but it was all madness down there. To begin with, I needed to find papers from the right decade.

It was a mess, though. I picked up one folder to see yellowed typewritten reports from the 1970s. Much too recent. I checked another folder, and then another. There wasn't much in the way of chronological order.

A rusty creak sounded behind me.

I turned, looking toward the back of the dim basement.

A narrow closet door was open. I hadn't noticed it

before, tucked beyond the built-in shelves and hidden behind bulky items like sawhorses and a stack of traffic cones. The closet was in a side wall, not the back wall, so I couldn't see into it without getting closer.

I stepped toward it, reaching instinctively for the flashlight at my utility belt, but it wasn't there because I wasn't wearing my gear. I hadn't wanted to look too loony when asking the local police for help, and I hadn't expected to encounter anything paranormal while digging through the town's old records during daylight hours. Maybe it was the ghost of someone who'd died of boredom among all this paperwork.

The temperature grew noticeably colder as I approached the open closet, weaving my way among the junk of decades past. I kept my distance from the closet itself, approaching along the wall opposite it.

The ceiling bulb nearest the back of the basement didn't do much to cut the gloom. It sputtered, close to death.

It was a narrow closet, but almost eight feet tall, and deep enough that I couldn't see much as I tried to peer into it.

Something moved in there. I couldn't see it, but I heard it, a metallic clank like a hammer striking metal.

Then it dropped onto the floor and came my way.

A tin can rolled across the concrete, spilling out a trail of rusty nails as it spun toward me. I stopped it with the toe of my boot.

The ceiling light bulb finally went out with a crackle, leaving the back area of the basement in shadow, like darkness had flooded out of the closet. I couldn't distinguish the darkness within the closet from the darkness around me, but I kept staring in the same direction, waiting for my eyes to adjust, waiting for whatever lurked in the closet to make its move.

As my vision finally adjusted, I discerned two circular shapes with dark spots in the center, faintly visible near the top of the closet.

Eyes. A pair of eyes stared at me from the closet, but they were too high up for any normal person, as if the entity within were giant-sized. Ghosts can take any form, really. Most tend to wear a version of their appearance in life, but others take different forms, often horrifying ones, whether by choice or because their self-image is monstrous rather than human. Truly old spirits may have shed their humanity altogether, twisting over the centuries into demonic shapes.

I stared back, torn between my desire to learn more about the case and the reality that I had no defenses on hand.

Avoiding any sudden moves, I backed away from the closet and toward the rickety stairs, which seemed impossibly distant.

The eyes in the closet didn't blink.

Footsteps approached.

"Hey, it took him forever to work the French press, but it's not bad." Stacey clomped down the stairs, a mug of coffee in each hand, utility belt strapped on, tactical flashlights holstered at her hips. "No French fries, but he has *beaucoup de* Hot Pockets if you're really…" She seemed to notice that I wasn't there, at least not in the lighted portion of the basement. "Ellie?"

I worried that speaking, like moving too fast, could potentially trigger the entity into moving, but I didn't have much choice. "Stacey, lights! Now!"

Then I bolted toward her, to the extent that I could

bolt without tripping and falling on the clutter. I figured if I was going to yell, I might as well put some distance between myself and the ghostly eyes.

"Oh, cripes, hang on." Stacey set the coffee mugs down on the basement stairs and drew her flashlights. The process seemed to stretch out forever, though it was probably just a few seconds.

I tripped over a stack of files on the floor, knocking them over like a snow heap. I lost my balance and landed on one knee.

Stacey's double-barrel flashlight blast filled the basement with white light, revealing the scattered files and piles of debris. The tin can marked where I'd stood, the long trail of nails behind it too rusty to glint even in the bright light. It had seemed like a pretty clear threat to me, rolling the can full of tetanus-riddled sharp points in my direction.

Nothing stood in the basement behind me. If the entity had pursued me, then the intense lights had driven it back.

"Thanks," I said.

"You got it." Stacey passed me a flashlight. "What happened?"

"The closet opened. Watch out for nails." I approached the closet again, armed with the power of light this time, and told her what had happened.

Finally, I reached the closet and pointed the light inside.

The eyes shone back at me, reddish.

Stacey gasped. "Is that what I think it is?"

"Yeah," I replied, seeing it clearly at last.

"It's even more awful in person."

Feeling a mix of relief and embarrassment, I stared

at the red glass eyes and filthy, dusty pink hide of the
Easter bunny costume from the old pictures, the one
that had probably given kids more nightmares than
happy memories. It had been stuffed onto the top shelf
of the closet, facing outward. The mask's actual
eyeholes appeared to be the wide nostrils of the bunny's
nose, below the glass eyes, which were just for show. I
wondered whether the costume maker was malevolent,
wanting to scare kids, or just had poor costuming skills.

"Is everything okay now?" Stacey asked.

"I'm not sure." I moved closer to the closet,
watching my step so nothing stabbed me through the
foot. I peered into the second shelf, the one below the
costume, which held a rust-splotched hammer and a
few loose nails. "The can must have come from here.
The shelf runs all the way to the brick wall of the
foundation, but there's nothing but cobwebs back there.
I suppose a rat could have knocked the can over—"

"Oh, please, let it be a ghost and not a rat," Stacey
whispered, looking at the heaps of files we needed to
search. Many were large enough to conceal a rat's nest.

"—but there would be little rat-prints in the dust."

"So a ghost threw the nails at you?" she asked in a
hopeful tone.

"Maybe." With the flashlight beam, I traced the
course of the spilled nails, then shook my head. "We
should clean these up so nobody steps on them. Let's
watch our backs down here."

Chapter Fourteen

"I'm still not finding anything about Solange," Stacey complained an hour later. We'd swept up the nails with a dusty broom we'd found, and then kept digging through files. We'd located police paperwork dated with the correct year, but nothing mentioning our missing girl.

"We have to wrap it up soon. Dave and Nicole are expecting us." I glanced toward the closet door, making sure the rabbit costume wasn't getting possessed and starting to move, like I'd kept imagining since discovering it.

We were just about to call it quits when Stacey shouted.

I turned, worried something had crept out and grabbed her, but she was waving a stained manila folder in my direction.

"Got it!" she announced.

"Are you serious? I'd given up on finding anything

today." I took the folder, laid it on an old desk we'd partially uncovered, and carefully opened it.

The file contained a few faded photographs, including the one of Solange that had run in the local paper. Others showed the girl at a younger age. She was usually with her mother, Aurelie, whose haughty beauty and French name would surely have made her an exotic presence in the rural mill town, even in her threadbare Depression-era day dress.

"So that's the lady who ran the boardinghouse," Stacey said. "I wonder what happened to her."

"Take pictures of every page." I pulled out my phone, while Stacey drew out a pocket camera with a much higher resolution.

The police notes stated that Aurelie was a young widow originally from Tours, France. Aurelie had moved to America with her young daughter Solange, arriving at the port of Savannah. She eventually found steady work in Timbermill, cooking and cleaning at the boardinghouse for its elderly owner, a much older widow named Ida Collins, who perhaps took sympathy on Aurelie.

The last page in the file was folded in half. I opened it gently, trying not to tear the fragile yellow paper. A photograph slid out and landed face down on the floor.

We looked at the paper first. It was full of scrawled, jotted notes, like a small addendum to the main file about the missing girl:

Also missing – Raynard, 7 – second child of Aurelie, disappeared one week later

"Wait, a whole other kid went missing?" Stacey asked. "How is that a footnote?"

I picked up the photograph from the floor and turned it over.

The boy in the picture stood alone, dressed in a bowtie, suspenders, and flat wool cap, his eyes huge and frightened, like he was scared of the camera or the photographer. He might have been six or seven in the picture. While Solange and her mother were fair-skinned and light-haired, the little boy in the picture had dark skin and curly black hair.

"Different fathers, you think?" Stacey asked.

"And the local police and newspapers clearly thought one child was more important than the other." I took a snapshot of the photograph and the accompanying paperwork with my phone. "Raynard. That sounds a lot like 'Rainy,' doesn't it?"

"The invisible friend from the spooky sheet trick?" Stacey asked.

"And if Andra finds it hard to say French names like 'Solange' and 'Raynard'—"

"Then maybe she simplifies them to Sunny and Rainy."

"But that still leaves open the question of why they went missing, and why Solange died, and whether this has anything to do with the 'Jack' character that the kids seem afraid of—"

The closet door slammed wide open against the basement wall, like a hurricane was blowing through.

I turned in time to see the can of nails, which we'd gone to all the trouble to gather up, hurtling through the air toward my head.

"Look out!" I moved to protect Stacey while also

turning my back toward the closet to protect myself. I really should have ducked instead, because the can cracked into the back of my head. Starbursts exploded behind my eyes as I staggered.

The nails exploded from the can, showering us with sharp points.

"Ellie! Get down!" Stacey shouted, though I was already off balance and drifting down to my knees anyway.

I heard the whooshing sound of something approaching from the darkness. The entity was making its move.

Stacey gripped her tactical light with both hands like a baseball bat. She swung it at a small, dark object that came flying toward us. My blurred vision finally registered that the old hammer had been flung through the air, in the general direction of Stacey's ribcage, which it could definitely damage at that speed.

I held my breath as her flashlight swept toward the hammer, momentarily blinding me with light, so that I heard the crunching impact rather than saw it.

Stacey let out a pained grunt and stumbled into me, dropping to join me on the floor.

At the same time, something crashed into the desk where we'd been working, scattering the files on the missing children.

"Did it get you?" I started checking her for injuries.

"I got it." She held up her flashlight to show me the deep dent in its side and gave me a pained half-grin. "Whacked it with everything I had. I think I pulled something in my side though, yikes. How's your head?"

"Fine," I said, though it ached. I pushed my way up, trying to ignore my throbbing head, and shone my light toward the closet door.

"Let's get out of here, Ellie," Stacey said.

"In a second. I want to see it if I can." I looked on the desk, where the hammer had landed after Stacey struck it out of the air. "Nice batting skills, by the way."

"Thanks! I was a Wildcat back in Montgomery. Fifth-grade softball champs? Surely you've heard of us."

"I may have seen something about that on ESPN." I advanced toward the closet door instead of taking the stairs out of the basement. Stacey sighed and followed me.

We looked inside, and the Creepster Bunny stared back at us, but the attacking entity had fled the scene.

Footsteps thudded on the stairs.

"Hey, or maybe howdy, y'all." Chief Tyler came about halfway down the stairway before stopping. "I heard some loud noises. Everything copacetic? I mean, y'all folks doin' all right 'round these parts? How's that?"

"It's pretty non-copacetic, actually," I said, while Stacey and I hustled toward the stairs. "To be honest, I think you might have a ghost problem. I would not come down here at night, or alone. And watch out for rusty nails."

We climbed up past him, leaving him to survey the messy basement, which was only messier after our visit.

"Well, I'll be," the young chief said, almost to himself as Stacey and I returned upstairs. He repeated the phrase, testing different ways of drawling out the syllables. "Weeeellll, I'll be. Well, I'llllll be." Then he cleared his throat and followed us up.

Chapter Fifteen

Stacey and I hurried out of the building, lest anything more be flung at us. The back of my head was tender, but it wasn't bleeding, so things could have been worse.

"So is the whole town haunted or what?" Stacey asked.

"Maybe. I wonder if it was stirred up by our investigation."

"You think that was one of the kid ghosts? Or maybe Jack?"

"We don't know anything about 'Jack' except some graffiti and what the younger kids said."

"Basically, we don't know jack about Jack."

"But we need to." I headed for the Red Caboose hair salon. "Maybe the coffee man's hairdresser with all the local stories is on duty."

As we approached, the glowing OPEN sign went dark. Through the plate-glass window, I could see a lady at the front desk, ringing up a customer while chatting rapidly. The desk lady was tall, her hair long and black with bold streaks of metallic red. Her face was wrinkled, like she was more elderly than her heavy-metal hair color implied.

The bell on the door jingled as I opened it.

"Oh, sorry, we're closed!" the lady at the desk said. "I can make an appointment in just one sec, as soon I get done checking her out, how would that be?"

"Thanks," I said.

"Can we browse?" Stacey asked, angling for a nearby display of hair-care products.

"Please do. Everything on the top shelf's ten percent off."

While Stacey did that, I looked along the walls, taking in the detailed work of the wainscoting, where floral designs were carved into the top rail.

"We'll see you next month," the desk lady told her customer. Then she called over to Stacey, "Anything I can help you with, hun?"

"We're looking for Dorothy," I said.

"That's me, I'm Doro," she said. "You want an appointment?"

"I heard you were sort of a local historian," I told her.

"Historian? I don't know about that." She chuckled. "But I am from Timbermill originally, and there aren't many of us around."

"She knows *everything* about Timbermill," said her customer, who was gradually drifting toward the door while checking her phone. The customer was thirtyish, dressed in yoga pants, and her just-styled hair looked fantastic.

"We're studying local legends," I said. "This may sound crazy, but have you ever heard stories about a ghost who comes out of cabinets? Called Jack? The other side of town has some graffiti about it."

"Ugh, they need to knock down everything on the other side of the tracks," the yoga-panted customer said. "But this side of town is *so nice.* We just moved here three months ago, and we love it. What's this about a ghost?"

"It's nothing," Doro said, but she looked suddenly nervous. "Just an old story the kids used to tell each other. Older kids love to scare younger kids, you know. You have a good night, Brooke."

"Oh, okay. You too." The lady seemed mildly disappointed as she left.

"Now, did you want to buy some of that product or not?" Doro asked Stacey. "I'd recommend the Golden Glitter shampoo for you. Goes real good with that shade of blonde."

"We'd definitely be interested in hearing about that ghost," I said.

Doro shook her head. "It's better to leave that in the past."

"But it's not in the past," I said. "I know people who just moved here, and their kids are already talking about it. They say Jack will come out at night if they don't take precautions."

"That's what we used to say growing up. They'd say Jack comes out looking for kids to steal at night."

"Do you have any idea where the legend came from?" I asked. "Is it based on something real?"

"It's not pleasant to talk about, I'll tell you that much." She turned off the salon's lights and opened the front door. Stacey and I stepped out to the sidewalk, and she followed, locking the door behind her. I guess Doro had decided it wasn't worth staying late to try to sell Stacey a bottle of shampoo. "Sure is nice out tonight."

"Was Jack involved with any kids who went missing?" I asked.

Doro narrowed her eyes at me. "You know more about it than you were letting on."

"Well, a friend of ours bought an old house in town, and we started researching it for her. We're sort of amateur historians."

"Which house?"

"It's on the other side of the tracks. We're trying to put the house's history together, and we've been reading through old issues of the *Timbermill Ledger*, but nothing's come up."

"Oh, I used to read the funnies in the *Ledger* every Sunday," Doro said. "One time they published a picture of me and my friends, after we won the scarecrow-building contest at the fall festival. I was in the very last class to graduate before they closed the high school."

"Why did they close it?" I asked.

"The town kept getting smaller, so I guess it was cheaper to bus the leftover kids to the county school. They closed the elementary school not long after. The town was dying. But now people are coming back."

"Maybe they'll reopen the schools," Stacey said, as if hoping to cheer her up.

"Or build a new one, more likely. Probably cheaper than bringing back the old places." She looked us over carefully. "Your friends have kids, huh? And they talk about Jack?"

"That's what got us started," I said. "We want to know if there's any sort of troubling history in their neighborhood. Anything someone would want to know if they lived there." I looked over at the Turntables Cafe. "Any chance we could bribe you with a cookie or a muffin?"

"Young lady, I don't do fifty-five crunches a day just to bury it all under cookie dough. But I wouldn't mind a chamomile tea. And bring it out here to me. I don't want the coffee man overhearing me and thinking I'm crazy. He's new in town, and he's not bad-looking."

"Stacey, can you take care of that?" I asked, not wanting to leave Doro out here waiting alone, in case she changed her mind and decided to leave. "And maybe a Nancy Sinatra for me?"

"Yeppers-peppers," Stacey said, skipping down the sidewalk toward the coffee shop.

"Does she always talk that way?" Doro asked.

"Kids these days, with their Pokémon and their cat memes. What are you going to do?" I shrugged, as if Stacey were four generations instead of four years younger than me. "But I am growing concerned that there could be something to this story of ghosts. Like Jack."

"That's one your friends really ought to know about." She sighed and sat down on a wooden bench, freshly painted bright purple as part of Timbermill's fun-and-funky restored downtown. "Just don't tell anyone you heard it from me. Not like you're going to run into anyone who cares, because almost nobody's left who's originally from here."

"Okay, no problem."

"I might have been eight or nine when I first heard of him," Doro said. "Down at the school playground. Kelly Mayhew said Jack crawled out into her room at night. Sometimes he'd whisper to her. She had this little carved rabbit she said he gave her, but of course it could have come from anywhere. Everybody said the only way to keep him out was to close up everything in the house. Every door, including cabinets."

"Whatever happened to Kelly?" I asked.

"She turned into a real troublemaker by high school. Smoking and drinking and finally ran off with her boyfriend, Andy Lumford. They moved out of town long ago, like most people with any sense. Wouldn't know where to find them now, or if they're even still alive. It's been a galaxy's age since I was in elementary school. Don't let the hair treatment fool you. Though I hope it does, since that's kinda the point."

"Your hair looks amazing. Did you ever hear about Jack from anyone else?" I jotted the names she'd mentioned on my pocket notepad.

"Lots of kids said they saw him, too, but it's hard to know who was telling the truth and who just made up stories. They say that's why Billy Traverton disappeared. Jack took him."

"Traverton? I saw that name recently."

"When I was eight, Billy was ten, two grades ahead of us. I remember the whole town searching for him. Then they just kind of gave up and moved on after a week or two. Like he'd never lived here at all. It was around the time people started hearing the mill might close. Maybe that's why everybody forgot him so fast."

"Did they ever find him?" I asked.

"Never did. To this day, nobody knows whether

he's alive or dead, like that poor cat in that scientist's box. His older brother Otis never really recovered. Said it was Jack that took him, but the adults figured Otis was crazy. The mill closed for good the next year, and nobody thought about that little boy again. Town started to die fast. The sixties turned into a bad decade for Timbermill."

"Otis Traverton still lives in town, doesn't he?" I asked. "Someone told us he was good at fixing things around the house."

"You don't mention to him or anybody that you heard this from me," Doro said. "Otis is from town. Don't tell him I've been talking."

"Of course." I decided to back off the Otis topic. "What else did people say about Jack? Were there any stories about where Jack came from, or what his motivation was?"

"Here we go!" Stacey emerged from the coffee shop with a multi-cup tray. She handed out paper cups in cardboard sleeves with the Turntables record logo. "One chamomile, one with sugar and cream for Ellie… just kidding, it's black…and whatever I got for myself." Stacey looked around for a nearby place to sit, didn't find one, and kind of awkwardly backed away to lean against a lamppost so she didn't loom over us on the bench.

"Thank you." Doro sipped her tea. "It's not bad, for something a man made. You want bad, try his muffins. I figure he's skating by on his looks."

"Doro's filling us in on the Jack legend, but remember, we can't tell anyone we heard it from her," I said to Stacey, mainly to keep Doro talking.

"That's right," Doro said. She drank more tea and

sat quietly for a while, and the town grew dark around us. We were running late to meet our clients. "Well, I don't know how much of this is real. But they say Cabinet Jack lived here in the old times when the town was big and new, instead of worn-out and broke. That was the magical time that your parents and grandparents would talk about. They say…and this is all worth what you paid for it—"

"Almost five bucks," Stacey said.

"My goodness. For a cup of tea? He must make a mint." She chuckled. "Making a mint from tea. Anyway, they say Jack was a carpenter, and could make fancy woodworking like the ladies of the day wanted for their homes. He built things all over town. The story goes that he was friendly and popular, carved little toys for the children. They called him Cabinet Jack, that was his nickname."

"Any idea of a last name?" I asked.

"I don't know, sorry. Again, I am not swearing any oaths about how real these stories are. Now, here comes the bad part. Jack dated this pretty widow in town, who had two children of her own. But she rejected him for another man, and Cabinet Jack turned out to be evil as sin. He murdered her children out of revenge. The men of the town didn't bother waiting for any judge or jury. They nailed Jack inside one of his own cabinets and buried him alive, so he'd die real slow and painful. And ever since, he stalks children around town, and takes them away in the night."

"Where did they bury him?" I asked.

"Some people say the town cemetery, but most say the swamp out past the mill, where Wandering Creek meets the Ogeechee River. The marshland goes on for acres. Jack could have run out of air and suffocated, or if the cabinet leaked, he could have drowned in mud."

"Can you name any other kids who were taken? Before or after Billy Traverton?"

"They say Timbermill used to have more kidnappings than most towns its size," Doro told me. "Now, I don't know if that's true or not, but it sure feels true, especially given how quick we all moved on from Billy. Like it was just a thing that happens from time to time, a boy disappearing. And like I said, the town unraveled after that. Everything started to go quiet. No more factories, no more trains. You could almost hear the weeds growing through the streets. Most people who grew up here didn't want to raise their children here. They all had reasons, but I suppose they all knew about Jack, waiting in the shadows. Didn't help that there were no jobs, of course. People were quick to leave and never come back."

"So why did you stay?" I asked.

"Where would I go? Anyway, I can't have kids, so I suppose I don't have to worry about 'em getting Jack-napped. I stayed here, took care of my parents 'til they passed, and I guess nothing much more ever came up for me. Kept the salon going through some lean years. That's something."

"Do you own the salon?"

"I inherited it by default. The previous owner— Bessie Porter, taught me everything I know—both her kids left town, and neither wanted to come back and cut hair. So when she passed, I took over the lease. And I'm still here, working 'til I keel over. I ought to retire, but business is just getting good. That's the wrong time to take your chips off the table. And it's why I'd rather you not go spreading these old tales around, either, but you do what's needed to protect those kids."

"And what is that?" I asked.

"Make sure they keep all the doors closed up tight. Every cabinet in the house. That's how I kept Jack away from me, and I still do it every night." She shook her head. "Why couldn't they have moved into one of those fancy new neighborhoods? My customer earlier was right. They really ought to just knock down the old places." Doro tossed her empty cup into an outdoor trash can, then stood and yawned. "That's really all I've got to say about it. It's getting late. I got a steak marinating at home, so I'd better get to it."

"Can we get back to you if we have more questions?" I asked.

"To be honest, I'd rather you didn't," she said. "I'd prefer not to speak about this again. And remember... let's pretend I never did."

She took out her car keys and walked toward the handful of cars parked near the front of the salon.

Chapter Sixteen

We were running so late that Dave was already taking the younger kids through the nightly cabinet ritual.

In the front parlor, with the door to the foyer slid shut, Stacey showed Nicole the videos she'd clipped out from the previous night. Nicole watched the cold spots in the closets with some interest, but looked startled when they reversed course before disappearing.

"What were those?" Nicole asked.

"It could be two entities, or two portions of a single, larger one," I said. "Maybe Andra's two invisible friends."

"Sunny and Rainy? *Are* they real?" Nicole asked.

"There were two kids who lived in this house, a sister and brother named Solange and Raynard. Their mother ran the place on behalf of the owner and did all the cooking and cleaning. Both kids went missing in 1938, and at least one died. The girl. She was twelve."

"How did she die?"

"We're still piecing that together. There's not much in the local newspaper archives or the police files."

"Except for a really aggressive ghost who throws hammers and nails," Stacey said. "The basement of your town hall is haunted, just as a local insider tip. They say you can't fight city hall, but this one picked a fight with us."

"Yeah, that did happen. It inflicted minor injuries."

"That is something I will take note of," Nicole said, warily, like she wasn't quite sure she trusted our word.

"All this seems to fit with a local legend about a ghost called Cabinet Jack," I told her. "According to a person who grew up here, the local kids were scared of Jack decades ago, when the town was still thriving. They had the same rules as your kids, closing the cabinets all over the house before going to sleep."

"All those years ago?" Nicole hugged herself as if cold, though the house was still warm from the earlier summer sunlight.

"Jack was supposedly killed by a vigilante mob when they discovered his crimes, possibly the murder of those two kids who went missing. If the newspaper editor and local police were sympathetic to these vigilantes, that could explain why the official records are so scarce."

"Because the whole town killed him and covered it up," Nicole said.

"If that's what happened, then it's the origin of the Jack legend," I said. "Adults probably didn't want to speak about any of it again, so the only history of it circulated as rumors among children, until the town shrank so much there weren't any children left to hear it."

"Until we moved here," Nicole said. "With our children."

"I have to wonder if other new families are experiencing these things, but their odds might be lower because—"

"Most people are moving into the new neighborhoods," Nicole said. "Meanwhile, nobody lives on our street. Except Otis, whose yard isn't having a great effect on the property values."

"Otis?" I asked.

"The overgrown house down on the corner. You can barely see it through the trees. The old man there came over and said he could help us with any repairs around the house. But Dave and I do that ourselves, just like when we restored our house in Kansas City. Hiring help blows up the budget and cuts into your resale margin. Anyway, the man seemed desperate for work, but honestly, and I hate to say it, he also seemed like a strange hermit. He was disheveled, his beard was tangled, he kind of smelled, and I just didn't want him in my house. If I didn't have my kids to think about, I might have hired him for some yard work out of charity, but…" Nicole shrugged. "I try to avoid him. I don't check the mail or go out front if he's out walking the neighborhood."

"Is his last name Traverton?" I asked.

"Yes," Nicole said. "I looked up the property records…so I could search his name and see if he had a criminal record, honestly. But he didn't, and that house has been in his family since it was built in 1921. His grandfather was one of the original owners of the mill, the managing partner who ran things. His father published the town paper, back when there was one. So I don't want to complain about him, really, because he belongs here, and we're the outsiders invading his neighborhood. But we're going to fix it up. The values will go up as the neighborhood improves. There's a lot of neglect and absentee ownership, but I think the real danger is in moving too slowly, because smart investors are already starting to look at these properties." She looked among the high cabinets and wooden storage nooks that ran just below the ceiling. "They're so unique."

"They say Jack was an expert carpenter in life and worked on houses and buildings all over town," I said. "If he was real, this could be his handiwork."

"Oh. Gross," Nicole said. "So what do we do now?"

"We have to learn more about who Jack was, and whether his ghost has ever harmed anyone," I said. "There was a kidnapping about two decades later that local kids blamed on Cabinet Jack, but we haven't researched it yet. I'd like to expand our observation tonight by setting up gear around the second floor, in your least used rooms up there. We might catch some more evidence. Speaking of which…" I took a deep breath and nodded at Stacey.

"Yeah." Stacey reluctantly queued up the clip of the mirrored armoire from Nicole's room. "We kinda caught this, too."

Nicole's jaw dropped as she watched the door swing open several inches, revealing clothes swaying on their hangers inside. "This happened in the middle of the night? While we were sleeping in there?"

"It looks like that door was left ajar. When you

watch it in slow motion, you can glimpse the entity who opened it."

"Do I want to see that?" Nicole asked.

"It's entirely up to you."

She looked over her shoulder, as if to make sure the doors out of the room were closed, or maybe to see if Dave would return from putting the kids to bed, which he didn't.

"Fine." Nicole turned back to the screen. "Show me."

Stacey played the slow version. The pale, misty hand, smooth and featureless as a white glove, pressed its palm and fingers against the inside of the glass. Then, in the background, the wispy oval form suggesting a face became faintly visible.

The video paused at the moment of maximum visibility for the ghostly evidence, as Stacey had set it to do.

"That's awful," Nicole whispered. "That's in our room. Can you send that to Dave's phone?"

"Of course." Stacey went to work.

"I don't know if I can sleep in there tonight," Nicole said. "Do you think it's safe?"

"You've been safe this long," I pointed out. "But if you did want to move to a guest room, we could set up more gear in your room for the night without intruding on your privacy too much."

"I think we'll do that. There's an extra double bed in the guest room. It's not terribly uncomfortable if you're desperate and tired enough. I'll tell Dave." She sighed and began to type on her phone.

Chapter Seventeen

Upstairs, Stacey and I worked as quietly as we could because the younger kids were already in bed. We mostly communicated with Nicole using silent gestures as we stuck microphones and cameras into her room and others around the second floor.

We were startled when we opened the door of a narrow windowless slot of a bedroom near the attic stairs, which had surely been the cheapest room to rent on the entire floor in the boardinghouse days.

A pale girl shrieked at us from the shadows, and I jumped back.

"Penny? What are you doing here?" Nicole leaned in to see her daughter, dressed in a white nightgown, kneeling on the floor by the bed. The bed was built into the wall, barely large enough for one person, its posters carved into horse's heads at their tops.

Penny appeared to be rummaging through one of several little fairy-sized doors built into the side of the bedframe.

"Uh, what am I doing?" Penny asked. "Maybe trying not to be bored for five whole minutes? I'm just looking around."

"What's in your hand?" Nicole moved forward. Stacey and I hung back, keeping our distance from any emerging family drama.

"Nothing." Penny closed the small door. "Just looking for interesting junk. This whole house is basically a junkyard full of junk, if you haven't noticed."

"And what did you find?"

"Nothing. Just this dumb thing." Penny finally opened her clenched hand. She held a ring, skillfully carved from cypress wood to look like a chain of tiny round flowers, with one large flower bud on top like a jewel. "I mean, I wouldn't wear it to school, but it's okay."

"And who gave you this?" Nicole touched a necklace Penny wore, tucked mostly into her nightgown, made of large hand-carved beads etched with flowers, rabbits, and butterflies, the same motif as the girl's tiny bedroom off the playroom downstairs.

"Nobody *gave* it to me." Penny pulled it back and tucked it away. "It's more junk from around the house. You never ask about the toys that precious little Andromeda gets from *her* imaginary friends."

"Do you have an imaginary friend, too, Penny?" Nicole asked.

"Ugh." Penny covered her eyes as if embarrassed by the question. "I'm not a little kid, Mother. I just mean, the more doors you open, the more little things you find. Can I go now? Are you all done invading my privacy yet?" She glared at us. "When are *they* leaving?"

I smiled and stepped out of sight, pulling Stacey along with me, down the dark passage to Jack's stairs.

We climbed up into the large attic bedroom, illuminating the area with our flashlights.

While Stacey replaced batteries in our gear, I poked and prodded around, looking in doors and drawers, inspecting again the sprawling roots and limbs of the bizarre bed with its tree-trunk headboard. The forward roots of the tree design created an almost cage-like environment around the bed, arching along either side of the bed as posters and rails, as well as arching overhead like a canopy.

I crawled onto the creaky, bare platform where the mattress would have gone. I had to advance on my hands and knees to crawl between the rootlike projections above and on either side. It was almost like entering a cave between the roots of a giant tree.

Several little round doors were built into the backs of the headboard's rootlike projections, visible only from the vantage of being in the bed. I rolled onto my back so I could open them and check the compartments, but I found mostly dust.

"All set," Stacey said. "Are you, uh, taking a nap there, Ellie? Because I would think that bed pretty much guarantees nightmares."

"Yeah, and the lack of any mattress or pillows doesn't add to the comfort—"

"Look out!" Stacey yelled as something scraped above my head.

I looked up to see a hidden panel sliding open in the headboard's central tree-trunk feature, right in line with my skull.

Something blurry came tumbling out and fell toward my face.

I flung myself to the side as far as I could, but those stupid root-like sculptures barred me from moving too far. The falling object cracked into the platform behind me.

"Oh, my gosh," Stacey whispered. "Did it...get you?"

"No." I tried to turn for a look at what had nearly fallen on me, but it suddenly felt like an invisible hand was pulling my hair, hard. "Ow! I think I'm stuck."

"Oh, that's lucky. It only got your hair." Stacey crawled toward me across the bed platform.

"I wouldn't call it lucky." I lay there while she pried something loose from behind me, with a sound like splintering wood.

"Wow. That's a...thing," she said.

With my hair free, I could finally twist around and see what she was holding. It looked like a hatchet, but with the rust-coated blade rotated sideways. Several of my long black hairs were stuck to the blade's edge.

Looking down, I could see where it had landed, leaving a small gash in the platform, with an alarming amount of my hair strewn beside it.

"I see what you mean by lucky." I picked up the long black locks. "I'm guessing it did not give me a great haircut."

"More of a hairchop, really." Stacey looked at the back of my head and grimaced. "I'm sure a good stylist can fix it. Too bad Doro doesn't want to speak with us again. But, hey, no blood, and it didn't bash your skull." She looked over the tool with the short handle and sideways hatchet blade. The cutting edge was beyond dull, but the weight could have done real damage to my skull and brain.

"That concealed panel opened itself." I sat up and looked into the compartment. Other tools were hung on small hooks inside, knives and hand scrapers gone to rust. We took them all out. "There's no knob or latch. You just have to know where it is and how to open it."

"You think this is Jack's stuff?" Stacey found a cardboard box where we could store them, while I kept looking at the hidden panel.

"It could be. It's also hard not to notice this is the second time we've had rusty old tools thrown at us tonight. In the police basement, it happened right after we mentioned Jack and the two missing kids. And now we're in Jack's room, according to the kids. And it's the place where they found the Jack graffiti." I looked at the freshly painted white wall.

"You think Cabinet Jack is following us around town?" Stacey asked. "And throwing stuff at us?"

"Maybe." I rapped my knuckles up and down the headboard's trunk, then moved on to the wall paneling. "I wonder if there are any more hidden cabinets."

"I'll help you look." Stacey began walking along the built-in woodwork, knocking on the back walls of shelves and cabinets. "Open sesame," she whispered, more than once.

"Abraca-doozle," I said, checking my area.

A few minutes later, after I'd checked several other spaces, I heard an interesting hollow sound at the back of the closet with the forgotten shirts and ties.

"I think I've got something." I knocked around with my knuckles, then tried pushing in different spots. The back panel didn't budge, so I kicked it, which also didn't help. I traced my fingers down along the back corners.

"Finding anything?" Stacey whispered, coming up behind me.

"There's no solid wall behind here. If I could just —" My fingertip found its way into what looked like a shallow knothole, an imperfection left over from the original piece of wood. Maybe that was how it had begun its life, but now it was something more.

Using the finger-sized hole as my handle, I slid aside the back panel of the closet, opening a window to a dark space beyond.

Chapter Eighteen

"What's in there?" Stacey asked, shining her flashlight over my shoulder.

"Looks like another cabinet." I moved aside the dishware and crockery that blocked the way on the other side, doing my best to keep quiet, and also not break any of the fragile stuff.

Then I climbed through into the cabinet on the far side. It was cramped, a dusty wooden tunnel through the attic's inner wall.

A closed square door waited ahead, and I pushed that open. I had to stop and awkwardly twist around, scrunched inside the cabinet, so I could bring my legs to the front before I could drop out of the cabinet and into the room beyond it.

The space beyond was cluttered with forgotten furniture.

"What's over there?" Stacey asked.

"The rest of the attic. Do yourself a favor and come

through feet first."

While Stacey slid out of the cabinet, I found the stairs at the attic's far end, leading down to the second floor. These stairs were wider and much better lit than the ones we'd taken up to Jack's room. The electricity in the main attic worked fine.

"That was weird," Stacey said, dusting herself off as she joined me at the head of the stairs. "Why would you want a secret passage from one part of the attic to the other?"

"Maybe you want to sneak out while people think you're home." I started down the stairs.

"Maybe it was for when he went out kidnapping and murdering kids," Stacey said.

I opened the attic door and stepped into the upstairs hall.

Nicole, on her way to the guest bedroom, shrieked at our sudden unexpected emergence.

"How did you...?" She looked toward the back hall, in the direction we should have come from.

"Sorry!" I said. "Jack's room connects to the main attic. Convenient for sneaking in and out. Also, this rusty old tool leaped out at me." I held it up.

"It nearly bashed her skull in." Stacey added. She carried the box of other smaller, rustier tools. "It looks like someone couldn't decide whether to make a hammer or an ax, so they ended up somewhere in between."

"That's a hand adze," Nicole said. "An antique woodworking tool, good for stripping things down to a smaller size."

"Like my head, for example," I said.

"An adze, huh? Good thing you knew that." Stacey

sounded impressed, looking over the rusty tool.

"You don't restore a house from 1855 without learning a thing or two about obsolete techniques," Nicole said. "And maybe I watch home-restoration shows semi-obsessively. I might have an actual HGTV addiction problem. I subscribe to their plus content, is what I'm saying."

"Is everything okay with Penny?" I asked.

"Of course not. She's always upset about something. But she's finished with that little room if you still want to set up there." Nicole eyed the adze. "That fell on you? Are you hurt?"

"Only my sense of style." I turned to show her my damaged hair. "And honestly, that wasn't one of my stronger points in the first place."

"That sounds scary."

"I'll be fine, but you and your family should avoid the attic until further notice."

She nodded. "The kids aren't supposed to go up there anyway, but I'll remind them tomorrow. I'm probably going to bed now, but text me if you need me. I haven't been sleeping well lately, so there's a good chance I'll still be up."

"We'll try not to bother you," I promised.

While Nicole went on to join Dave in their temporary room, Stacey and I wrapped things up inside, including a few microphones in the attic that would hopefully help identify which kid had been whispering strange things late at night.

Then we retreated outside to the van, waiting as the hour grew late and the house grew dark and quiet.

We watched the silence and the shadows. In the attic, in the rooms and closets of the second and first floor, little stirred beyond the occasional spider or palmetto bug. The microphones around the attic let us hear every creak of the house settling, every footstep of someone getting up for a late glass of water.

Midnight came and went, and still there was no activity, not even the hesitant cold spots from the night before. Certainly no doors pushed themselves wide open. In the master bedroom, we'd moved the night vision camera so we wouldn't lose sight of the mirror if the armoire opened again. Maybe we'd get a clearer look at the entity's face this time.

Occasionally, I checked the tender spot on the back of my head where the can had hit me. A swollen knot had formed there, just in time for it to become more visible to the world thanks to the adze chopping through my hair.

"I'm going in," I told Stacey after another uneventful hour had passed. "I need to stretch my legs."

"Ooh, me too."

"Wait here and watch my back."

"Fine, but if my legs cramp up from going unstretched, I won't be able to run in and save you."

"I'll accept that risk." I stepped out of the van and walked up to the dark house.

I opened the front door as quietly as I could, wincing at the slight groan of the hinges and the creak of the floorboards beneath my boots.

The playroom was my main destination, but I took the most circuitous possible path there, walking through the parlor and then the dark, windowless back hallway carved out of once-grand rooms. I looked into an empty guest bedroom, a bathroom, and the laundry room, which smelled of dampness, detergent, and bleach.

I moved on, glancing into the kitchen before finally arriving at the playroom. I felt chills walking in there, though not literal physical ones, just my psychological response to the memory of the sheet-shrouded ghost.

Keeping the overhead light off, I studied the room in the moonlight from the window. The room was messy, with abandoned toys and a half-solved puzzle on the floor, but everything that I could see looked fairly normal.

The stage-curtain sheets still hid the back half of the room. I approached the turtle-print one that had been inhabited by the ghost and slowly reached up to grab its edge. It wasn't moving, wasn't giving me any indication of trouble lurking behind it, but I felt some uneasy anticipation as I drew it aside.

Nothing waited for me behind the curtain, as far as I could see.

I knelt to look into each of the small sleeping rooms, then decided to crawl into the one decorated with butterflies, flowers, and rabbits.

I closed the pint-sized door behind me, shutting myself inside. At least this one had a window. I wasn't sure I could have handled the other sleeping room, sitting in pitch blackness in a house with multiple ghosts, especially since Andra said Rainy was less welcoming to visitors. Accordingly, I'd picked Sunny's room.

"Ellie, what are you doing in there?" Stacey asked.

"Fishing for answers." I took a voice recorder from my belt and waved it at the night vision camera.

"Ooh, good luck. Let's hope you get something. But

nothing, you know, *too* scary."

"I'm hoping for the same." I leaned back against one wall and slid down to sit on the floor. There was barely enough room to stretch out my legs. I hoped the poor kid who'd lived here hadn't been claustrophobic.

I placed my EMF meter on the floor beside me so I could watch for temperature changes and electromagnetic fluctuations, then sat quietly, waiting to see if any paranormal activity arose on its own, perhaps stirred up by my presence.

Finally, I started asking questions, in Ouija-board fashion. "Is anyone here?" Long pause. "Can you hear me?" Another long pause. "This is a pretty room, isn't it? Do you like it here?" I closed my eyes and imagined the girl's grainy gray picture from the newspaper, the cheerful smile she'd given the photographer, the happy energy that had seemed to radiate from her. She'd been twelve when she died, after disappearing from home for more than a week. According to the legend from Doro, the kids had been murdered by Jack—talented carpenter, but also a murderous psycho stalker.

Looking over the figures carved into the bedpost— a striped butterfly, a hopping bunny—I whispered, "Did Jack make this for you?"

I shivered, and this time it wasn't nerves. The room felt colder, and my meter confirmed a drop of three degrees.

"What about this?" I touched the toy chest, etched with similar animals and flowers, then opened it to reveal the locomotive and rabbit wearing its little top hat. "Did he carve these?" I paused. "Did you once live here?" The EMF meter indicated an increase in electrical activity. Plunging ahead, or perhaps out on a limb, I whispered, "Is your name Solange? Solange Tondreau? Was this your room? Was Andra's playroom your mother's room?"

The temperature dropped fast, the summer night turning into winter in an eyeblink, mist forming around me as the thick soup of Georgia humidity condensed from the air, frosting over the window, blotting out the moonlight and dimming the little room.

The window curtain twitched as if stirred by a breeze.

Then it swelled toward me as a shadowy form filled it, rising from the bottom.

It was solid darkness, the size and shape of a child, standing just inches away, enshrouded by the thin window curtain and silhouetted against the frosted windowpane.

"He knows you're here," she whispered, her voice flat and raspy, like a dull knife scraping a block of ice. Her whole presence was like ice, chilling the tiny room, making me shiver.

"Solange?" I asked. She didn't reply, so I said, "What happened to you?"

"He said he loved us. He lied." Her face behind the curtain was barely visible, like a smooth mask of black silk. I couldn't see any features. It was unnerving. I had to resist the instinctive urge to kick out at the apparition or crawl away in fear through the small door.

"What did he do to you?" I asked.

"The same as he'll do to you," she whispered. "He'll make you his."

"Did Jack murder you?" I asked.

As if in response, something thudded against the inside of one of the room's little cabinets, carved with the image of a butterfly perched on a flower. It was like an animal trying to escape. Then the other cabinet door shook, its knob and hinges rattling.

"Jack's coming," she whispered. "Someone called for him."

"How can I stop him?" I asked. "How can we help you?"

"Close all the doors tight," she whispered. "Or he comes out at night."

As if responding to her words, all the little doors trembled, with rat-like scratching sounds behind them.

"Stacey, did we close everything upstairs?" I whispered into my headset microphone, but there was already a sinking feeling in my gut.

"Uh, I think probably, let me look...and no. We left the closet with the hidden door open in Jack's room after we crawled through it."

The rattling and scratching of the cabinets stopped abruptly. I looked to the shadow girl enshrouded in the sheer curtain.

"Jack's here," she whispered.

Then she vanished, and the curtain fell back into place against the window.

The small door through which I'd entered shuddered, and I turned toward it, startled. I hadn't expected Jack to arrive from there, but I supposed it was a door he'd carved.

I went for my flashlight, but a man's ice-cold hand reached out and grabbed my forearm from out of the shadows.

The pale hand had emerged, impossibly, from the open top of the large, hand-carved toy box. I could see part of the arm attached to it, clad in a moleskin work shirt with a wooden button at the wrist.

The hand was strong, gripping me so tight I thought I could feel the thin bones creak inside my forearm. It yanked me toward the toy box, where the smiling rabbit carved on the front seemed malevolent now, reminding me of the creepy bunny from town hall who'd presided over the egg hunts of yesteryear.

I looked inside, but the toy box seemed to brim with an inky darkness, showing little beyond where the arm emerged. It was cold in there, like an ice box instead of a toy box, sucking out what little heat remained in the room.

"Ellie, are you okay?" Stacey asked over my headset. "What's happening?"

"Shh." I grabbed my tactical light from my belt but kept it dark. Breaking away from the apparition would be nice in the short term but would also cost me a chance to learn up close.

The cabinets rattled again.

"Let me in, little bunny." An oily voice floated up from the darkness of the toy chest as though echoing from a cavern or a deep well. "I made a special present for you. Don't you want to see? Let me in...let me in... let me in..."

"What do you want, Jack?" I asked, in the most authoritative voice I could fake at the moment.

His grip didn't loosen, but he stopped pulling me for a moment, as if my question had caught him off guard.

I leaned closer to the toy chest, staring hard into the darkness within, straining to see anything.

"The new girl," the voice echoed up from inside. "I like new girls."

"Show your face, Jack," I said. "Stop hiding."

"Let me in, and you'll see all of me." One of the cabinet doors rattled again, then fell silent. "Go on," he whispered.

I looked at the door, inscribed with a sunflower, and considered it, but shook my head.

"I don't think so." I pointed my flashlight into the toy box and clicked it to life, flooding the interior with searing full-spectrum white light.

The inside was...very strange.

It looked as though the toy box had no bottom and overlaid an open hole in the floor, which was impossible because there was no such hole.

Within that impossible hole was an impossible tunnel made of disjointed planks and beams. The smells of sawdust, burning wood, and hot coal rose from inside.

The man in the tunnel, holding tight to my arm, must have been Jack. He looked dried out, almost like he was mummified, his lips peeled back from his dry teeth and black gums in a freakish grin. His pale eyes shone with malice.

He didn't respond well to the light. The evil entities hate the light the most. Sometimes I think they resent being forced to see themselves, to be made even momentarily aware of what they are. There's also the more basic electromagnetic interference that the light can bring to such entities, disorienting them, scrambling their focus.

I barely had a glimpse of him before he vanished like smoke, his grip releasing me. The toy box lid slammed shut. When I opened it again, my flashlight revealed the normal interior that had been there before, the forlorn wooden rabbit lying on its back like the locomotive beside it had run it over.

Sliding the toy box aside, I touched the floorboards and found them as solid as ever.

"Everything still okay in there?" Stacey asked over my headset.

"It's fine now," I said. "I saw him. He's definitely a danger to this family. We have to get rid of him."

Chapter Nineteen

That was enough excitement for one night, at least for me. I crawled out of the small door and hurried through the kitchen and dining room and, finally, out the front door. On the porch, I took a deep breath of the night air, as though the atmosphere inside the house had grown thick and sour.

"You sure you're not hurt?" Stacey hopped out of the van to meet me. I walked down the porch steps to escape the shadow of the house.

"I'll be fine. It's a sign of progress when something attacks from the shadows, typically."

"Then I'd say we've made amazing progress tonight," Stacey said. "If we make much more, we'll be leaving in an ambulance."

We returned to our uncomfortable seats in the back of the van, facing the array of small monitors displayed there.

"The rest of the house looks calm," Stacey said.

"I'm really worried for that family now. It's almost unnerving to see only the empty rooms and not be able to check on the people in there."

"I've got audio of Dave snoring from one of the attic mics, if you'd like to listen to that. And of the teenage boy grunting and lifting weights or something in his room."

"No, thanks. What we need is solid facts about Jack and who he was in life. Then we can try to trap him."

"Jack facts." Stacey nodded. "Like where he's buried?"

"That would be good to know. Doro said the vigilantes likely buried him alive somewhere in the swamp."

"And they probably didn't commemorate the site with a historical marker."

"They didn't even commemorate it with a police report or newspaper article. The whole town just collectively shoved it under the rug."

"But then Jack came back," Stacey said. "Seeking revenge from beyond the grave by preying on the local children? That kind of thing?"

"That's how it looks to me."

"Something's happening." Stacey pointed at spikes in the visual graph of the audio feed from one of the microphones. She turned up the audio so we could listen.

The sound was slow and methodical, a low scratching or scraping. Stacey looked puzzled by it. I wasn't sure what it was, either.

"It's from the microphone above Jason's room," Stacey said.

We listened to the scraping for a long, quiet few

minutes.

Then a child's voice whispered, "I like it. But it's not easy…" The kid's voice continued, along with the scraping and scratching. "I was bleeding last time, so be more careful."

"Sounds like the same kid from last night," Stacey added. I nodded in agreement.

More long minutes passed where the kid occasionally muttered quietly. The scraping continued.

"When can I carve something for me and not her?" There was a long pause. "I already told you. A Groot. I already found the right limb." Another pause. "Well, *I* know what he looks like. I just need a little help."

"Who do you think he's talking to?" Stacey whispered.

"If he's getting carving lessons, it must be Jack," I said.

"Do you think that's where Penny's mysterious wooden jewelry is coming from?"

"Maybe."

"Ow!" the boy said. "I want to go to sleep." He paused. "But I don't want to finish it tonight." Another pause. "Stop it, that's scary. I told you not to do that! Go away!"

"Let's go." I jumped out through the back door of the van and raced toward the house, not waiting for Stacey to catch up.

I barged through the front door and took the stairs two at a time, up and around to the second floor, where I ran to Jason's bedroom door and turned the knob.

Locked.

I shook the door in its frame a few times, uselessly, then knocked as softly as I could, which is not a very effective way to knock. I didn't want to wake up every kid in the house if I could avoid it. No response came, so I tried knocking a little harder and saying Jason's name a couple of times.

We'd charged inside with a gung-ho attitude after hearing the kid freak out on the audio, but now I wasn't sure about the right approach. Kicking his door open would be fastest, but could also add extra unnecessary fear and trauma to his night.

Picking the lock was a quieter option, but not the faster one. I knelt, drew out my picks, and got to work at the brass keyhole. Stacey arrived a moment later.

"It's so quiet in there now," she said, leaning her ear against the door. "I hope he's okay."

I finally popped the lock and pushed open the door.

Jason's overhead light was off, but there was a glow on the far side of the bed from the open closet door. We couldn't see inside the closet from the hallway, though.

"Hey, Jason?" I stepped into the room. He wasn't in his bed, or at the drawing table, or anywhere I could see him.

We circled around the bed, and finally I saw him, but the sight wasn't particularly reassuring.

The ten-year-old crouched on the hardwood floor, facing into the closet, where he'd moved the lamp from his nightstand. We could only see the back of his head, his long dark hair tangled from an earlier sleep, like he'd awoken in the middle of the night, or something had woken him.

His shoulders and arms moved methodically, in time with the rasping, cutting sound we'd been hearing over the microphone in the attic above him.

"Jason?" I repeated. "Can you talk to me, pal?"

Nothing—he just kept on cutting and scraping the unseen object in his hand.

I remembered how we'd heard something from this closet when Nicole had first shown us the room, just before the older girl Penny arrived angry at her mother for talking about her.

Moving closer, I took a deep a breath, then placed my fingers on Jason's shoulder. He felt cold, which was alarming.

"Jason!" I said, louder than ever.

He twisted around, his eyes glassy and dark, his face expressionless and pale as a corpse.

In one hand, he held a half-carved wooden bracelet with an occult-like pattern of stars and moons.

In the other, he held a short, sharp carving knife, which he slashed in my direction.

"Hey!" I jumped back and collided with Stacey, then mumbled an apology to her as I drew my flashlight and blasted Jason with it.

He covered his eyes with the back of his knife hand. "You should leave," he said, in a voice deeper and flatter than it should have been.

"What are you making there, Jason?" I asked. "Who's the bracelet for?"

"Not you."

"Well, now I'm heartbroken. Can I see it?"

He tossed it into a large, dusty wooden box in the closet in front of him. The box held an assortment of blades, a sharpening stone, sandpaper, and scraps and chunks of different types of wood, as well as a spray bottle of rust remover.

Jason slammed it shut.

"I guess that's a no," I said. "That's too bad, Jason. I

was very impressed with your work."

"Jason's asleep now." Jason stared at me, his gaze as fixed and unblinking as a reptile's.

"Yeah, I was afraid you might say something like that." I crouched down next to him, imitating his stance. I clicked off the flashlight and casually held it in front of me, ready to fend off another knife attack. "So, who am I talking to? Jack? Are you forcing Jason to make things for you?"

"He wants to learn," replied the thing inside Jason. "A talented apprentice."

"Well, he's not yours to apprenticize," I said, wincing as I heard that surely incorrect term escape my lips. "He's only ten, for one thing—"

"A fine age to begin."

"—and for another, you're some kind of dead thing that needs to move on," I said. "There's a future for you on the other side. I promise."

If my words meant anything to him, he gave no sign. Ghosts tend to be pretty good about staying in denial about being dead.

"Let him go, Jack," I said, in as commanding a tone as I could assume. I wished I'd known his last name, or anything substantial about him, anything more than a vague town legend. Calling an entity by its name can give you some leverage over it, or at least hold its attention for a moment. "Leave the boy alone. Leave this house. You don't belong here, Jack, not anymore —"

Something sounded in the hallway, maybe a footstep. I nodded at Stacey, and she ran to check it out.

When I turned back, Jason's face went slack, as did his grip on the knife. The handle looked antique, made of antler, but the blade was sharp and gleaming.

Movement deeper in the closet caught the corner of my eye. A section of the closet wall toward the back swung inward. Maybe it had been slightly open before, but I hadn't had much of a chance to notice, with the distraction of the attempted stabbing and such.

I clicked on my light and pointed. There was definitely a small door concealed in the wall of Jason's closet, but I wasn't going exploring until I confirmed that Jason was not planning to sneak up and stab me in the back.

"Hey, Jason?" I asked.

"Huh?" he asked drowsily, blinking. He noticed his hunched, squatting position, like a caveman tending a fire, and frowned and dropped to the floor, stretching out his legs. "Did I sleepwalk?"

"Kind of. Do you remember what you were doing?"

"I dreamed someone was teaching me to carve. Not my dad." He looked at his hands, dotted with fresh wood shavings, then at the box in the closet, and the strange little doorway that had opened. "Is this still the dream?"

"Jason!" Nicole ran into the room, followed by Stacey. They must have encountered each other in the hall.

Jason leaned against his mother and closed his eyes as she embraced him.

"What's going on, Jason?" she asked. "Why are you awake?"

"I'm tired." He slid away from her to sit on the bed, then lay down across it. "Please close the closet door."

"Got it." Stacey swung it shut.

"No, I mean…the *other*…closet door." Jason lay still, eyes shut like he'd been drained by a vampire, or more likely a predatory entity.

"What happened?" Nicole asked, looking to me and Stacey. She wore checkered pajama pants and a faded t-shirt that read *5K for Heart Disease*, with the blue Pagonis Realty peacock logo among the sponsors.

"One of our microphones picked up Jason talking to someone who wasn't there, like an imaginary friend," I said.

"Jason? He doesn't have imaginary friends. He likes to draw cartoon characters and movie superheroes."

"He sounded frightened, so we ran in to check on him. We found him here." I opened the closet, still illuminated by the lamp on the floor, causing the hanging clothes to cast high, weird shadows on the ceiling.

"What is that?" Nicole looked at the rough-hewn box on the floor.

"He was working with these tools." I picked it up and opened it for her. "Making little carvings."

"Since when? Where did he even get these?" Nicole picked up the antler-horn whittling knife that Jason had almost stabbed me with.

"He may have found them somewhere in the house," I said. "And freshened them up with the rust remover and sharpening stone there."

Nicole replaced the knife and picked up the partially carved bracelet. "That looks like the other weird things Penny had. Did *Jason* carve them? He shouldn't be playing with those kinds of tools. He had some scratches and nicks on his hands the other day, but he said he just got them playing in the yard."

"It seems like Jason is being taught by an entity in this house," I said. "Maybe the carpenter, Jack."

"The one who…" Nicole glanced at Jason, seemingly asleep on the bed, and lowered her voice. She made a cutting motion at her throat with the wooden charm bracelet. "…those children?"

I nodded. "When we started to talk to Jason, the panel in the side of the closet blew open. Like someone we couldn't see was escaping through there."

"What?" Nicole looked and saw the strange opening in the closet wall. With all the other craziness happening, I couldn't blame her for not noticing it sooner. "I didn't know that was there," she said.

"Maybe it's where Jason's been keeping these carving supplies." I set down the box and stepped into the closet, kneeling to peer through the open panel.

My flashlight revealed a low, narrow passageway, twisting away at odd angles between the walls of the house. There were even a couple of light bulbs along the path, mounted on the inside of wall studs and connected by visible wires, but they didn't respond when I tried the switch.

"What is this?" Nicole whispered. "Where do you think it leads?"

"I'll check it out." I moved ahead, turning sideways to fit, twisting and ducking in a couple of spots where it was so low I had to crawl. It reminded me of the tunnel of irregular, mismatched bits of wood I'd glimpsed through the toy box when Jack grabbed me.

I reached what looked like a dead end, but there was a low tunnel that branched off at an angle to one side.

To my other side was a door, wider and shorter than a normal door, set a couple of feet above the floor instead of lined up with it, as though it had magically floated up along the wall.

I slid open the latch and pulled on the round peg of the doorknob, swinging open the door.

The oddly elevated door was made of dark, heavy wood, as was the rest of the enclosed, closet-sized space on which it opened. Clothes hung from the rod, including a couple of blue blazers.

Sliding the clothes aside, I stepped through and pushed open the door on the far side.

It opened onto the master bedroom. I was coming through the same way as the entity who'd opened the armoire in the night. Our cameras on their tripods stared back at me like one-eyed, three-legged aliens as I emerged from the armoire.

"Where does it lead?" Nicole's voice asked behind me. She carried one of Stacey's flashlights, followed by Stacey, who carried the other. Apparently, they hadn't been able to resist exploring the newly revealed passageway, either.

"This one goes to your room." I stepped back in from the armoire, letting her have a look.

"What about that tunnel?" Stacey pointed her flashlight near the floor.

"It looks like I'm about to explore that, unfortunately." I sighed and dropped to my hands and knees.

Crawling through the tunnel, I half-expected the cold, calloused hand to reach out and grab me again, the wide, smiling face to emerge from the shadows ahead. The tunnel of wood was so tightly confined that it felt like a trap waiting to spring, especially as I advanced deeper into the dusty hole, avoiding rusty nails that jutted out here and there like medieval anti-intruder devices.

I found another knob on the wall and pulled open a low square panel, which opened onto the back of a deep cabinet. I reached through and opened the cabinet door onto a view of a small, dark room.

Again, our own cameras looked back at me. It was the windowless bedroom where we'd found Penny with the carved jewelry.

"I'm starting to notice a pattern here," I called back to Stacey and Nicole, who'd both decided not to crawl after me down the creepy woodwork tunnel at this time.

"Should I…come in there?" Stacey asked, in a tone that made it clear she would rather not.

"No, that might get a little crowded." Instead of exiting into the cramped bedroom, I continued onward, through the tunnel between the walls.

The crawlspace terminated at a built-in ladder, leading down through a square opening to the first floor, into darkness below.

"Meet me downstairs," I called back to Stacey and Nicole.

Then I started down the ladder, going deeper into the hidden spaces of the house.

Chapter Twenty

The ladder brought me to another unpleasantly cramped space. I found the nearest way out, another odd-shaped door that took me into the coat closet on the first floor, underneath the stairs. Yet again, I found myself in another of the house's trouble spots, our cameras looking back at me.

Stepping around the cameras, I opened the coat closet door and stepped out in front of Stacey and Nicole, who jumped as they reached the bottom of the stairs.

"How did…?" Nicole looked from me to the top of the stairs, as if I might have invisibly streaked past them.

"There's a ladder between the walls," I said. "Someone was very interested in being able to move around this house without being seen. There could be more of these hidden passages. Maybe they were built as the house was subdivided during the boardinghouse years."

"But why?" Nicole asked.

"That's a good question, and I don't have an answer for it. But if the renovations were done by Jack, maybe he built the hidden doors and secret tunnels. He could have worked them in while chopping up the rooms for the owner."

"And then what? He crawled around spying on people while they slept?" Nicole shivered, probably remembering the ghostly face and hand from her mirrored armoire door.

"Possibly," I said. "And it looks like he's still using those hidden passages now, as he haunts this house. They could serve as liminal spaces for him, where he crosses back from the world of the dead."

Nicole looked up along the grand, showy staircase, with its monumental posts, recessed panels, and intricately decorated balusters. "The woodwork is half the reason I wanted this house so much. Now we discover it's the handiwork of a murderer. A *child* murderer. Even just from a real estate standpoint, this is a nightmare."

"I'm concerned that Jack might be taking control of Jason," I said. "Maybe it started with just his hands, teaching him to carve." I told her the entity had seemed to speak through Jason, claiming Jason was asleep.

Nicole looked understandably shocked.

"This whole move was a mistake," she said. "I thought a big change would be good for us, and I wanted to finally feel some real independence from my family for once, from my older sisters, from everyone else always thinking they know what's best for me. Now I just want to run home to them and admit I was wrong." Her eyes shone with tears. She wiped them away, but she couldn't wipe the worried, frightened expression from her face. "Should we move back?" she asked me, her tone desperate.

"I...can't tell you what major life choices to make," I said, feeling sorry for her and somewhat panicked at her turning to me for life advice. Death is my usual focus; when it comes to living, I'm a little clueless. "If there's somewhere else you and your family can stay while we investigate, that could only reduce the risk to them."

Nicole seemed to think it over, frowning deeply. "We can't pack up and go back to Kansas City. We already spent weeks split up among my sisters' homes. I don't think they'd welcome us back, especially if we showed up with no plans, no idea what to do...and no money for a place to live, since we're making payments on this house..." She shook her head. "We're trapped."

"If you stay here, you could consider changing your sleeping arrangements so nobody's alone at night," I said.

"Personally, I don't think I'll be sleeping again tonight," Nicole said. "Maybe not ever again, in this house."

"We'll work to make it safe again for you and your kids," I told her. "I promise." That was the best promise I could make—that we'd work toward it. I couldn't see the future, so I didn't know whether we'd succeed, or whether the house would ultimately have to be abandoned to its dead inhabitants.

The night was drawing to a close, anyway. Nicole hurried back upstairs to check on Jason. When she confirmed via text that he was still asleep, not awake and wielding a knife again, Stacey and I eased out the front door.

We left as the sky lightened from black to purple. We'd learned a great deal from the night's observation, none of it reassuring. The entity we faced was strong and dangerous, and I wasn't the least bit comfortable leaving our clients alone with it, even during the day, without Stacey and me watching over them like low-rent guardian angels.

Chapter Twenty-One

I spent the morning at home, sleeping like the nocturnal weirdo that I am, while normal people were getting up and going to work.

Stacey met me at the Bull Street Library. We had lots of old newspapers to dig through in search of whatever information about Jack still remained, so we split up the years around 1938 before sitting down at the microfilm machines.

Stacey did her best to not look sullen about it. Historical research wasn't her favorite part of the job; it was maybe her second least favorite aspect of the work, after getting attacked by monstrous things in dark basements. Maybe she even preferred the monster-in-the-dark encounters over the research.

Much time passed as we loaded film, skimmed pages, made notes, occasionally sent something to the library's printer...and repeated.

"It's the bunny!" Stacey announced at one point,

indicating an article about the town's Easter celebration in 1938. The tall, creepy bunny with the glassy eyes stood at the bandstand on the town green, surrounded by a group of well-dressed children, boys in coats and ties, girls in dresses and ribbons.

A longhaired blond boy in a patched coat who looked thirteen or fourteen stood closest to the rabbit. The youngest kids kept their distance, their eyes on the straw basket of goodies in the rabbit's paws, their faces showing fear of the disturbing holiday creature despite its gifts.

"That's not really what we're looking for, Stacey."

"Or is it?" Stacey pointed to a girl in the crowd. "Does she look familiar?"

"Solange! Good find." In the picture, Solange wore a dress and a ribboned hat, and beamed at the creepy rabbit, not scared of him at all. "I don't see her younger brother here...actually it's all white kids, isn't it? Maybe Raynard wasn't allowed."

"Aw, poor Raynard." Stacey moved the microfilm to show me another page of the paper. "Look at the headless bunny here."

The picture did indeed show the same bunny with his head removed, tucked under his arm, revealing a man with a toothy ear-to-ear smile that made my stomach lurch. His eyes looked straight out from the picture, straight into mine, and for an awful moment I saw another version of his face, withered and mummified, and felt his cold, calloused hand clamped tight around my arm.

"That's him," I said. My eyes flew to the caption: *Local carpenter Jack Macgill hops into the holiday spirit with local children. Also pictured: Gabriel*

Baylor, Macgill's apprentice.

Jack's big bunny paw was around the shoulder of the same blond boy from the previous picture, who smiled and held up a toy-sized carving of a rabbit wearing a comically askew bowtie.

"That looks like it could be from the toy box in the playroom, doesn't it?" I asked. "Kind of a similar style?"

"Totally similar. Is he the entity that grabbed you?"

"That's him." I looked at Jack's light-colored, amused eyes, the wide smile, and imagined the current mummified version crawling through the hidden pathways of the house, watching the family members by night, stalking their children. "We have to get rid of him. Rip him out of there by the roots. Whatever those might be."

"Sounds like a plan to me," Stacey said. "Well, more of a metaphor than a plan, but it's a start."

I skimmed the article about the town's Easter events, slowing when I read the relevant portion.

Carpenter Jack Macgill returned for his third year as the children's beloved Easter rabbit, with a basket of toys and treats, before the Easter egg roll on the green.

"I enjoy it as much as the children do," said Jack, who carves toy rabbits to give out along with the candies. "I look forward to having

children of my own someday,
but I suppose I'll need a wife
for that."

The article went on to detail the egg hunt, school band performance, and other Easter festivities.

"I could definitely see that guy as a murderer," Stacey said. "He has that Slenderman vibe."

"Now we have his name. Jack Macgill. Great job, Stacey."

"So, we're done?"

"No, we now have even more leads to research."

Stacey groaned and slouched in her seat.

"The reward for good work is more work," I reminded her.

"Seems like a flawed system." She sat up and resumed searching.

The library printer hummed and rolled out a copy of the article, complete with the black and white images of Jack, both with his rabbit head and without.

We kept digging. Apparently, Jack loved the holidays, because another article showed him constructing a team of wooden reindeer on the town green, near a windowless gingerbread-style shack. A sign on a candy-cane post read *Santa's Workshop.*

From the Christmas article, we gleaned that Jack had learned his trade up north, in Rhode Island, but "was now a transplanted Yankee with no designs on leaving the South."

Further searching revealed no more articles about Jack, not even around the dates when Solange and Raynard disappeared, or even after Solange's death.

We did turn up more missing kids in the years

following Solange's death—and Jack's, if he'd died at the hands of a vigilante mob like Doro had said. There seemed to be a missing kid every year or two through the 1940s and 1950s, which seemed like a lot for any small town. One was Angela Kilborne, twelve-year-old daughter of the police chief, one of his seven children, who disappeared three years after Solange. About a year later, there was a memorial ceremony for the missing girl, who had never been found.

The missing kids' ages ranged from six to thirteen. Three of our clients' children fell into that range.

The most recent case we identified was Billy Traverton, age ten, vanished in 1960. Again, there was no obituary, just a memorial notice several months later. This was the younger brother of Otis Traverton, the fix-it man recommended by the Turntables Cafe owner.

Altogether, we collected the names of a dozen kids who'd disappeared without ever being found.

"Where did they all go?" Stacey whispered. "How does a ghost make a whole kid disappear?"

"No idea." I thought about it. "I've heard of ghosts taking objects and hiding them somewhere else in the house. I also read about a case in the *Journal of Psychical Studies* where objects would disappear for months or years, only to show up in plain sight again. And others where they were found in a seemingly impossible place, like inside a locked drawer, or between the walls during a renovation years later."

"So, they'd be taking objects over to...the other side?" Stacey asked. "Like, the *other* side? And back?"

"These researchers speculated that certain entities can move physical objects through space and time in ways we don't understand."

"Let's hope they can't," Stacey said. *"Now* are we done here?"

"For now, yes. I think it's time we paid a visit to Otis Traverton. But first, the coffee shop."

"Music to my ears." Stacey wasted no time hopping to her feet and gathering up microfilm to return to the reference librarian.

I collected our printouts. I could have sworn the old photograph of Jack was staring right at me over his wide grin until I covered up that particular page, then reshuffled the stack to bury it deep.

Chapter Twenty-Two

"I thought this place was abandoned," Stacey said quietly.

We could barely see Otis Traverton's house through the tall trees and overgrown, interwoven shrubs in his front yard. We approached up the driveway, then followed steppingstones through the undergrowth to the front door.

Like the other houses in the neighborhood, it had elaborate woodwork, with rows of decorative posts and spandrels on the porch and upper balconies, and intricate geometrical flourishes around every window, giving the whole house a sort of fantastical look that was enhanced by its bright green and pink colors, which had been recently painted. Despite the thorny wilderness of the front yard, Otis's house itself was in good repair.

The only exception was the front door, made of horizontally striped aluminum.

"What's with the door?" Stacey murmured.

"Maybe it's some kind of extreme security thing," I said. "Don't make any sudden moves around him."

We climbed up the front porch steps and rang the doorbell.

"Ready with the bribes?" I asked Stacey.

"Of course." Stacey carried a paper box containing Marvin Gaye raisin muffins, as well as a to-go cup of Low-Fats Domino coffee, decaf because it was late in the afternoon. The coffee guy had assured us these were Otis's favorite items at the Turntable Cafe. We'd stocked up there partly to make it clear that we'd been sent by the coffee man, someone Otis already knew, in case he was wary of strangers. "Who could resist these okay-looking muffins?" Stacey asked.

The curtain moved, then the aluminum front door rattled and raised. It was a roll-up door, the kind usually found on garages or storage units, but roughly the size of a regular door. I'd never seen one at the front of a residential home before.

The man behind it was elderly, lean, with thick glasses, wispy white hair, and a tangled, not particularly clean beard. He wore overalls and a long-sleeve checkered shirt even though it was June, as well as scuffed brown work boots.

"What can I do for you?" His eyes went to the takeout box in Stacey's hand.

"Are you Otis Traverton?" I asked.

"Yes, ma'am. Is that for me?"

"Yes, sir." Stacey extended the box toward him. "Marvin Gaye raisin muffins and a Low-Fats Domino."

"I don't recall ordering anything from Walt. And I wouldn't order coffee and muffins for delivery, 'cause I ain't rich. And if I had to eat one of his muffins, I'd pick the Chuck Blueberry."

"They're more of a gift," I said. "We're studying some history of the town, and we've heard you're an expert."

"Ain't much to be an expert on, but it's true I've stuck around. Wasn't smart enough to clear out like everybody else."

"What made you stay?" I asked.

"Wishful thinking." He shook his head. "Trying to hold together a town that was determined to fall apart. Well, time makes fools of us all. How many muffins have you got there?"

"Four," Stacey said.

"I won't eat that many. I suppose y'all can come in if you want to share them. I can tell you what the town used to be like, or at least how I remember it, but the memory gets foggy with time. Remember that when you're old—if you can." He cackled and stood aside to admit us.

The interior of the house was similar to our clients' down the street, full of embellished woodwork and paneling along the front hall, and decorated woodwork all the way up the stairs, which were long and straight instead of wrapping around like at our clients' house. Green, tree-filtered light flooded in from high windows at the back of the house.

The space under the stairs was walled with cabinets and cupboards, all of them nailed shut.

"Excuse the mess," he said, though there really wasn't one, just a lot of dust. "I've been remodeling. Real slowly, over many years. More open space, more light. Clear out the cobwebs." He looked around at the cobwebs in the upper corners. "Well, architecturally. I grew up in this house. Belonged to my granddad originally, built in 1911. It's almost as old as the mill itself. It takes some doing to keep these old places standing. Done a lot of it myself. A few other houses on the street, too. Folks inherit 'em but don't want 'em, and they have me keep an eye on 'em, keep the roofs patched and the rats out. I also caretake the town cemetery, to the extent anyone does, but nobody pays me for that."

We passed through a doorway with bare hinges at one side and into a front parlor with a stiff, formal feeling, very different from the TV room at our clients' house. The bookcases were heavy with leatherbound volumes. A finely sculpted mantelpiece framed the fireplace; its supports looked like oak trees.

"I don't care for these muffins as much as Walt thinks, but I don't have the heart to tell him." Otis sank into one of four stiff, high-backed chairs around a table in front of the fireplace, perfect for having coffee or tea with friends, or reading a book alone. He opened the box Stacey had placed on the table and lifted out a raisin muffin with a resigned look on his face.

Stacey and I took one each, at his insistence. As Otis had indicated, they were okay, or maybe a step or two below that.

"That coffee shop used to be a butcher and deli, run by the Powalski family," Otis said. "They would never have believed you could run a whole shop just selling coffee. Records, maybe, once upon a time." He sipped the coffee and shrugged, as if ambivalent about how that tasted, too. "I believe I've seen you down at the new folks' house."

"Yes, we're looking into the history of their house, too. We understand it was a boardinghouse for many years."

"That it was. Most of the big places got chopped up into lots of little rooms to rent during the Depression. Including my family home here, for a time, and that helped us hang on to it during the lean years. The house you're asking about belonged to the widow of a mill manager."

"I read it was managed by a woman with a French name…" I flipped through my notebook. "Aurelie Tondreau. Is that right?"

"She ran the house for the widow Collins. Cooking and cleaning. Apparently Mrs. Collins saw her as sinful, which meant it was fine to work her to death and treat her with contempt." Otis set his muffin down with only two tiny bites missing, as if he found either the muffin or the history of the boardinghouse distasteful.

"I read an old newspaper article that said her kids went missing."

Otis looked at me. His fingers, wrinkled with age and thick with callouses, pinched off some raisin muffin, crushed it, and rolled it into a doughy ball. "That was the beginning of the end for the town. They say it was the mill closing, but the mill wasn't everything. The town gave up its soul, or at least became something different. I wanted to tell that new family all this, but how do you start? I'd just sound crazy. I tried to get to know them first, but I don't meet new people all that much, and I suppose I'm out of practice. I either can't say nothing at all or I won't stop running my mouth."

"What did you want to tell them?" I asked.

"Those kids you asked about, the housekeeper's kids. They were kidnapped and, well, there's no good way to say it. I certainly don't care to talk about it, but I need to figure out how to explain to that new family, somehow." He dropped his doughy ball onto the muffin wrapper and pinched off another piece to roll up, with no apparent intention of eating it.

"They know us," I said. "If you tell us, we can tell them."

"Will you? What I have to say isn't good news at all."

"Were the kids murdered?" I asked.

He nodded. "The girl first, then the boy about a week later. They were taken in the night. Later they were found buried out in a field that had been clear-cut by the timber company, all the trees reduced to stumps for acres around. They were in shallow graves, holding little toys that a carpenter who lived in their boardinghouse had given them. That's who folks suspected of the murders, that carpenter. Jack."

"Why him?"

"The story goes, he was having a romance with the French lady who ran the place. But she dropped him when she got a better offer."

"Ooh, juicy gossip. What was the better offer?" Stacey asked.

"Her boss, the widow Collins, passed away and left the house to her nephew Charles, who was well-established in Watkinsville, with farmland and a feed store and a few other interests. Well-to-do. I suppose he noticed Aurelie was a pretty and hardworking lady, and she noticed he was wealthier than average, and so she soon accepted his proposal of marriage. And this jealousy awoke something evil in Jack. When the French lady spurned him, he did those awful things to her children as revenge. It's hard to understand evil like that."

"Was the carpenter arrested?"

"He should have been." Otis sipped his decaf and grimaced. "But the crime was so terrible—children murdered—that the men of the town went ahead and sought justice with no judge needed, you might say. They went to Jack's workshop. He was renting space at the woodworking factory, making cabinets there. He and his apprentice, and a few other workmen, installed a lot of the interior woodwork in this neighborhood." He pointed to the row of cupboards along one wall… which, I couldn't help noticing, were all nailed shut.

"What happened at the workshop?" I asked.

"They found the adze he'd used to murder the children. It had been washed, but still stained with blood. They ended up nailing him inside a big cabinet he'd just made. They got shovels, and they buried him alive. They say he kicked and hollered the whole time."

"Where did they bury him?"

"I always heard it was in the swamp, down where the creek meets the river," he said. "Away from town. It's soft, easy to dig a hole fast."

"Could you tell us exactly where he's buried?" I asked.

"No, like I said, some of this is just what you hear. It ain't necessarily true. I wouldn't go out in the swamp, though, unless you're a fan of gators, snakes, and skeeters."

"I am definitely not." I took a slight breath, then pushed things a little further. "There was graffiti in the boardinghouse. Apparently, it gave the kids nightmares. It was about keeping your cabinets closed, or someone called Jack would come out. We've seen it around town, too. Do you think there's any connection?"

"Growing up, all the kids knew about Cabinet Jack. They'd say keep everything closed, your cabinets, your closets, any dark spaces in your home, or Jack would come out at night. Sometimes kids would dare each other to leave things open on purpose, and invite Jack in. You'd say, 'Come out and play, Jack.' And sometimes…you'd see things."

"Like what?"

"Kids said when they left things open at night, in the dark, if they watched long enough, they'd see a face looking back at them. Sometimes, they said, he'd grab you and try to take you with him."

"Did he ever do that to you?" I asked.

Otis looked at me a long time, as if deciding whether to go on. Finally, he looked at the floor. "No. It was my younger brother he was after, Billy. Billy would go around and make sure everything was closed up at night. I used to make fun of him for it. I'd open things back up just to scare him. Sometimes I even called for Jack, because that would *really* scare him. I knew the stories, like every kid in town, but didn't really believe 'em. Or you could say, I didn't believe 'em soon enough."

"What changed your mind?"

He hesitated again. "I'm only going to tell you this because someone has to watch out for those new kids. Cabinet Jack took my brother. I know, because I saw it happen. Nobody believed me, except for other kids. Not my parents or the police. The adults said I was just telling stories to get attention."

"I think whatever you saw must have been real," I said, hoping to encourage him to open up.

"It must have been awful, losing your brother," Stacey said. "Mine died when I was a kid, too."

He looked up at her, then back down, and nodded. He didn't really seem frail, despite his age, but did seem worn down and tired.

"Anything that you tell us could end up helping to protect the new family," I reminded him.

"I know it." He took a breath. "Our parents were gone that night. Not out of town, but at a big Christmas party at the mayor's house. It was a Friday night, only two days until Christmas. Christmas Eve Eve, you might say. Back then, the mayor would have a big shebang, and my family were sort of big wheels for a small town. My mother and father went and left us alone. I was twelve, my brother was ten."

"Did you have any boarders living at the house then?"

"Oh, no, not here. My family had boarders during the Depression and the war, but by the time my brother and I came along, things were rebounding, the newspaper was doing well, and we still owned shares in the mill. I don't mean to brag. There's nothing left to brag about now. I just mean those were good days, happier times for the town and for my family, right up until it happened.

"My brother and I stayed up late, since our parents weren't home yet. We played just about every game we could think, running around the house pretending to be pirates, cowboys, soldiers. A house this size made for a grand playground, at least when no adults were around to holler at you to quit carrying on.

"I said we ought to play hide and seek, but Billy didn't want to. It was late, later than we'd ever stayed awake before, and dark as sin outside. And cold. It's always cool on Christmas, sometimes chilly, but that year it got down below freezing.

"Anyway, I insisted on it. Billy was scared. I knew he was scared of Cabinet Jack, but he didn't say it aloud that night. He knew I'd just make fun of him.

"So I made him hide, and I counted to a hundred, then started searching for him. I checked every closet and spare bedroom, of which there used to be many on the second floor. I've since knocked out the walls from the boardinghouse days, restored the original larger rooms.

"I heard Billy yell from his bedroom—it was more like a yelp, like a dog getting kicked. I opened his door and walked in there thinking I'd won the game.

"Billy was in there, but he wasn't alone. Somebody had him. A full-grown man, tall. He wore a leather workman's apron with all these big, dark stains. He had a big smile, too big, not the smile of a decent person. His hand covered my little brother's mouth, and my brother was struggling, but Billy wasn't a very strong kid. He was kinda sickly, kinda scrawny. Our dad always told him to eat more and bulk up.

"They were in Billy's closet. The guy uncovered Billy's face long enough for him to scream again, and then the guy closed the door from the inside.

"I can't say how long I stood there, looking at the closet door, waiting for it to open again, waiting for an adult to show up, waiting for something to happen. I didn't know how to react. Finally, I thought I should go get a weapon, so I ran to my room for my baseball bat.

"The walk back to Billy's room, and up to his closet door, seemed to take hours. I was scared to open that door. I thought I'd find my brother dead, and then I'd be next. I knew then that Cabinet Jack wasn't just a rumor from the playground, he was real and haunting this town. And what good was I against a man who could return from the dead?

"I opened the door and drew back quick, getting into my hitting stance, ready to swing at Jack like he was a fastball across home plate.

"But there wasn't anybody there, not anymore. I swung anyway, I was so worked up. There was nothing to hit, just Billy's clothes, hanging there. I knocked 'em aside with the baseball bat, but Billy and the man had both disappeared.

"I ran all through the house, shouting for my brother, but he was gone. I was alone. Sooner or later, I ran outside, still with my baseball bat, and I ran down the street in my pajamas in the freezing dark to the mayor's house.

"The town spent Christmas Eve and Christmas Day searching for my brother. Nobody really believed my story about how he disappeared into the closet. Some figured the kidnapper took off with Billy while I ran to get my bat, but that's just not possible, since we would have crossed paths in the hall. Most people figured I made it up based on the local legend, and Billy actually ran off."

"Did they ever find your brother?" I asked.

"We never did. Never heard from him again." Otis crushed a particularly large hunk of muffin in his fingers. He'd worked his way through most of the muffin, crushing and crumbling nervously without eating, leaving broken muffin bits on one side of the plate and a pyramid of raisins on the other.

"That must have been really hard on you," I said.

"The whole family," he said. "And the town worried for him that winter. Then came the rumors about the mill closing, and those consumed everybody, especially once they turned out to be true.

"When the mill went, most of the town went, like lights burning out over the next few years. The *Ledger* folded in time. My daddy never really had much heart for the newspaper after Billy disappeared. I grew up and moved out of town, but when Daddy passed, I came back just for a little, for the funeral and to sell this house, so I thought. But one night, sitting here alone, I tore into Billy's closet, I mean hammer and crowbar. I can't say why, only I'd never been able to stop thinking about it. It was my fault Jack came for Billy, you see. I was the one who used to call for Jack, though I didn't really mean it.

"Then I found it." He cleared his throat. "I am sorry. You were just here to talk about town history. Not my problems, or this rickety old house."

"No, please continue," I said. "What did you find?"

"A little door, I suppose you'd call it, in the back paneling of the closet. It latched from the inside, so we'd never discovered it by accident. When they divided this into a boardinghouse, slicing up big rooms to make little ones, somebody left spaces between some of the rooms, and strange ways to get there, trap doors and hidden entrances in cabinets and closets. I looked into it, and a lot of the work was done by a carpenter named Jack Macgill. That was Cabinet Jack, I believe.

A real person. He worked on this house, and the house of your friends down the street."

"Why would he build those secret places?" I asked.

"Personally, I think it was to rob people," Otis said. "Remember, most of the big houses had boarders at the time. Some were travelers and itinerant workers passing through town. If you stole a little here and there, especially from the drunks who didn't track their spending too well, you could turn quite a profit over time. There's ways in and out through crawlspaces and under the porches with all the fancy millwork. Jack could get in and out whenever he liked."

"So that's it? Just to rob travelers?"

"People were desperate to get by during the Depression. Maybe he liked the challenge of building it all, too," Otis said. "Maybe he liked secrets. Maybe he liked to spy on people, one of them Peeping Toms. He liked having his own ways in and out, that's all we can know for sure. And I wasn't crazy. There was a secret way out of that closet."

"But if he died decades before he took your brother, and turned into this ghost stalker," Stacey said, "why would he need to use a hidden door?"

"Because my brother wasn't a ghost yet, was he?" Otis said. "He took him whole, body and soul. If you ask me...Cabinet Jack's ghost uses those hidden passages and doors as his way around town. That's what I think, after all these years of thinking. That's why I stripped all of it out of this house. Knocked down walls upstairs, opened it all back up, lots of light, no more dark spaces. Haven't quite finished down here yet. It takes money to do it right, and you got to think about resale value. Got the rest nailed shut in the meantime."

"And Jack doesn't bother you here?"

"He does not. But then again, I'm no kid, which is his usual prey, so maybe he's just not interested in me. Anyhow, I couldn't sell the house to any other person in good conscience until I did what I could to remove the danger. I always meant to sell it, but I didn't really have anywhere to go. I'd started college but didn't finish. My daddy, he could read Latin and Greek. He would have been ashamed of me, but he didn't care about much by the time my higher education came falling down. I never kept a good job, but I'm all right with my hands, and I fell into keeping things up around town as people moved away. Like these houses around us. After a while, I saw the whole town was going to fall apart if nobody took care of it."

"Do you know why there wasn't a trial for Jack?"

"Well, he was a Yankee, so that didn't help him much. And the crime was so awful."

"We've looked at the newspapers from that year, and we didn't find anything about this. Not the murders of the missing children or Jack's death."

"You wouldn't, would you? Because my daddy kept it out of the paper. The real story would have implicated a number of men in town. Influential men. And there was a sense that justice had been carried out, that Jack needed killing after what he'd done to those children. Is this really what you came here to learn about?"

"It sounds like an important story," I said. "Maybe one that shaped the whole history of the town."

"It's why every kid who grew up here was eager to leave," he said. "And most did, especially if they had children of their own to think about. If you tracked them down, I doubt they'd ever tell you they were scared of Cabinet Jack. They'd probably just tell you the town was running down, getting poor. Running out of ink, my daddy used to say. And that's true, too. But I think Jack killed this town, just as much as the mill closing did. And maybe the taint of that vigilante justice, too, even if it was understandable. If towns have a soul, ours was stained with blood."

A silence hung in the room after that. I leafed through my notes, and finally asked, "Do you have any idea what happened to Aurelie Tondreau, the mother of the two children Jack Macgill murdered?"

"Aurelie married Charles Collins after he inherited the house, and they moved to his home in Watkinsville. You can imagine she'd want to leave the town where her children were murdered. The Collins family continued to operate the boardinghouse as absentee owners. They eventually let it go to the county for unpaid taxes."

"Have you ever worked on our clients' house?"

"Yes, ma'am. For the Collins family. Charles and Aurelie's grandson used to pay me to keep it up, though I only met him once in person. I've worked on every house on this block, one time or another. Speaking of which, I have to pick up some things from Gnann's Fix-It in Springfield before they close. I'd better shake a leg, because mine don't shake too fast these days."

"We don't mean to keep you." I got to my feet. "Is there anything else you'd recommend to help keep the new family safe?"

"Rip out all of Jack's handywork. I'll come day or night to help them with that particular job. And until they do, close it all up tight, every night."

We left through the front door, into a dark, cloudy evening with a light drizzle of rain, and followed the steppingstones away from the porch. Soon the house was out of sight, concealed again by the woods behind us, like one of Jack's hidden passageways.

Chapter Twenty-Three

"Do you think Jacob will check out that swamp with us?" I asked.

"He will if I ask nicely. When do we want him to come?" She brought out her phone.

"Tonight would be best, if you can sweet-text him into it. Tomorrow night would be second best. The night after that—"

"Third best. Got it." She started thumbing her message.

I texted Nicole and Dave, letting them know we were returning.

Out on the weedy neighborhood green, Lonnie and several other teenage boys played a fierce game of soccer, one team shirtless so they could tell each other apart.

"That kid's the only one who seems to be adjusting to the move," Stacey said, as Lonnie hip-checked a smaller kid, knocking him to the dirt and stealing the ball from him, then shouting obscenities at the fallen kid and giving him the finger.

"Yeah, Lonnie seems well adjusted." I looked at the edge of the green and saw Penny under the branches of a dogwood tree full of white blooms, leaning back against the trunk. One of the local boys had split off from the game to chat with her. He was on the shirtless team, and muscular, wearing only a thin, gold-colored necklace and standard black soccer shorts. He stood in a dominant pose over Penny, his hand planted on the trunk behind her, fencing her in with his arm. A tattoo of a skull and roses adorned his bicep. Penny's previously tangled hair was brushed and smoothed now, her smile red with lip gloss. "Looks like Penny's making friends."

"Ooh, maybe she's adjusting, too. I wonder how Nicole will like the guy's tattoo and nose ring, though —"

"Penelope!" Nicole emerged through the front door, framed by the lavishly ornate millwork of the porch. The densely packed balusters and spandrels seemed to form a kind of cage around her. "Come watch Jason and Andromeda!"

Penny glanced over at her mother, but quickly resumed talking to the boy, smiling at him, and pulled out her phone and typed with her thumbs.

"Now, Penelope!" Nicole shouted.

Stacey and I slowed our approach, not particularly wanting to stand in the middle of any fighting.

Penny gave the boy a long, close hug, as though he were leaving on some year-long voyage across the seas.

"Penelope!" Nicole called again.

Penny drew away from the boy and glowered the

whole way home, her face crimson. Her angry expression was an identical-but-younger reflection of her mother's.

"That was so embarrassing!" Penny hissed as she stalked toward the porch.

"Well, you have to look after your—" Nicole said.

"Make Lonnie look after them for once!"

"He is making friends right now."

"What do you think I was trying to do, before you embarrassed me to death?"

"Penelope—"

"Stop calling me Penelope! I'm not some old Greek lady waiting around for her husband to stop cheating on her with witches and princesses." Penny stormed up the stairs past her mother. "You should hire a babysitter! And pay them a living wage!" She slammed the front door on her way inside.

Nicole rolled her eyes and looked down the steps at us. "I've done the math. There will come a time when, for just a few months, all four of them will be teenagers, all at once. When I imagine this time, I imagine something like the city of Pompeii when Vesuvius erupted."

"That sounds a lot like my family growing up," Stacey said. "Except with more boys."

"I can't imagine." Nicole looked out at her purple-haired, dirt-crusted son grunting and kicking his way through a pack of local guys. "That one better rinse off before he steps inside. I have to keep a hose on the side of the house for him. Have a seat. Dave's coming in a minute."

We took the outdoor lawn chairs. Nicole brought out a glass pitcher of lemonade and poured cups for us without asking, more or less forcing us to consume the cold, delicious stuff.

"How's Jason?" I asked.

"He won't say much," Nicole replied. "He says he found the tools and taught himself. We took the tools away, of course."

"What does he say about the ring and necklace he gave to Penny?"

"He says he carved them for practice, and he didn't give them to Penny, he just left them sitting out because he didn't care what happened to them once he was done. He's like that with his pictures, too. I've caught him throwing amazing drawings in the trash when I tell him to clean his room."

"Did he have anything else to say about Jack?"

She shook her head.

"Penny is not being cooperative," Dave said as he stepped out. "I had to turn on the TV to keep Jason and Andra occupied. They're watching some anime thing that I really can't follow. I think it's about octopuses who live on a spaceship."

He sat down, and we hurriedly caught them up on what we'd learned so far—Jack's name and history, including the picture of him in the bunny costume with his too-wide smile. They looked aghast to learn about the spate of missing kids in the town's earlier history, and particularly horrified when they heard about Otis watching his brother disappear into the closet.

"Otis recommends you tear out all the cabinets and secret passageways as soon as possible, and open up all the rooms. Remove all of Jack's woodwork from your house," I said. "In the meantime, I wouldn't leave any of your kids alone at night."

"We're making them double up," Dave said. "I already dragged Andra's bed into Penny's room, and Jason's into Lonnie's. Penny's angry about it. Lonnie isn't, but only because he doesn't know about it yet."

"Wait until they notice I dug out the old baby monitors," Nicole said.

"Maybe we won't mention that," Dave suggested. "But we'll be listening."

"Sounds good," I said. "Any chance we could speak to Jason? Away from the other kids?"

"If you can get him to talk, go ahead," Nicole said.

"If he's not himself, or if he has another episode like last night, we may have to speak to someone who specializes in removing possessive entities."

"You're talking about an exorcism?" Dave asked.

"Do you really think Jason needs that?" Nicole sounded skeptical but looked worried.

"Not if he's still in control of himself. But he needs to learn to block out the entity, and never let it take control of his hands again. Because it's possible this entity wants to move toward complete possession."

Both parents looked aghast.

"Our best bet for changing the situation is finding Jack's body," I said. "If we can exhume his remains and put them to rest, that could force him to move on. Local stories indicate he's somewhere in the marsh where the creek meets the Ogeechee River, but apparently that's a fair amount of ground to cover. We've reached out to a psychic to walk that area with us—"

"He's coming tonight." Stacey peeked at her phone. "In about an hour."

"So we'll do that," I said. "Then return to our nerve center in the van to monitor your house during the late-night hours."

"And we will totally not get swamp mud on your floors," Stacey said. "We have backup shoes, because we're always searching for clues in haunted forests and damp, foggy graveyards and stuff. Or there might be a pond where someone drowned long ago, that kind of thing."

"You can use Lonnie's hose if you need to," Nicole said, almost mechanically, all color drained from her face. I wished we'd had better news for her.

The front door creaked open. Eight-year-old Andra stood inside the screen door, dressed in polka-dotted pajamas and clutching Carrots the stuffed rabbit.

"Daddy, can we check the cabinets?" she asked, her voice quiet and plaintive, like she was afraid of what she was asking.

"Of course." Dave stood and yawned. "Where's your brother?"

"He doesn't want to. He's drawing. Can the ghost investigators come, in case Jack jumps out?" Andra looked at us. "You can shoot him with lasers or something, right?"

"We can probably run him off if we see him," I said. "Stacey, why don't you join them for cabinet check? I'll talk to Jason."

Stacey and Dave joined Andra inside and closed the door.

"So how much danger are we really in?" Nicole asked me, her voice low.

"The more we learn about this entity, the more dangerous it sounds," I said. "Until we can get rid of it, I would take those rules from the local lore as seriously as Andra does. Keep everything closed tight."

"I can't believe this is real." She looked at her older son, still playing as the last of the daylight faded beyond the empty house across the street. "This place was supposed to be safe. A good investment in our future, security for our kids, the perfect small-town life near a lovely city. And then living the dream turns out to be a nightmare."

She took the empty lemonade pitcher and returned inside.

Chapter Twenty-Four

I knocked on Jason's door, and it drifted open, since he hadn't closed it all the way. All the lights in his room were out except for the one over his drawing table in the far corner, where the ten-year-old boy hunched, scribbling with a pencil.

"Hey, Jason?" I said, doing the best soft, gentle, motherly type voice I could manage to summon. "It's Ellie. How are you?"

He didn't stop scribbling, and he kept his back to me, just like the previous night.

"Uh, Jason?" I moved into his room without waiting for an invitation, approaching him through the darkness. "You doing okay there, kiddo?"

He kept scribbling.

I reached out and gently touched his shoulder.

He spun toward me rapidly, his eyes and mouth wide, and let out a piercing shriek.

I covered my ears and backed off, checking his

hands for weapons. He didn't have a knife this time, but his pencil looked pretty sharp.

"You scared me!" he yelled.

"Sorry!" I said. "I was talking to you for a minute there—"

"But I was *concentrating*. I can't hear anything when I'm *concentrating*." He dropped his pencil and hurriedly covered the drawing, leaving only scribbled darkness visible around the edges of his hand.

"I didn't mean to scare you. I just wanted to ask about the carvings you did."

"I'm not allowed to carve anymore. Mom and Dad took all the stuff. I was getting good, too. I was going to make a Groot."

"Was there someone teaching you how to do it?"

He shook his head.

"Are you sure?" I asked. "Nobody taking control of your hands, guiding you?"

He hesitated, then shook his head, but very slightly.

"Well, if someone was, you would want him to stop, because he might try to take over more than your hands. And he might not let you have control again. But you can keep him out if you want."

"How?" he whispered, looking toward the closet door. It was closed.

"Imagine there's a door that leads in and out of your mind," I said. "You have complete control of it. When you close it, no one can—"

"What kind of door?" Jason squeezed his eyes tight, as if concentrating on picturing what I was describing.

"A thick, solid—"

"Can it be one of those castle doors with spikes on

the bottom?"

"A portcullis. Sure. Your mind is a castle, and you control the only door in or out—"

"And there's archers and catapults."

"Right. So—"

"A dragon lives in the cave under the castle, and he's my employee."

"Awesome. And anytime you want, you can kick out anyone who doesn't belong in the castle of your mind and slam that door shut. You always have the power to say no."

"And send my dragon after them."

"Absolutely."

"Because it breathes out Force lightning." He opened his eyes. "Are all ghosts bad?"

"No, not all. But all of them are out of place. All of them need to let go of this world, of their past, and move on."

"What if one is your friend?"

"What kind of ghost is it?" I asked.

He shrugged.

"Jason," I said, "was it Jack teaching you to carve? Did he show you where to find the tools?"

"I think I want my mom."

"Okay. She's in her room." I walked with him to the hallway, but then he bolted toward the master bedroom. "I mean the guest room! Sorry!"

He turned and ran to the correct door, slamming it behind him after he found his mom.

I never said I was great with kids.

Now that he was gone, I could finally see what he'd been drawing—an open doorway, a skeletal figure with long, stringy white hair standing beyond it, peering out, and darkness behind it.

As I looked closer, though, I saw the darkness was actually a mob of shadows gathered closely behind the figure, as if preparing to follow it through the door. I thought of the mob of vigilantes who'd buried Jack alive.

I had to feel bad for any kid who saw such things, whether real or just in his mind.

Through the open door to his closet, I spotted several new nail heads in the closet wall. It looked like Dave or Nicole had hammered the hidden panel in Jason's closet permanently shut.

Figuring my clumsy attempt to talk to the kid had probably done enough damage for one night, I headed back downstairs to wait outside for Jacob's arrival.

Chapter Twenty-Five

It was well after dark when the headlights of Jacob's Hyundai appeared down the street.

The night had gone quiet, aside from the chirping insects, after Lonnie and his friends departed the neighborhood green for destinations unknown. If the teenage boy had returned inside the house, he hadn't done so through the front door, though there were other ways inside. Perhaps some of them had been known only to Cabinet Jack.

Stacey and I hopped out of the van to meet Jacob as he parallel-parked behind us. Our vehicles were the only two on the street.

"I told you to wear crummy clothes for the swamp." Stacey greeted him with a quick kiss, and I glanced away momentarily, toward the clients' house, where most of the windows had gone dark.

"I am," replied Jacob, despite his business casual wear. "This shirt's missing a button, and these khakis are a little frayed around the left pocket."

"Wow, and you haven't thrown them out yet?"

"I also brought the big guns." He pulled out a pair of thick-rimmed glasses held together by duct tape. "You know I only break out these monsters for special occasions. So where do we enter this swamp?" He glanced around like he expected a sign or gate, or maybe a neon arrow.

"We'll start at the creek by the old mill and head toward the river," I said. "It's not a long walk from here, and we can pass through the empty part of town."

"That'll be scenic," Jacob said. "Or bleak, based on what I saw driving in."

"Bleak," Stacey assured him.

"You know, I honestly don't think I've ever heard of this town before, and I've lived in Savannah most of my life," he said.

"It was basically empty until recently," Stacey said. "Maybe not a total ghost town, but at least a zombie town. Undead but aimless."

"Not a vampire town, then," Jacob said. "Vampires always seem to have clear goals and solid plans for attaining them."

We set off along the crumbling sidewalks, out of the mostly empty neighborhood and through the blighted side of town. The empty diner, gas station, and shops were like the hollow remnants of civilization in some post-apocalyptic world.

"So we're heading toward the train tracks to search for a dead body," Stacey said. "Kinda like *Stand by Me*."

"Except there's only three of us, and we're not kids," I replied.

"And we're probably not at the beginning of a complex and troubling coming-of-age story," Jacob added.

"I just hope there's no leeches in the swamp," I added.

"There could be," Stacey said. "Freshwater leeches are very common in Georgia."

"Ugh. Thanks for mentioning that," I said.

"We'll be fine, Ellie!" Stacey patted my arm. "We're not going into the creek, right? And it's not like they'll fly out of the water and latch onto us. Not unless they're some new kind of mutant jumping leech. Though you never know what might evolve."

"Are we stopping here?" Jacob slowed as we approached the rusty gate of the town cemetery.

"We certainly can," I said. I hadn't been planning to visit tonight, but I'd meant to do it at some point, since the obituaries indicated that some of the people we'd researched were buried there.

"Ooh, is something tugging your psycho-senses?" Stacey asked.

"It's just a feeling." Jacob unlatched the gate, which wasn't locked, and swung it open.

The cemetery was somewhat better maintained than the buildings around it. Stately oaks, beautiful mimosas, and crepe myrtles with crinkly purple blossoms shaded the graves. Otis dutifully kept the grass mowed and the largest weeds pulled, though it still had a rough quality from being maintained on a volunteer basis by one aging man. Ivy had taken over some of the trees and headstones, a difficult invader to vanquish.

We followed Jacob toward a stone wall that divided

off a smaller section of the cemetery at the far end. We kept our flashlights off, relying on the thin moonlight and whatever inner senses of Jacob's had drawn him here.

He walked along the dividing wall, which ran unbroken from one side of the cemetery to the next. There had to be a separate entrance somewhere for the smaller section.

Stacey and I kept our distance to avoid distracting him. I tried to read the gravestones we passed, but it was too dark without my flashlight.

Jacob slowed as we approached the far end of the cemetery, the entrance gate a distant memory through the forest of trees behind us.

I felt a tingle along the back of my neck, like someone was watching me from behind. This was pretty unsettling, considering Stacey and Jacob were both in front of me.

Turning quickly, I thought I glimpsed something moving among the shadowy gravestones under one giant old magnolia tree, but it was gone before I could focus on it. It could have been a large animal or a small child. I wasn't entirely sure which would be worse to encounter in the cemetery of a haunted town after dark.

"Here we go," Jacob murmured. He stopped at one small gravestone. "This is her."

"Who?" I asked.

"The one who's been whispering to me," Jacob said.

I knelt by the stone and brushed dirt away with my fingers. I didn't dare click on a light for fear of chasing off the spirit that was speaking to Jacob, but I had trouble reading it in the dark.

"What's she whispering?" I asked.

"She's not happy about this." Jacob touched a low, saggy point in the stone wall, where the stones had eroded and cracked a bit more than elsewhere, and the moss looked thicker and heavier. Jacob brushed pebble-sized chunks off the top of the wall, sending a tiny avalanche down to the earth.

"She doesn't like the wall falling apart?" I asked.

"The opposite. She hates the wall." He brushed away more off the top, deepening the eroded sag next to the gravestone.

"Maybe we shouldn't vandalize the cemetery, though?" Stacey whispered.

"It's fine. This cheers her up. You know the 'something' in the Robert Frost poem that doesn't love a wall? That's her, in this case." Jacob brushed away more, larger chunks. "She's just a kid. She's got...oh." He went silent, staring at a space beyond the gravestone where I knelt.

That goosebumps-up-my-neck feeling returned.

"What? Is she...getting closer?" I whispered.

"She was murdered. She's all hacked up." Jacob said.

Then he turned away and climbed over the wall, leaving Stacey and me standing there with the invisible murdered girl.

"Um, Jacob? Are you ditching us?" Stacey asked. "Or are we all supposed to jump the wall? What's happening?"

"Huh," Jacob replied. Actually, it didn't sound much like a reply at all, more like he was talking to himself. It was hard to see him in the gloom. "There's someone else over here, who also doesn't love that wall. It's segregating…I mean, separating…" Jacob looked around the smaller patch of cemetery where he stood. "No, 'segregate' was right. The wall separates the dead by race. How old is this cemetery?"

"Probably as old as the rest of town," I said. "1911, 1912."

"Okay. Well, there's a kid right over here with the same opinion as the girl. They're buried next to each other, but with the wall in between. He's…someone murdered him, too. It looks like big chunks were torn out of him."

I winced, thinking of the adze Jack had used to murder the kids, the sharp sideways blade cutting deep and wide.

"Is that why their spirits are here?" I asked. "The wall?"

"They're also unsettled about their violent deaths, which is definitely understandable. Was their murderer never brought to justice?"

"It's a gray area," I said, thinking of the vigilante mob that had buried Jack alive. It wasn't a civilized form of justice, but certainly he'd paid for his crime— assuming he was actually guilty, which hadn't been established at trial. There weren't even police records about the events, just tales handed down, which could easily have become as distorted as the original message in any game of telephone. Perhaps the mob justice and subsequent burying of the truth left the kids' ghosts unsettled, tied to the earthly plane along with their murderer, haunting their old home, desperately seeking playmates among the living while they waited for things to change. "Will they say who their killer was?"

"He was a man they trusted. And…now they're

off." Jacob clambered back over the wall, pausing to kick loose a few more stones from the top before he returned to our side. My feeling of being watched had gone away.

I turned on my flashlight, finally reading the headstone, though I was pretty sure I knew what I'd see.

SOLANGE TONDREAU
1926 - 1938

Pointing my flashlight across the crumbling wall, I saw a matching headstone on the opposite side:

RAYNARD TONDREAU
1931 - 1938

"The wall's between the siblings," I said. "They had to be buried apart."

The three of us stood there quietly for a minute.

Before leaving, we each knocked a few more stones off the low point in the wall, wearing down the barrier a little more.

Chapter Twenty-Six

The stone walls of the empty mill loomed like a castle in the night. We kept to its shadows, not sure whether we might run afoul of trespassing laws. We may not have been on Chief Tyler's good side after wrecking his basement. The "hey, it wasn't us, it was the ghost" excuse doesn't always work, even when true.

We followed the overgrown railroad tracks past the empty mill.

Ahead, the trestle bridge leaned sharply in the sloshing waters of the creek, which had clearly eaten away at the wooden lattice of supports over decades of neglect. The chain-link fence with the warning signs blocked us from crossing the bridge, but I certainly wasn't planning to try.

I drew out my flashlight and started into the swampy wilderness that began across the tracks from the mill ruins.

Then I noticed I was the only person heading into

the marsh.

"Uh, hello?" I turned back to see Jacob staring at the chain-link with all its warning signs in a way that made me very uncomfortable. Stacey, still beside him, returned my look of worry.

"Your little dead friends from the cemetery," Jacob said. "They're back. They're telling me that what you're looking for is across the bridge."

"What do they think we're looking for?" Stacey asked.

"They don't want to say. But they think you know."

I walked around the side of the bridge and pointed my flashlight across the creek, illuminating the sluggish, potentially alligator-infested black water below and the leaning structure of the bridge above.

"It kind of looks like a death trap," I said. "With leeches."

"The boy and girl seem to think it's safe to cross," Jacob told me.

"They're already dead, though," Stacey said. "So that could skew their perspective on safety. Can't they just give us clues or riddles or something?"

He shrugged. "They insist it's what you're looking for."

"Which is exactly what someone operating a death trap would say to lure in new victims." Stacey shook her head.

I looked across the black water of the creek to the cypress swamp on the other side. It wasn't exactly the Golden Gate Bridge, but we'd have to walk a good thirty feet or more across the deteriorated bridge to reach the far bank. The "far bank" itself was a hazy concept. Presumably there was some sort of solid ground over there, among the muddy water and snaking willow roots, but I couldn't see it from where I stood.

"There must be another way around," Jacob said.

"If we go west, we'll hit the Ogeechee River, which is even wider. East…" I pulled out my phone. "Even if we drove the van, we'd be looking at a long hike from the nearest paved road trying to get around to the other side." I put it away and took a deep breath. "I'll cross first. If the bridge holds me, y'all follow. If it doesn't, consider rescuing me from the creek after I fall. And help me remove all the leeches."

"I should go first, actually," Jacob said. "So the local Deadites can tell me where to get off the tracks and slog into the swamp."

"If anybody's breaking their limb on the decaying bridge to a haunted swamp, it's going to be me," I said. "It's almost exactly the way I've always pictured my death. It's fate."

"I may have better health benefits, though." Jacob was an accountant at a CPA firm by day, which was possibly the least psychic-y job I could think of, but life could be strange like that.

Rather than continue debating, I jumped onto the chain-link fence and climbed, using the barrier as a ladder, reversing the intentions of those who'd built it. It wobbled as I scaled over the top and clambered back down on the other side.

"This is why it's hard to win an argument with Ellie," Stacey said, shaking her head at me.

"I'll be fine. Probably." I followed the railbed to the edge of the creek, where only wooden cross-ties remained like sagging, deteriorated wooden stepping stones ahead, a view of the black creek in between them. "Okay, Sunny and Rainy. Show me the way."

If any helpful spirit guides were tagging along as I crossed over, they certainly didn't make themselves known to me. Ghosts supposedly hate to cross running water, which is a major part of why many homes in Savannah, including the interior of my apartment, are painted a hue known as haint blue. Does it help? I don't know, but I need all the help I can get in the don't-haunt-me department.

Maybe ghosts made an exception about running water if there was a bridge, though, and particularly a bridge like this, which looked like it belonged more in the land of the dead than that of the living.

I avoided broken ties as I moved out across the bridge, step by hesitant step. Some ties felt dangerously spongy beneath me. My view of the creek widened. I could see the gap in the woods where it flowed away into the west, and also how the thick trees and undergrowth grew right up to the water and over it, concealing almost all the solid ground.

"Watch your step up here!" I called back to Stacey and Jacob. "Only about one in three crossties seem safe."

The wind picked up and the bridge creaked. It swayed beneath my feet, as though made of rope and planks instead of water-rotted timbers. I looked for reference at the massive tree trunks on the far shore, trying to see how far the bridge was swaying, but I couldn't tell because the night wind was whipping those trees around, too.

I held still, like a deer that just heard a twig snap, and braced myself as best as I could for a fall.

Then the wind and the bridge both settled.

I kept going, though the supports creaked and groaned beneath me as if the whole rickety structure might give way.

Gradually, I crossed into the shadows of the trees on the far bank. Shining my light past the edge of the tracks, I saw limbs and roots, plants growing atop plants, but no obvious bare ground on which to walk. The tracks were still elevated on posts, indicating soggy ground below, but I'd entered the swamp beyond the creek.

"Over here," a child's voice whispered.

I automatically pointed my flashlight toward where I'd heard the voice. This wasn't actually the best response, since I didn't want to chase off any supernatural entities who might be trying to communicate with me.

My beam found no one there, but it did land on a gap between a pair of tree trunks, a sort of gateway into the deeper swamp.

I dropped into a patch of high weeds and landed awkwardly in knee-deep muddy water, which splashed all over my jeans, shirt, and face. At least I'd managed to land on my feet, though I wobbled before gaining my balance.

"Hello?" I sloshed forward to the gap between trunks, my light pointed straight down now to minimize the risk of chasing off the entity. I couldn't turn it off altogether, though, because then I'd be walking blindly.

No response came. Ahead lay a narrow pass between trunks thick with moss, a barely visible walkway through the vegetation, if you didn't mind low-lying limbs, thorny vines, and thick, resistant undergrowth.

"Hello?" I went out on a limb. "Solange? Raynard?" No response. I tried another limb. "Aurelie?"

A large splash sounded behind me. I jumped and pointed my light.

"Ellie?" Jacob hadn't landed as luckily as me, more on his hands and knees. He pushed himself to a standing position, even more muddy than I was, and fished his flashlight out of the shallow water. "Oh, good. We didn't hear you announce you were leaving the tracks. You just kind of disappeared."

"I'm still alive. I heard something in the woods and was trying not to run it off."

"Stacey, we're here!" Jacob held up his flashlight like the Statute of Liberty to create a beacon for her, like I really should have done for him instead of chasing strange voices into the swamp like a will o' the wisp.

I pointed my light ahead, through the pair of tree trunks. The way forward, the way of the whispering spirit, promised more treacherous footing, roots and weeds and pools of water. Thick, wild plants completely obscured the ground, hiding any distinction between earth, mud, standing water, and moving water. Witch alder shrubs, their leaves dark green and tough for the summer, helped block the way. Colonies of pitcher plants stood like veiny red and green cobras reared up with their mouths open, waiting to lure in hungry insects with deceptive promises of sweet nectar, only to eat them alive.

Surely nothing similar was happening to us, as we allowed ghosts to direct us across a perilous bridge into a deeper swamp.

"Wow, this is gnarly." Stacey arrived along the creaky railroad bridge. When she dropped the few feet to the knee-deep water below, Jacob was there to steady her after she landed, but he got a fair amount of mud on her in the process. She leaned into it, though, probably enjoying the whole muddy wilderness scenario. Wading among snakes and alligators while avoiding any semblance of climate control is her idea of a perfect vacation. "Nice catch," she told him.

"Yes, you are." He leaned in for a kiss.

Deciding that I'd rather hang out with the invisible whispering dead child than witness this, I returned to the narrow pass through the swamp, weaving and pushing my way through the undergrowth.

"Wait!" Stacey called after me, quite a number of seconds later. "Is that even the right way?"

"It is," Jacob told her.

"Then she shouldn't be in there alone."

I pushed onward, not bothering to answer them. Maybe my silent disappearance into the swamp would get them moving faster.

The path forward became less obvious, if it existed at all, and I stopped to wait for them to catch up.

"There you are!" Stacey announced as her light flooded my general area, lighting up the cypress bark around me like it was daytime.

"Took you two long enough," I said. "Jacob, which way?"

"We're on the right path." He closed his eyes for a long moment, then opened them and took the lead, ducking under limbs and crawling through mud and muck.

"I kind of expected the woods to be a little thinner,

considering there was a timber mill nearby for about fifty years," I said.

"The mill's been closed for decades, though," Stacey said. "That's plenty of time for trees to grow back."

"Maybe you kids could keep it down back there," Jacob said. "The voice guiding me is very faint."

"Copy that," Stacey replied. "Ellie, we have to cut the chatter."

"I heard him," I said.

Ahead, Jacob turned off his flashlight, as if he could somehow find his way forward better in the dark. I didn't ask questions, not wanting to break his focus, or risk Stacey implying I was some kind of chatterbox, which I found ironic coming from her.

"Up here," Jacob murmured, shoving his way forward as the swamp seemed nearly impassable.

We followed him through, getting muddier by the minute. Everything in the swamp was damp from the recent rain. Wet leaves and branches brushed and scratched at my face like unwelcome fingers.

Jacob had found something of a clearing, full of trees that had broken and fallen many years ago and had since grown thick coats of moss and fungus. The trees at the edges had grown in, their branches reaching out to claim the empty space left by the fallen older generation of trees.

"Here," he said softly.

"Here what?" I asked, after a respectful pause, and not the kind of short, impatient pause a chattery person would give.

"This is where the girl's leading us," he said.

"Solange? From the cemetery?" I asked.

"No. Different girl, about the same age, with a fainter presence." Jacob walked over to a spindly black gum tree and touched the damp bark. "Here. This is where she's buried."

"Who?" I asked.

"This girl who's been guiding us. You came here to find her grave, didn't you? Right? Some missing girl? Red hair, very muddy? That's who I've been following." Jacob looked between us.

"We're searching for the grave of an adult man," I said.

"But we're flexible," Stacey added.

"She was murdered like the other kids," Jacob said. "Big pieces of her just…cut off. Peeled off. Her killer buried her out here."

"What's her name?" I asked.

"She's communicating in images and feelings, not words. She's pale, lots of freckles, red hair. Middle school age."

"That could be Angela Kilborne," I said. "The police chief's daughter who went missing—"

"Yep," Jacob said. "She grew a little sharper and clearer when you said that."

"Can she tell us who killed her?"

Jacob opened his mouth, then clapped a hand over one eye and dropped to his knee like he'd been struck in the head.

"Jake!" Stacey ran to his side.

"Leave him alone!" I shouted, sweeping the area with my light, reaching for the speaker on my belt.

"It's…okay," Jacob said. "Her answer was just kind of forceful. She showed me her death. He slipped into her room in the middle of the night, grabbed her, and pulled her away through a cabinet in her wall. Then he killed her. So, yeah, experiencing all that at once kind of knocked me over."

"I'm sorry," Stacey said.

"I'll be okay." Jacob rose to his feet and pointed. "He buried her here, at the base of the tree. Dig and you'll find her."

"Well, it's not what we expected, but it'll be good to put one victim to rest, at least," I said.

"She's not the only one." Jacob clambered over a fallen trunk and waved his hand over another spot, like he was testing it for heat. "There's a boy here. Eight, nine, maybe ten years old." He walked slowly around the upturned, overgrown roots. "And here. A girl. And there's another kid's ghost…and another one…what is going on? Stacey? Ellie? It's *Daycare of the Dead* out here."

"This is where he brought his victims," I said.

"Yeah," Jacob said. "I think maybe they were all killed by the same guy, because they died in the same way."

"They need a proper burial somewhere," I said. "Maybe the police chief can help us. Let's mark each grave."

"I'm on it." Stacey drew red flags mounted on thin metal stakes from her backpack. We'd brought them to mark the murderer's grave if we found it.

She followed Jacob, planting them where Jacob directed her, but she only had ten, and Jacob found two more bodies. We marked the final two with heaps of stones that we dug out of the wet earth.

At last, the grim work complete, we found ourselves back near the point where we'd begun.

"You definitely earned your psychic fee this time, Jacob," I said.

"Am I getting paid for this one? That's always a plus." He looked down at his mud-crusted shirt. Despite his surface-level good humor, he looked pale, plainly disturbed by finding so many young murder victims. "I'll...have to add a clothing allowance to my rider."

"I warned you," Stacey said. "Let's go hose off."

"Wait." I looked back at the flags we'd planted. Most were out of sight from where we stood, but I pictured where they were, and the pattern became clear. "They're in a circle."

"Roughly, yeah," Jacob said.

"Did we check the center?"

We looked ahead at the place where the rotten trunks were piled the thickest.

"There's no spirit calling me there, but I'll look." Jacob walked ahead, fighting the undergrowth. He climbed up onto a fallen trunk and walked atop its slippery, mossy surface, his arms wide for balance. Stacey and I helped light his way.

He reached the top and knelt, closing his eyes. He touched the dead trunks, their rotten innards long exposed to the rain, the thick colonies of mushrooms and fungus feeding on their decay.

"There's something," he said. "Someone. But not the same kind of victim as the others. He was...I think he was buried alive down here. Like he was sealed inside a coffin and just buried. Only it wasn't a coffin, because it was too small. He was cramped up inside. A slow, slow death. Awful."

I couldn't help feeling a rush of hope. Maybe we'd

found Jack at last, but the presence of his victims' bodies in a circle around him raised new questions.

"Can you tell us what he looked like?" I asked.

"It's not as clear. Like I said, he's not eager to reach out to me like the others. He's older than them, though."

"How much older?"

"He was maybe…thirteen, fourteen, fifteen when he died." Jacob said, which threw off my line of questioning.

"Wait," Stacey said. "It's another *kid* down there in the cabinet? It's not…uh…you know…a non-kid, by any chance?" She stumbled, trying out of habit to avoid leading questions.

"Definitely not an adult," Jacob said. "He was hit with a crowbar, bound and gagged, and thrown into the cabinet."

"By who?"

"The same guy as the rest. Then he was carried here and buried by a group of guys. He could hear their voices. He was kicking, trying to shout to them, but the more noise he made, the more they shouted him down. They sang drunkenly as they buried the box. The more mud they piled on, the less he could hear them. Eventually, he could only hear silence, and dripping mud, and his air began to run out." Jacob's hand recoiled from the mushroom patch, and he opened his eyes. "He's trying to return home, to continue life in some form."

"Back way up," I said. "You're saying there's a teenager down there who was murdered by the same guy as the rest of these victims? You're sure about that?"

"Yeah, why? Wouldn't it be weirder if it was a whole other murderer?"

"So, wait," Stacey said. "If it wasn't Jack that got buried here, who was it? And where did Jack get buried? Or was Jack never buried alive, and the local legends got confused about who was? Because either they're confused or I am."

"Who's Jack?" Jacob asked.

"A murder suspect," I said.

"Big smile? Leather apron?" Jacob asked.

"That…sounds like him," I said.

"He always smiled when he killed the others," Jacob said. "But not this one. He didn't smile when he put this older one in the box."

"His apprentice, maybe. What did the teenage boy look like?"

"I'm not seeing him as clearly as the others. He's keeping his face away from me, like he regrets opening up to me at all. His hair's long, blond, and tangled, like he's not overly into the whole grooming thing."

"Can you ask him—"

"He's gone again. He avoids this place, where he suffered and died, but it sometimes draws him back."

"So where does he go the rest of the time?"

"Probably somewhere he cared about in life. Maybe his old home. That's the first place I'd look."

"Do the others buried here know they're dead?" I asked.

"Yeah, they've figured that one out. They're much less emotional than the first one, really kind of restrained for kids. They're just sort of hanging out by their graves, watching us. But they aren't saying much. Maybe there's bits and pieces of those victims' souls here, residual hauntings, spiritual afterimages. Still best to help them move on, though."

"Just to be clear, though, you haven't encountered the actual ghost of that murderer?" I asked.

"So much for avoiding leading questions," Stacey said.

"Not so far." Jacob looked between us. "Is that what you were hoping to find? The murderer's ghost?"

"His body, actually," I said. "He was supposedly buried in a cabinet out here. But someone else is buried there instead."

"But then where's Jack buried?" Stacey blinked a few times. "And how did he die? And when? And where? And who did it? And why?"

Jacob shrugged. "If I run into him, I'll ask."

"But he…has to be dead, right?" she asked. "Ellie?"

"If he was still alive, he'd be more than a century old," I said. "So I'm guessing he's dead."

"But…" Stacey trailed off, looking as dissatisfied as I felt with this new but incomplete information.

"The kid ghosts are going to ground, like they're done talking with us. Or maybe they're afraid." Jacob looked back in the direction from which we'd arrived. "Something's coming."

Even I could feel the approaching cold like a falling frost. Thick fog formed from the heavy, humid summer air, filling the swamp with winter-white clouds that blotted out any light from above.

Chapter Twenty-Seven

"Lights off," I whispered.

"Are you sure?" Stacey whispered back as we clicked off all of our flashlights.

"Keep them handy, though," I added, staring into the approaching cold. The fog coiled and curled in thick tendrils, twisting through the woods like mystical, ravenous wild vines, like the ivy growing out of control in the town cemetery, swallowing everything.

We fell silent as footsteps approached. They were barely audible, moving slowly, in no hurry at all.

I tensed, waiting and watching, my heart loud in my ears. Maybe it was the town police chief, here to arrest us for trespassing.

A dark figure appeared in the fog, walking toward us along a broken, fallen, fungus-covered trunk. He was tall, thin, featureless at first. As he drew closer, I saw he wore a flat cap and a workman's shirt. Over this was a leather carpenter's apron with pockets and loops holding tools—files and rasps with rough steel teeth, sharp awls and chisels.

He carried a claw hammer at his side.

"Jack?" I asked. "Jack Macgill?"

The figure did not answer, just kept walking toward me.

"Ellie," Jacob whispered. He wasn't far away, but his voice sounded distant. "This guy is evil. And strong."

I nodded. "Everybody hold steady," I whispered.

The figure's face became clearer as he approached, thin and dry, as if mummified, the skin peeled back to form a wide, unsettling smile. The smile was an unwelcome sight. I wanted him to look worried, afraid, anything to indicate we might be close to defeating him.

"It's time for you to move on, Jack," I said. "Leave this town alone. You've had your revenge. More than enough. We're going to help you move on and get free of all this."

When the entity spoke, his voice sounded wet and oily like when he'd grabbed me before.

"I have already moved on."

"No, you're still obsessed with this world. You did horrible things in life. You don't want to continue in death. Everyone who tried to kill you is long dead. Who did they bury in that cabinet, Jack? Was it your apprentice, Gabriel?"

Jack's smile slipped away. "They took him from me."

"You killed him," I said. "You struck him with that crowbar and nailed him inside. They buried him while you got away. You let Gabriel die in your place. You didn't like doing it, but you did it for your own survival. It certainly took the sunshine out of your smile, though."

"I punished them all." I didn't like how he seemed to be drifting closer to me, especially with the hammer in his hand.

"Yes," I said. "Your revenge is done. Surely you've punished every family by now. Most of them are gone from this town, scattered to the wind. You could be free like them."

"I am more than you know," Jack said. "When I brought the first of the twelve here to the swamp, strange things approached me. Spirits of decay, welcoming my offerings. They gave me the power of doors and doorways, of coming and going, so I could take the children and never be caught."

"Are you dead or alive, then?" I asked.

"Death is only another door."

"Well, it's one you need to pass through. And close it behind you this time."

He said nothing. His silent smile made me shiver, as did the bitter cold that had taken over the swamp. If it grew much worse, ice would start to form in the stagnant pools of black water.

"And what did these sacrifices gain you, other than the ability to collect more sacrifices?" I asked. "Because it seems to me you lost your body and your soul."

"All that I made contains a little of my soul. This town is my body, and my resurrection is at hand."

"Depart peacefully, or I will force you to go." I said that like I had any idea how I would actually do it. I knew I would die trying if it came to that, though—

Jack reminded me too much of Anton Clay, the old slave-master spirit who'd killed my parents. Neither had any remorse for the pain they caused. Both seemed to delight in murder, and to grow stronger with each life they took.

"Something else is happening," Jacob warned me. "I'm not sure what, but it's big, and he's distracting us —"

"I will not depart," the shadowy specter of Jack said. "Nor will any of you."

"Ellie—" Jacob began, but then I saw them, heard them, and felt them.

The ghosts of his victims erupted from the dense fog around us. Dead children climbed out over and between fallen trees. Others slithered up from the ground, their voices like rustling leaves and creaking branches. As if they hadn't suffered enough when they'd died, they remained his possessions in the afterlife.

"They brought you here for me," Jack said in his chilly voice. "To my place of sacrifice, to join them in the earth."

Then he raised his hammer, and I tried to back away, but I was already struggling with three or four corpse-like children grabbing me, climbing me, biting me with their black-gummed mouths.

Jack swung the hammer, but not toward me. He buried the hammer's claw in the soft black bark of a long-dead cypress tree that must have once towered over the swamp, but its upper reaches had long since broken off and rotted into the mud.

He pried open a low door built into the tree, ripping open years of moss and fungus that had concealed it. The tree's interior was hollow, large enough for a man to stand inside.

He stepped through, into the darkness within. He closed the door most of the way behind him, and its edges again grew difficult to distinguish in the fungus-covered bark.

The apparitions of dead children surged around us like reanimated bodies raised from below by an evil spell. They grabbed us with their small, skeletal hands. Faces gone soft with decay, like forgotten Halloween pumpkins, drew close and snapped at us with sharp little teeth. They were hungry for our living energy, eager to tear us apart.

"Get back!" Jacob bellowed in a voice that I'd only heard from him occasionally, a powerful, commanding tone like he expected the spirits to obey. That's always worth a try. Jacob could add a little extra psychic oomph to it. I hoped it was working for him, but I couldn't really devote much attention to the matter because of all the hideous things attacking me at that particular moment.

A bony girl climbed up the front of me, her dark red hair full of swamp mud, her pale skin flayed in multiple places with long, deep adze wounds, her eye sockets hollow and bleeding, her mouth wide open like she was planning on sinking her mud-stained teeth into my face. I wondered if this was the one who'd contacted Jacob, who'd whispered for us to follow her.

I blasted her with three thousand lumens of white light from my flashlight, straight through her skull, or at least the mushy remnants of it beneath her rotten-paper skin. I got a pretty good look at the dark-jelly interior of her head as the light flooded through, and it was not pretty.

Stacey had activated her light, too, and we filled the air with sacred music to really create an unpleasant atmosphere for the vicious ghosts. The child ghosts weren't truly evil, of course, but under Jack's control, acting as extensions of his will.

I flipped through my playlist to find the children's choir songs I'd downloaded at some point. Kids sang "Dare to be a Daniel" over the speaker mounted on my belt. I assumed they meant the one in the Biblical lion's den story and not Daniel Tiger, the ambitious young predator who'd seized control of Mr. Rogers' Neighborhood.

The music and lights didn't send our attackers back into the ground, unfortunately, but they seemed to slow their attack. The cold little hands gripping our legs and arms loosened their grip enough that we could run.

Mud and swamp water and tree roots and undergrowth didn't add up to a great running environment, though. We all did a lot of staggering and crawling on hands and knees through damp earth.

The cold fog followed us to the train tracks. Stacey and I turned down the volume on our utility-belt speakers so we could talk.

"Who goes first?" Stacey looked up at the train tracks on their crumbling supports.

"We don't have time for that," Jacob said. "They're still coming for us. They're already getting resistant to your small defenses."

"If you've got any big defenses in mind, I'm all ears," I said.

"Distance is our best defense here." Jacob started to climb the wooden support structure like an awkward, slippery ladder with inconveniently large and widely spaced rungs. "Come on! I'm not kidding. Everyone together."

I pointed my flashlight back toward the woods. The fog was so dense I couldn't see much besides the scattered reflection of my own light.

"Ellie, we should go," Stacey said.

"I'm right behind you, but we do need to space ourselves out a little so we don't break the bridge," I told her. "Get going!"

Stacey nodded and climbed up the four feet or so to the tracks, then vanished into the fog as she started across.

I waited on the muddy, spongy ground, watching for any sign of further attacks coming from within the fog. The unnatural cold bit into my bones, but fortunately no vicious little elementary-school ghosts emerged to do the same.

Finally, after giving Jacob and Stacey time to get ahead, I turned my back on the fog and waded into the stagnant water by the bridge supports. I climbed the slippery, sagging wood of the skeletal frame, which wobbled in a way that was not reassuring.

At the top, I was careful to crawl out onto the railroad tie that looked least likely to crack under my weight. I rose to my feet and looked ahead, but the cold fog had come with us. I could barely discern a blonde figure up ahead as it walked out of sight.

That seemed like plenty of spacing to me, so I began to walk carefully as before, testing each tie before putting my weight on it, avoiding the obviously broken ones, though it was getting harder to see as the cold fog grew thicker and denser around me, the summer's steamy heat a painfully distant memory. I couldn't see the moonlight above nor the blackwater creek below, though I could hear water gurgling against the bridge supports.

The fog meant we weren't yet safe, weren't alone. Something was crossing over with us, not far behind me, perhaps already surrounding me.

As I stretched out my foot to step over an obviously bad rail tie, a pale little hand dripping with swamp mud reached up through the track and grabbed my ankle.

I cried out in surprise as the hand pulled my foot down through the tracks. My leg tore through the desiccated rail tie like it was paper, and I toppled forward.

I flung my arms forward across the newly created gap, toward the seemingly reliable, solid tie beyond. I caught myself with both hands, but the slippery wood cracked as I grabbed it. My flashlight spun away, down through the fog before splashing into the creek.

More cold, damp little hands, at least six of them, crawled like tarantulas over my legs and back and torso, grabbing me, pulling me down.

I crashed through rotten wood, into fog and darkness, surrounded by shadowy figures and childish giggles.

A diagonal brace broke my fall, though it nearly broke under me when I landed on it. I clung to it as it swayed, creaking. I couldn't see much, but I could see the brace was attached to a withered support post that looked like a pillar of black mush.

The crowd of cold hands clenched tight and pulled harder, their touch burning like dry ice, and I felt my energy and strength draining away. The little monsters were feeding on me. The ones I could see looked like the muddy husks of corpses, remnants of hair clinging to their skulls, their eye sockets hollow, their lips long gone, leaving permanent grins of sharp little teeth reminiscent of Jack, as if they were his disciples.

There were others I couldn't see, out of my line of sight, weighing down my back and shoulders and legs, preying on me.

I tried to climb back up the crumbling woodwork to the track above, but they wouldn't let me go. They began biting, insatiable, ravenous for the last traces of energy in my weary body and soul. I felt exhausted, like I'd aged years in a few seconds. My muscles were losing their strength, my eyelids growing heavy.

The water gurgled below, as if enticing me to sleep.

I forced my eyes open. Running water. If I could reach it, maybe I could shake the hungry ghosts loose.

When I tried to climb down, though, they held me in place, not letting me escape. Their whispering grew angry. I didn't have the strength to fight them.

There was clearly another, more dangerous way to get myself down to the running water, and it was perfect for my remaining energy level—let go and drop below. Such a simple, clear plan that it even rhymed, I thought with my exhausted clattertrap remnant of a brain.

If I was lucky, I'd land in deep, quick-running water that caused the ghosts to release me.

If I was less lucky, I could smash my skull into a rock, tree trunk, or one of the many missing timbers that must have fallen from the underside of the bridge over the years. At least that would take care of my headache.

That didn't even get into the large or venomous

forms of wildlife I might encounter.

"Ellie!" Stacey called back to me. Maybe she'd heard the crack of the railroad tie, or any screaming I may have been doing.

"Keep going!" I yelled as loudly as I could in my drained state, which wasn't particularly loud. My second attempt was even more pathetic, as I struggled to form the words "keep going" while yawning.

Then I let go and dropped below. Simple as an ad slogan.

Falling backward through the fog, I got a better look at more of the barely human, child-sized creatures that had been on my back. They scrambled to the remaining supports, not wanting to ride me down into the creek water, apparently.

I fell…and then I didn't.

The claw-like hands and sharp teeth remained sunk into me. The entities weren't letting me escape, but instead held me tighter, continuing their feeding frenzy on my basic vital energy, though at this point they were surely licking the bottom of the bowl on that.

From a distance, upheld only by shadows, it might have looked like I was levitating among the broken-down, timeworn infrastructure of the bridge.

"Come on," I grumbled. "Just let me go."

Their mouths, the ones that weren't biting me, smiled wickedly. Their deteriorated faces moved closer, their assortment of dead eyes and empty eye holes staring at me without blinking.

I twisted and tried to kick free. My boot passed uselessly through the nearest ghost, who looked like the zombie remains of an elementary-age boy with a flattop haircut. Maybe he'd been a pee-wee football player.

My kick continued onward and struck the crumbling support post behind him, and the post wobbled. The whole trestle structure around us groaned and shifted in response.

"Let me…go…" I whispered. "Or we all go down together." Well, I thought that sounded pretty gangster at the time.

If anything, they tightened their grips and moved closer, draining what little warmth I had left. My fingers and toes were completely numb, and the cold was working its way into my core.

"Fine," I whispered. "Be that way."

I kicked through them again, into the crumbling support, which responded with a deep, grinding sort of groan, like I'd really hurt its feelings.

I kicked again and again. And again.

Finally, it crumpled and gave way.

Railroad ties dropped down around me, one after another, decayed wood smashing into more decayed wood. Two lengths of old rail came down like long, sharp spears.

The bridge seemed as if it had been held together mostly by habit, and now that the habit was broken, it was falling to pieces, one loose, decomposed timber crashing into another, one rusty forgotten bolt after another shearing loose.

The entire trestle fell apart, and I finally tumbled free, falling toward whatever bone-breaking objects awaited in the water below. Even if I lucked into landing somewhere deep and safe, any part of the collapsing trestle could strike me from above.

Still, the swamp children had let me go, so at least I

could enjoy that relief for a few seconds on the way down to my exciting new future of pain, broken bones, and getting eaten by gators.

Someone caught me, though, and pulled me out of the landslide of broken supports and falling ties and rails. They somehow hauled me back up and onto the next solid tie, supported by the next trestle over instead of the one that was collapsing into the creek.

The track was broken now, with a sizable gap about halfway across the creek. I couldn't see much of the other side, where fog still shrouded the bridge. Screeches and howls of displeasure sounded from the shadows there, the kiddos furious they'd lost their feast. Not that I had much energy left for them to take from me. I felt like I was about to die from exhaustion and hypothermia. Exhaustothermia, they could call it on my death certificate.

Fortunately, the night air around me was warming, returning to proper summer temperature, and the fog was dissipating accordingly.

"Stacey?" I turned to see the blonde figure standing over me, the person who had, in an impressive show of courage and strength, grabbed me up and pulled me away from disaster.

It wasn't Stacey. It wasn't Jacob, either.

This discovery freaked me out, and I struggled to rise to my feet.

His ice-cold hand steadied me, easing me away from the precipice where the tracks now ended in an abrupt drop.

It was another dead kid, tall enough that I'd mistaken him for Stacey in the fog, though up close I saw his hair was longer than hers, a dirty blond crusted with swamp mud. To be fair, Stacey's hair had also been crusted with swamp mud last time I'd seen it. He was as clearly dead as the other kids, but at least he had eyes in his sockets. He wore a workman's cap and collared moleskin shirt, and a leather apron with pockets and loops.

"I've seen you before," I told him, my voice thick and slow. I thought of Jason's black-ink drawing, the figure with the long white or light-colored hair looking out through an open door, a horde of shadows behind him.

The apparition turned away, heading in the direction Jacob and Stacey had gone.

He faded out of sight, along with the last traces of the fog, all of it burned away by the summer night's heat asserting itself again.

A bright light like the headlamp of a train appeared down the tracks, seeming to bear down on me.

"Ellie!" Stacey shouted from behind the light. "There you are! It sounded like the bridge fell down."

"Yeah. I kinda knocked some of it down on purpose," I added, though actually I'd been shocked at the scale of destruction. That bridge had not been in good shape.

"You did? Why?"

"It seemed like a good idea at the time."

"Do you need help?"

"No, just get off the bridge. I'm coming."

I took a final look back across the creek. The bank of fog had retreated back along the bridge, toward the swamp, but it hadn't disappeared. It felt like the ghosts were still in there, watching us, perhaps waiting for their master, Jack, to return.

Chapter Twenty-Eight

We trudged home through the bleak and boarded part of town, past some anonymous former shops, their individual identities lost long ago along with their signs and window displays. I was exhausted and stumbled frequently. Stacey and Jacob helped support me, as they always do, in various ways.

I tried to mumble through an explanation of what had happened. Jacob filled her in a little on the supernatural side. He'd been able to witness aspects of it with his psychic abilities, even in the dark, though too late to act on it.

"They attacked her," Jacob told Stacey. "But one helped her."

"Which one helped?"

"Kiddo," I mumbled. "He needs shampoo." I was really, really tired.

"We'll put out an APB on that kid," Stacey said. "An All-Psychics Bulletin. Right, Jake?"

"If that existed, sure."

"Is anything after us now?" Stacey asked.

"Not yet, but I would never feel too sure in this town after dark." Jacob mentioned this as we passed the town cemetery again.

After what felt like thousands of years of walking, we finally reached our clients' neighborhood and our van. I sat and slumped on the curb beside it. Stacey gave me a long drink of distilled water from her Platypus collapsible water pouch.

"I'll text Nicole we're here," she said. "And I guess we actually should use the hose."

I nodded. Nicole had mentioned we could use the garden hose with the spray attachment on the side of her house, behind the privacy of several tall, red-blooming azaleas. I had figured a change of shoes would probably be sufficient, but plainly I had figured wrong, because we were muddy all over.

Stacey went first, then Jacob joined her, and I heard some laughing and splashing like maybe they were having slightly too much fun over there. I would have rolled my eyes if my eyelids hadn't felt so heavy.

Finally, Stacey returned, dressed in her backup shoes and clothes, her hair damp.

"Okay, so we aren't dripping mud anymore, but I still don't feel presentable enough to enter the clients' house," Stacey said.

"We'll stay in the van and observe tonight," I said.

"That was the plan last night, too."

"I'm much too tired to go charging in anywhere tonight." I yawned. "If there's trouble, just tell them 'don't go into the light' or something. Unless they're already dead, then tell them to do that. Easy."

I eventually took my turn with the hose, while Stacey saw Jacob off for the evening, since he had to get up for his job a few hours later. Nicole was right that the area behind the mass of azaleas was secluded, as long as the house next door was uninhabited, as it currently was.

Still, I hurried and put on fresh clothes while I was still damp. I was in complete agreement with Stacey about not wanting to encounter our clients anytime in the near future, especially since I was basically dead on my feet.

In the van, Stacey had turned on all the monitors and screens so we could look inside the house.

"You keep watch for activity," I told her as I stretched out on the drop-down cot.

"What are you going to do?" she asked.

"I'm going to review the details of the case very quietly to myself. I'll let you know when I'm done." I closed my eyes and fell instantly asleep.

Sleep didn't last long enough; it seemed like only a few seconds later that Stacey was nudging me awake.

"What's happening?" I muttered. I opened my eyes on monitors that seemed too bright, so I turned my head away toward the van wall. My head felt like it was full of concrete, or at least partially dried cement.

"It's nearly sunrise, so I figured we should head home."

"Yeah, good idea. You drive, I'll just lie here." I closed my eyes again.

"Ellie! You're forgetting about seat belt safety. I am not getting a ticket over this."

I groaned and forced myself to lumber up to the passenger seat up front. I managed to buckle the seatbelt after only four drowsy failed attempts.

"Now you can go back to sleep." Stacey pulled away from the curb, headlights illuminating the overgrown neighborhood around us.

"That's impossible until I eat something. Those monster kids sucked away every drop of energy I had." I touched my rumbling stomach. I was so hungry I felt emaciated, though I didn't look that way in the mirror on the back of the passenger-side sun visor. I just looked tired and pale, with enormous dark-purple patches under my eyes, somewhere between vampire and zombie.

"Okay, we can swing by the Turntables Cafe and see if it's open yet."

"A bagel or a muffin isn't enough," I said. "I was thinking more along the lines of a Pop's Pancake Platter at The Country Barn."

"Oh, no way. You couldn't eat all of that."

"I could. Maybe two."

"Don't be crazy. If you're sure that's what you want —"

"Yep."

"It's going to be about half an hour. The nearest Country Barn is off an I-95 exit on our way home."

"Of course it is. The Country Barn and an interstate exit ramp, name a more iconic duo." I stretched and took a deep breath. "Last night seems like a crazy nightmare."

"It was. And I still don't understand what happened way back in the past. I get that the men of the town nailed Jack inside the cabinet, and then Jack's apprentice rescued him."

"Maybe they left to find shovels or something," I

said. "Once they decided to bury him alive."

"Right," Stacey said. "But then the apprentice freed Jack, who was so ungrateful that he bound and gagged the apprentice—what was his name?"

"Gabriel. That's it!" I unbuckled my seatbelt and staggered toward the back of the van.

"Um, Ellie? Seatbelt laws? We are cruising down the highway here."

"I appreciate your concern." I opened my laptop bag and dug through a sheaf of papers we'd printed out at the library. When I found what I was looking for, I pulled it out and started toward the front of the van again.

Stacey slammed on the brakes, flinging me forward into the dashboard. Just ahead of us, a red Mustang cut sharply across our lane and squealed as it turned off down a side road.

"Sorry!" Stacey said, as I climbed into my seat. "But that's why—"

"Seatbelts, I know." I clicked mine into place, then showed her the printout. The image was from the *Timbermill Ledger* Easter article, with Jack Macgill in his unsettling bunny costume, his arm around a boy with long blond hair holding a carved rabbit. I read aloud from the photo caption, "Gabriel Baylor, Macgill's apprentice."

"He looks like a kid. I guess people started work young in those days."

"He's the one who kept me from falling at the bridge," I said.

"But why? What makes him different from the others?"

"Jack might have less control of him, for one thing.

Jack murdered all those other children himself, but he only assaulted Gabriel and tied him up. The actual murder was carried out by the vigilantes."

"Doesn't that mean Jack was actually alive when he was sneaking into kids' rooms and kidnapping them?" Stacey asked. "As revenge for his attempted murder?"

"Right."

"But why bury them in the swamp near Gabriel's body?"

"Because, at the time, the police chief and other town leaders wouldn't want anyone to search that area of the swamp," I said. "The body was still there, buried in the swamp, evidence of their crime. So when Jack needed a place to bury some bodies—"

"He put them in the one place where they would never go digging." Stacey nodded. "He used their own guilt against them. Hiding them in the town's blind spot. So is Jack...alive? Dead? Some in-between place?"

"I'm not sure we can trust his word, but it sounds like his series of child murders brought him in contact with something demonic. And now he has some kind of supernatural existence, and he's coming back to stalk the town, now that it's coming back to life."

"Well, *that* has to stop," Stacey said.

"Did you notice anything else unusual while I was asleep last night?"

"I caught part of a one-sided conversation from Penny's room," Stacey said. "I'll play it for you in a minute. It sounded like she was making plans to meet someone."

"If it's someone dead, that can't be good. Are you sure she wasn't talking on the phone?"

"I'm not sure anyone her age ever talks on the phone, but aside from that, no, I got the impression she was talking to someone in the room."

We parked at the Country Barn, marked by a glowing sign towering high above the interstate, the letters in its logo resembling crooked wooden boards. An assortment of ladder trucks, landscaping trailers, and police cars occupied the parking lot, people starting their workday with an early breakfast.

"Okay, my hunger pangs are developing hunger pangs, but let's hear it," I told Stacey.

We clambered into the back of the van, where Stacey drew up the audio clip on a tablet. It did sound like the older girl Penny talking, though much of it was inaudible even when Stacey cranked the volume.

"I do," Penny said on the recording. "But I know you're making my brother carve them, and that's kind of weird..." Pause. "Yes. I know you can't. You're like an angel. But I wish we could..." Pause. "Yes. I've picked. You'll see."

"Yeah, that all sounds pretty relevant," I said. "What did she pick? What's she talking about?"

"That's not clear. You can listen to the whole conversation, but I think that's the most critical—"

"Okay. Let's eat, then."

Inside the restaurant, surrounded by farm-implement décor and large photographs of old barns and bridges, I sank into the padding of the booth. It felt as soft and comfortable as a bed at the Four Seasons at the moment.

Coffee was out of the question, since I'd be sleeping at home soon, so I ordered a tall glass of tomato juice and, as threatened, the Pop's Pancake Platter, featuring heaps of pancakes topped with blueberries, strawberries, and sliced bananas. I didn't turn down the basket of buttermilk biscuits that the server offered, either.

"Wow, they really drained you," Stacey said, watching me slather butter and grape jelly on the flaky, steaming biscuit.

"Mm-hmm." I bit into it, feeling my mouth water and my stomach growl, as though a beast had awakened.

I ate my enormous breakfast as quickly as I could manage while trying to appear civilized. Stacey did her best not to gape at me over her fruit boat, a new menu item that involved canned-looking fruit served with cottage cheese in a bowl shaped like a canoe, a reluctant sop to people for whom deep-fried okra wasn't quite healthy enough.

Once I was as stuffed as a Thanksgiving turkey, I waddled back out to the van.

On the way home, I listened to the long version of the audio recording. Penny whispered about how she liked the jewelry, followed by something too low to hear. Then she went silent, as if listening. Then she giggled.

The giggling made me feel ill.

The sun was up, but its golden light felt overly optimistic, like it was offering false hope. I didn't know how best to proceed. I only knew that the situation was urgent, and time was running out.

Chapter Twenty-Nine

At home, I ended up talking with Nicole on the phone after she texted me for an update. I paced up and down the short length of my studio apartment, my cat watching from the couch.

"The victims' bodies need to be exhumed and given a proper burial," I said. "We should reach out to the police chief about that. The problem is, all we have is the word of a psychic, and that's not likely to get us far. I'll need more tangible evidence."

"It sounds like you're going to dig up one of those graves," Nicole said.

"I can't think of a more direct way to prove it, unfortunately. I'm concerned that these entities are developing relationships with your family. I can't guarantee that your home is safe for the time being. If you can't get your family out for a few nights, then continue to make sure none of the kids are ever alone, especially at night. Keep your bags packed in case you need to leave in a hurry."

"That's not exactly reassuring. I'll see what we can do."

"I'm sorry I can't reassure you more, except to say we're moving as fast as we can to find a way to banish this entity and get your life back to normal."

"I'm not sure it's ever been normal, but a closer approximation would be a nice change."

After Nicole, I called Michael.

"You know how they say your friends will help you move, but your best friends will help you move bodies?" I asked him.

"Oh, no," Michael said. "You've finally killed Stacey."

"Not yet, but I know where certain bodies are buried."

"So you're going into politics? Or blackmailing? Or both?"

"There's actually thirteen bodies."

He paused as that sank in. "That seems like a lot. I probably don't want to know why they're there. How are we moving them? Forklift?"

"I actually just need some tangible, photographic evidence, since most sane people aren't going to listen to my paranormal sources. We have to dig until we find a body and take pictures of it, so we can convince the town or the county to do the rest."

"That sounds…more reasonable, but still awful. So these are our date nights now? Digging up corpses?"

"Bones, most likely. In a swamp. And definitely not at night."

"It'll have to be tomorrow, then," he said. "We're already short two guys today, but I'm off tomorrow."

"Tomorrow it is, then," I said. "Wear your worst clothes."

"No way. I'm not digging up swamp mud in my Santa sweater."

"You can just burn that. Thanks, Michael."

I caught up on a few more hours of fitful sleep, with nightmares featuring Nicole's three younger children, Penny, Jason, and Andra, crawling out of the woodwork of their house, transformed into dead swamp creatures like the others. Fifteen-year-old Lonnie didn't show up, though, maybe because he was outside Jack's usual age range for victims.

About an hour before noon, I gave up on finding my way to the peaceful side of dreamland and made a strong cup of coffee instead.

I texted Stacey to let her know I was up and working. Then I opened the sliding glass door to my tiny balcony that seemed designed to fit just one lonely person and her cat. I stayed inside but hoped the fresh air and light would help chase away the darkness of my dreams.

Sitting cross-legged on my bed, I did the sort of preliminary research I could do from home, now that I had more ideas of where to look.

The Watkinsville newspaper, the *Oconee Enterprise*, had several articles in its records about local businessman Charles Collins. The archives had been digitized, so I could read them over the internet.

A wedding announcement from 1939 included an image of Charles Collins, who'd inherited the boardinghouse from his aunt, with his new bride Aurelie. Charles was a bit shorter than his wife, balding with thick glasses, and chubby in a way that his tuxedo failed to hide despite its best attempts. Aurelie was a tall, curvy beauty beside him, barely smiling while he grinned and beamed.

Birth announcements followed, three of them over the following five years. After the Depression and the war, Charles's feed shop had expanded into a tractor dealership. He later opened a drive-in hamburger stand.

Aurelie's obituary appeared in the surprisingly recent year of 1989. She'd gone on to a long life, outliving her husband by a couple of decades, leaving behind a sizable herd of grandchildren and even some great-grandchildren.

I wondered how often she'd looked back on her earlier life in Timbermill, on her two murdered children. Perhaps that period had grown to seem like a distant nightmare, forgotten in the busyness of daily life with her new family, but occasionally creeping up on her at unexpected times, reminding her of the horror.

Or perhaps she'd moved on altogether, keeping the past behind her, and that was why we'd seen no hints that she was still around, haunting the old boardinghouse where she'd once worked night and day while raising two children alone.

Searching the data-fusion database to which we subscribed—a resource used by law enforcement and insurance companies as well as licensed private investigators—I tracked down several of Aurelie's living heirs and found contact information for some of them.

I called those living heirs, mostly leaving voice mails since nobody answered my unknown number. One person was a lawyer in Virginia whose receptionist took a message from me. Her tone didn't make me hopeful about getting a callback.

Finally, Stacey and I returned to the town hall to visit Chief Tyler again. He barely had time to stash his game controller under his desk and turn off his desktop monitor when he saw us coming.

"What's up?" Chief Tyler stood up so quickly he nearly knocked over his can of Code Red. "I was just catching up on some paperwork, you know, cop stuff. Keeping the, uh, horses in the stable and the ducks in the pond. So how's it going with your…whatever you were doing?"

"We've actually learned a lot more than we expected," I said. "We even have an idea about where the missing kids might be buried."

"Whoa!" Chief Tyler gaped at us with Code-Red-colored teeth. "What missing kids?"

"A dozen kids disappeared from Timbermill, mostly in the 1940s and 1950s," I said.

"Ohhhh, you mean back in the day. You really freaked me out. I thought I was way behind on work for a second there. You mean these are cold cases? Like on that show, *Cold Case Files*? I thought you were doing research type stuff for investors."

"It led to more," I said. "The first two kids were taken from the boardinghouse we're studying, and we think the killer lived there in the attic bedroom. The kids lived there, too. Their mother did all the work around the place. The murderer moved away after the town leaders tried to kill him, but he came back every couple years to kidnap and murder their children as revenge."

"Are y'all for real?" Tyler looked between us like we were a pair of his fraternity bros pulling a prank.

"Naw. Come on, now."

"Have you really never heard of the missing children?" I asked. "Or Cabinet Jack?"

"Is that like a...carjack?"

"You can read up on the missing kids if you like." I unzipped my laptop bag and passed him copies of newspaper articles that we'd printed out.

He flipped through them, skimming but not really reading. "This is some heavy, heavy baggage, town-wise. Did they ever catch the murderer?"

"No. They thought they did, but they were wrong."

"So, like, some innocent person got arrested for it?" He continued pawing randomly through the printouts like he didn't really want to read any of them.

"Nobody got arrested. Some of the townspeople caught the murderer and tried to bury him alive out in the swamp. But he managed to escape at the last second and substituted someone else to die in his place."

"This is so wild." Tyler sat down at his desk, his gaze flickering to the game controller plugged into his PC like he wanted to get back to it. "I mean, uh...well, I'llllll be." His Andy Griffith voice was getting better.

"Like I said, we think we know where to find the bodies." I edged toward the basement stairs. "If we could look through the missing-persons records from those decades, it would be a big help."

"Y'all left it a wreck last time." He stood and folded his arms.

"We found it a wreck, too," I reminded him.

"It's such a big help to us." Stacey smiled and shot him a pair of finger guns. "You are the *man*, Tyler."

He cast a worried look after us as we approached the stairs. He lifted the phone off his desk as we descended out of sight.

Down in the dim, chaotic basement, our first stop was the closet at the back. The creepy, buck-toothed bunny head stared at me when I opened the door.

"You want to put that in a ghost trap?" Stacey asked, as if reading my mind.

"It can't hurt."

"Seems like grasping at straws to me," she said. "Or maybe whiskers."

I touched one of the bunny mask's short, wiry whiskers. "It's pretty bulky. Maybe we could just cut off an ear to bait the trap."

"Or a foot," Stacey said. "You know, like a lucky rabbit's foot?"

"Why not?" The costume didn't have feet, but it had grimy glove-paws. I carved one of these away with a pocketknife and stuffed it into my laptop bag. Walking out with the whole thing would have been hard to explain to Chief Tyler, and anyway, it wouldn't fit into a ghost trap.

A hand-carved rabbit wearing glasses and a fedora, similar to the one Gabriel had been holding in the newspaper photo, sat on the shelf under the costume. I grabbed that too.

Then we dug into the really fun stuff—trying to find records about the missing kids, our search guided by the newspaper articles we'd already found.

The cases shared clear similarities. The kids had all vanished at night, when they were presumably home and asleep. Often the window was left open. I wondered if that was an intentional misdirection by Jack, or maybe that was how he entered homes where he hadn't previously built secret doors. Of course, sleeping with a window open at night in hot, humid Georgia wouldn't have been unusual in the days before air conditioning.

In most cases, a search party was formed but found nothing. Now we knew the searches had been steered away from the place where they might have found the victims' bodies, by men afraid of exposing their own crime of vigilante murder.

As it turned out, we only found files from about half the missing-person cases we needed before Chief Tyler returned, trudging down the stairs with a hangdog look on his face.

"So, hey," he said, "I hate to, uh, rain on your barn while you're still building it, or whatever, but I called Wet Willie's uncle—I mean, Mr. Dalton—and he talked it over with the town council. They're saying maybe this isn't such a good idea."

"What isn't?" I asked. "Solving cold-case crimes?"

"Right. Well, not so much that as throwing, like, a big spotlight on the whole thing. They're working hard to get people to move into all these new developments and stuff. They don't really want Timbermill to be known as the child murder town. People might start calling it, I don't know, 'Murdermill' or something." Tyler looked momentarily pleased with himself, then blanched. "Don't ever repeat that word, okay? And don't tell them I made it up."

"The cases are public knowledge. I showed you the newspaper articles—"

"Yeah, but I never heard of that stuff before today, really. The bosses are kinda saying, hey, maybe we should just leave that dog out in the woods where nobody can see it, you know?"

"We won't take much longer down here," I told him.

"Nah, actually I have to give y'all the boot, pronto. And I can't help you anymore. And I'm supposed to find out exactly who you're working for."

"I'd prefer to keep our client anonymous," I said.

"Right, so you're going to have to get out of here. Like, now." He gestured at the door. "So, this is me, escorting you out."

"Who could say no to the police chief of Murdermill?" I asked, and he winced.

He followed us up and out of the basement, then toward the door out of the police station, like a dog herding sheep.

"Y'all come back now, you hear?" he said as we stepped out, but then he frowned. "Except maybe don't. Maybe just stay out of town and leave this alone. Wet Willie's uncle sounded real serious about it. There's no need to go searching for honey in a hornet's nest, folks." He turned away, closing the glass door behind him.

Chapter Thirty

"I have a funny feeling the chief's not going to welcome our evidence of dead bodies in the swamp," Stacey said as we walked away from town hall.

"He won't welcome it, but he won't be able to deny it. And if he still doesn't help, we'll go over his head."

"You mean talk to Wet Willie's uncle?"

"I was thinking county or state authorities, but sure, we could try the town council first. We still need to dig up some evidence before that."

"And by evidence, you mean bones." Stacey grimaced.

"We're just taking pictures," I assured her.

"Of bones. That we have to dig up."

"Between the police chief kicking us out and Michael being unavailable for grave digging today, my afternoon plans keep hitting dead ends," I said.

"We could grab dinner at the Soup & Spuds." Stacey pointed to a restaurant down the way, not far from the Turntables Cafe and Red Caboose Salon. "I assume they have soup."

"And spuds," I added.

"There's hardly a mystery we can't solve together."

We had a light dinner of salads and soups—tomato bisque for me, vegetables and noodles for Stacey. It was neither bad nor great. Maybe the spuds were the place's true specialty, but we didn't try those.

The sun was setting by the time we reached the clients' home, its low-burning reddish light reflected by the elaborate tree-limb spandrels and balusters of the upper and lower front porches. Across the street on the little neighborhood green, a soccer ball lay abandoned, along with a couple of t-shirts and Monster Energy drink cans.

Dave answered the front door with a distant, puzzled look on his face, like we were complete strangers, or perhaps door-to-door salespeople.

"Hi!" Stacey said, responding to his strangeness with an extra helping of smiles, as if she could lift him into a better mood with enough mental effort.

"Oh, yeah. I almost forgot about this." He looked back over his shoulder, as if to check whether any kids were nearby. He seemed like he was drifting mentally.

"Is everything okay?" I asked.

"It's Lonnie," Dave said. "He and his friends were lifting weights in the basement, and I guess he tried to bench press too much—he likes to show off in front of the other boys—and it fell on him. We've been at the hospital all day. I finally brought the kids home. Nicole's still there."

"Oh, no! Is he hurt?" I asked, though the general answer to that was pretty obvious.

"The x-ray showed a fractured sternum, and he's still under observation. They're doing a CT scan next, maybe an angiogram. There's some risk of organ damage." Dave looked like he wanted to cry, but he bit it back. "Sorry, in all the chaos we forgot we had this haunted house stuff going on, too. Maybe you two should take a night off."

"I understand," I said. "But after what we witnessed at the swamp—"

"We won't be going anywhere near the swamp," Dave said. "I'm sure the ghosts and goblins can wait one more night. We all need to rest and have some normal family time tonight."

"These entities are strong and dangerous."

"I get it. We'll call you when we're ready to continue. Good night."

He closed the door, shutting us out, and his family inside.

Though not all his family, as it turned out.

As Stacey and I slunk back toward the van, we heard voices from that secluded area of the side yard where we'd rinsed off swamp mud.

I motioned for Stacey to wait, then I crept closer, listening through the thick hedge of blooming red azalea bushes.

"…that doesn't make any sense, Caleb," Penny was saying.

"Someone else was down there with us," a boy's voice said. Kneeling and looking through the branches, I saw the teenager Penny had been speaking with before, the boy with the nose ring and the skull and roses tattoo. He'd apparently come back to collect his shirt from the neighborhood green, though he twisted it nervously in his hands rather than putting it back on. He also hadn't collected any of the Monster Energy drink cans from the lawn, I noticed.

"Okay, fine, who was down there?" Penny asked.

"I don't know! I just saw his hand reach out and push. Rusty was spotting your brother, but he was running his mouth and barely looking. And then this other guy was just *there*, like he'd been there all the time. He pushed it down on your brother like he wanted to hurt him. It's dark down there, so I couldn't see his face real well. Then I yelled at him, and that's when I saw he was some stranger, and he just gave me this creepy smile. Then he was gone."

"He ran away?"

"No. Like he wasn't there at all."

"So what? You think my house is haunted?" Penny asked.

"Maybe."

"I think I know where there might be a ghost," she said. "Want to come inside with me?"

"No! I'm never going in that basement again."

"Not the basement. It's a bedroom upstairs. Come on."

The boy called Caleb looked like he was wrestling with some strong feelings on both sides of that choice. When Penny started toward the back door, he followed.

"Do I text Dave to let him know she's sneaking that boy into the house?" I asked Stacey when I rejoined her at the van. "Or stay out of their business because he wanted us gone for the night? I don't want to be nosy, but then I am working as a detective for the parents…"

"We don't technically know that she's *sneaking* him in," Stacey said. "There's nothing supernatural about that. It's out of our job description."

"Except they're looking for ghosts, so it is," I said.

"I don't think that's what either of them actually have in mind, Ellie."

"I'll let Dave know," I said, taking out my phone and thumbing a message. "And I'll have to repeat what the boy said about the disappearing man who pushed the weight down onto Lonnie. So much for winning Penny's trust."

Then we drove away. I had profound misgivings about leaving the family alone with the supernatural threat, but we couldn't very well hang around their house against their wishes. That sort of behavior could get us fired, and even lead to embarrassing stalking charges and restraining orders.

"I wouldn't have hurried through my soup and salad if I'd known we had the night off," Stacey said. "What should we do? Some glow-in-the-dark bowling, maybe?"

"We could go to the office and review the accumulated data so far."

"There's definitely a ton of that. Now I wish I'd gotten one of those big baked potatoes with sour cream and chives. Oh, well."

We moved quickly down the country highway, making great time because all the evening traffic flowed in the opposite direction, out from Savannah. They were commuters driving home from city jobs to their suburban chateaus in Timbermill's newly built neighborhoods, clueless about the darker hidden history of their picturesque new hometown. The town council and sheriff didn't seem particularly keen on letting them hear about it, either, at least not until all the pricey new developments were sold off to unwary homeowners, and a new generation of families and children had rooted themselves into place, waiting to be harvested by Jack.

Chapter Thirty-One

In our workshop at the office, Stacey and I divided up all the unexamined footage and data from the boardinghouse.

For the next couple of hours, we were each in our own world of headphones and screens, uneasily sifting through the collected sights and sounds, watching cold spots arise and vanish late at night, listening at hints of whispered voices, creaking floorboards, the occasional tapping of rain.

When my phone rang, the vibration in my pocket almost startled me out of my seat. I glanced at Stacey to see whether she'd seen me jump, but she was absorbed in her own audio and video. A banshee could have screamed right behind her and she wouldn't have heard a thing.

I didn't recognize the number—or the area code, really—but I answered, hoping it wasn't another bot trying to sell me a car warranty. "Hello?"

"Hi, this is Deborah Collins, returning your call from earlier. My receptionist said you're doing some genealogical research involving my family?" She was the attorney who lived in Virginia.

"That's close. We're researching the history of a house where your ancestor, Aurelie Collins, lived before she was married. She ran a boardinghouse in the town of Timbermill, Georgia."

"How did you know I was the family genealogist?" Deborah asked.

"I didn't. I tried to contact any of her living descendants that I could find. It sounds like I got lucky."

"Someone would have had you call me eventually. Aurelie was my great-grandmother."

"That's great. We learned Aurelie had two children who died young—"

"Solange and Raynard." The woman's voice tightened. "This is not a pleasant part of our family history at all. Why do you want to know about them?"

"For the family who lives there now," I said, since that seemed the best way to get her to open up about her tragic family history. "They've moved in with their children, and they're trying to understand their new home."

"I'm sorry to say it, but the history of that house is tragic. My great-grandmother worked hard there during the Depression, cooking and cleaning for all the guests, and she lost her first two children, as you know. What you may not know is that the children died violently."

"Did they die in the house?" I asked, like I was clueless.

"They were kidnapped, then murdered in the

woods, I believe. Imagine the terror they must have suffered. I'm sorry you have to break this news to the new family."

"It is shocking," I said. "Do they know who did it? Or why it happened?"

"It was a man she was dating. She broke it off to marry my great-grandfather. She was right to end it, because her ex-boyfriend turned out to have true evil inside him. I don't think she ever suspected that her children were in danger, though."

"I'm glad we finally reached someone who knows about all of this," I said. "So what do you know about this man who committed the crime?"

"Not very much, to be honest," she said. "It's not a branch of our family's history that I've gone out of my way to study. It's just so awful, and at the same time, obviously none of us are descended from those poor children."

"But you seem to know a lot."

"Just what's in the letter. It was found among her papers when she died, and of course I've ended up with it."

"What letter?"

"It's one she wrote to her children after she was engaged to my great-grandfather but before she married him. I think she may have meant for the children to read it when they grew older. Or maybe it was her way of working out her feelings before explaining her upcoming marriage to her children. We have names and dates and addresses, but really the letter is all we have to show us what was going through Aurelie's mind."

"Could you send us a copy of that?" I tried to keep my voice steady and neutral, like this request was no big deal, but deep down I knew I would drive hundreds of miles and break down her front door to rip that letter from her hands if it had any chance of helping us protect the Brown children.

"It's very fragile." She sounded uncertain, and that made me nervous.

"Even just a snapshot with your phone camera would be great," I said, trying hard not to angrily demand it from her. She didn't understand that lives were on the line, and I would sound crazy if I tried to convince her. "We'd all really appreciate it. It would really help us."

"I can do that. You know, it's funny you would call…"

"Why's that?" I asked after she trailed off.

"I only met Aurelie once, when I was a toddler, and I barely remember that. But I had a dream about her last night, or maybe the night before. Out of nowhere."

"What happened in the dream?"

"I don't remember my dreams very well, either. She was very worried about a door being left open, I think."

"What door?"

"All of them," she said. "That's what she was saying. She wanted all the doors in the house kept shut. It was her house, but not the one I visited in Watkinsville. It's strange how that can happen in dreams, isn't it? The house that's unfamiliar but is supposedly your home. I don't know. That's all I can tell you. I hope for the best for that new family living there. Tell them to be careful. It's an old place, with unhappy memories. I have to go now." She ended the call abruptly.

The story about Aurelie's dream appearance left me

in a little bit of shock. I jotted everything down in my notebook.

I began to wait nervously for Deborah's pictures of the old letter, worried she'd changed her mind about sending them, or would simply put it off until she forgot about it.

The pictures arrived a few minutes later, though, and I quickly alerted to Stacey to take off her headphones.

"Did you find something good?" she asked.

"See if you can guess who wrote this letter." I zoomed in on the image of the yellowed, handwritten page that Ms. Collins had sent, and I began to read aloud from my phone, scrolling slowly with my fingertip. "My dearest…Solange and…Raynard—"

"A letter? Where'd that come from?"

"I've been getting into all kinds of crazy research while your back was turned," I said. "Anyway, want to listen?"

"Of course." Stacey rolled her chair over to sit across from me, then put her elbows on the table and her chin in her hands like a kid waiting for story time.

"You are…the…twin?" I paused my slow scroll across the zoomed-in image, squinting at the faded cursive writing. "Yeah, twin. You are the twin… lights…of…my…life…the…sun…and…moon…"

"That's enough." Stacey held out her hand. "Fork over the phone and I'll blow it up on the big screen."

I started to give her the phone, but then it erupted in my hand. Dave was calling.

"Hey, Dave, you can't give us the night off and then expect us to be on call," Stacey said when his name popped up on my screen.

"I guess we have to take this." I drew the phone back from her and answered it.

"Andra's missing." Dave sounded out of breath. "I've been searching for her everywhere. Nobody's seen her in a couple of hours. I've called the police, but maybe you can help."

"We will definitely help." I jumped to my feet, gesturing for Stacey to get moving. "We're in our Savannah office, so it's going to take at least half an hour for us to get there."

"Thanks." Dave hung up without another word.

"Savannah office?" Stacey asked. "You make it sound like we have multiple offices. If there's one in the Caribbean, I'm putting in for a transfer."

"Andra went missing," I told Stacey as we hurried to the van. Worry knotted my insides. I wished we hadn't left Timbermill.

"Little Miss Magic Show disappeared? That's terrible!" Stacey climbed into the van with me, and I pushed the remote to open the garage door at the back of the workshop. It rattled and clunked its way up, revealing a drizzling night outside. Rain was never far away along the humid subtropical coast.

The rain grew heavier. We drove out of town as fast as visibility, physics, and the law would allow, or maybe just a little bit more than that. I sped up as we left the city for the countryside, the old, equipment-heavy cargo van chugging through the weather as best it could.

"Tell Dave to have the police look in the swamp." I passed Stacey my phone.

Stacey gaped, turning pale. "You don't think Jack's already taken Andra out there and…and…"

"Someone should definitely go look. But they'll have to go the long away around, because I broke the bridge."

"Should that someone be us? Should we go there instead of the house?"

I wrestled with that, because I wasn't sure. "We don't know if there's even a path through the woods to the burial site. We'd have to follow the old railroad tracks. Pull up a satellite map and see if you can figure out the best place to start from the other side. But text Dave first, because the local police might know a better approach."

"I doubt Chief Tyler knows much about the back ways and footpaths around town, but maybe he knows someone who does." Stacey began typing the message to Dave.

Ahead, lightning cracked across the sky. I was driving us right into the storm.

Chapter Thirty-Two

The town of Timbermill lay dark and empty, torrents of rain pounding the rooftops and sidewalks. The storm had knocked out all the power, including the traffic light in the center of town.

Every shop was closed, and we didn't see a soul. That was surely normal at midnight on a weekday, but it made the downtown feel abandoned and empty.

The refurbished, gentrified new appearance of the town had largely vanished with the loss of light, every sign fallen dark, the woodwork and bricks looking aged and worn instead of vintage and charming, as if it had reverted to a ghost town once again.

"Even the town hall's gone dark," Stacey whispered as we passed the quaint brick building.

Crossing the old tracks was no longer like traveling through time from the present to the past. In the absence of light and life, the entire town felt unified again.

Our clients' neighborhood was aglow, not from the houses or streetlamps, but from two police cars pulsing blue law-enforcement strobe lights through the heavy downpour. Both cars had their headlights on, and one cruised slowly down the street, peering into yards with a spotlight. Another officer in a bright yellow raincoat walked the neighborhood green with a flashlight.

Chief Tyler stood on the front porch, the hood of his official yellow raincoat pushed back, his hair rumpled as he kept passing his fingers through it, looking panicked, busy on his police radio.

"I didn't know this town had this many cops," Stacey said as we pulled up to the house.

"Don't forget the chief told us to leave town like some Old West sheriff."

"And here we are, back like an unwanted boomerang he tried to throw away."

I parked behind the police car marked CHIEF OF POLICE. We grabbed our rain jackets and backpacks of gear before jumping out and running through the flashing, rumbling storm.

As we stepped out of the torrential rain and under the shelter of the porch, Chief Tyler looked us over— Stacey, then me, then Stacey again—but he didn't offer up any tidbits about how we looked wetter than a couple of fresh-caught catfish, or some other attempt at retro-television folksiness. He looked angry.

"Oh, it's the 'detectives.'" Chief Tyler wagged his fingers in sarcastic air quotes and moved to block our path to the front door. "Mr. Brown tells me you're the reason their house is full of cameras and microphones. He says you've convinced him the place is haunted, and that, big surprise, he needs to pay y'all a bunch of money to deal with it. Is that about the, uh, long and short of it?"

"They contacted us about these problems," I said.

"Ghost problems?" He rolled his eyes. "You can't come around here harassing my citizens with this garbage. We're a nice, quiet community."

"We've dealt with several cases like this before, unfortunately," I said.

"Uh-huh. Yet somehow you never mentioned any of that when I let you poke around the town archives. You told me you were representing real estate investors."

"That wasn't a lie. They are working to restore the house, as an investment—"

"It wasn't exactly the whole truth, though, was it? Then you talked about some alleged kidnappings from a hundred years ago—"

"Alleged? You have files about them."

"Maybe so, maybe not, but letting y'all down there was the real mistake. I'm doing what I should have done in the first place and having a junk removal company take everything out of that basement. Polish up the woodwork, fresh paint, boom—new private office for the town chief. There's even a room for a couch for my bros when they visit."

"You can't just throw out the town's history!" I said.

"Whatever. Here's what I think. You two keep going on about these missing kids. Then the girl disappears, *right* after y'all leave town. Like, *right* after. Pretty big coincidence."

"Are you accusing us of kidnapping Andra?" I asked.

"Then later you'll rescue her and be the big heroes

who charge a big fee."

"We're not con artists!" I snapped.

"Like I'm going to believe you." He called over to his deputy, a thick guy with a mustache and a slow gait. "Go check that blue van."

"Excuse me?" I said.

"If you're going to drive around in a big windowless van, don't be surprised when people ask you questions after a kid goes missing." Chief Tyler smirked as he watched his deputy open each door of our van and check inside for kidnapping victims.

While the chief watched that, I dodged around him and rang the doorbell.

"Hey!" Tyler barked after me, but it was too late. Dave was already opening the door, Jason clinging close to his side, dressed in pajamas, shivering despite the warm weather.

"Oh, good, you're here," Dave said. He was dripping wet, like he'd been out in the rain already and hadn't bothered with an umbrella or jacket.

"I wouldn't put too much trust in these two ladies," Chief Tyler said to Dave. Behind him, the other police car reached the end of the neighborhood and drove away, turning off its blue flashers.

"Where's he going?" Dave asked.

"Traffic light's out downtown," Tyler said. "Someone has to direct traffic until power is restored."

"There's literally nobody out driving around downtown," Stacey told him. "It was completely deserted."

"Ma'am, please calm down and let me do my job here," Tyler said to Stacey, in something close to a flat, official-sounding tone that wasn't very Andy Griffith at all.

"You need to check the swamp," I said.

"I already explained that," Dave said. "But he didn't send anyone."

"Yeah, we have a lot happening with this storm," Tyler said. "Not a lot of resources to deploy, either. This town is not prepared for an emergency."

I held back my impulse to make a snarky comment about how the police chief probably had some responsibility for emergency preparedness. The chief was already ready to throw us out of Mayberry, as soon as his answer to Barney Fife was done bumbling his way through our van.

"Is Lonnie still at the hospital?" I asked Dave.

Dave nodded. "Nicole's with him. The hospital's moving at a typical glacial hospital pace. I told her not to drive through this storm even when he gets released, just wait for the weather to calm down." He shook his head. "I haven't told Nicole about Andra, because she needs to stay there with Lonnie. She can't help from there, so she'll just worry. I'll deal with this myself. But I do need help." He looked among the three of us, two paranormal investigators and a young police chief who would probably rather be playing Frisbee golf. "Please."

"We'll keep looking." Tyler pointed at Stacey and me. "But you two need to stay out of my way. They're trouble, Mr. Brown."

"Even if they are, we need all the eyes and ears we can get," Dave said.

"We can stay inside the house for now, Chief," I said, in a sinking voice that implied I was surrendering to him. "If that keeps us out of your way."

"Well, good." Tyler sounded uncertain. He was going along with what I wanted, but I was trying to give him the exact opposite impression, that he was bossing me around.

"You should also follow up on the swamp," I advised again.

"Right, because we're going to hang out in the swamp during a storm looking for a kid who disappeared miles away, and who nobody saw going into the swamp," Tyler said. "That's definitely happening. Let me invite the whole county in on that."

"Maybe you should," I said.

"You stay here like I told you." Tyler pulled up his yellow hood and walked out to join his deputy, who'd finally stopped rummaging through our van.

Stacey and I followed Dave and Jason into the cabinet-lined foyer dominated by the wraparound staircase.

"When was the last time you saw Andra?" I asked.

"In her older sister's room, going to bed after her nightly cabinet check. Penny was still up reading, but now she says she fell asleep and didn't see where Andra went. I've searched the whole house. Andra's not here."

"The house may have more hidden spaces than what we've found," I said. "Jason, do you have any ideas where she could be?"

"No…" He looked at his dad. "Unless…"

"Is there something you haven't told me, Jason?" Dave asked.

The quiet ten-year-old boy looked like he might cry. "Maybe she went with Sunny and Rainy."

"Her imaginary friends?" Dave asked.

"Maybe they're not that imaginary. They're too

good at magic tricks," Jason said.

"Where would they take her?" I asked.

He shrugged. "I don't know. In the olden days, didn't they go down to the basement during a storm? Maybe there."

"Why didn't you say anything about this before, Jason?" Dave asked.

The boy covered his face with his hands. "I don't know. I'm just guessing!"

"It's okay," I said. "We'll start looking where Andra was last seen, though. Is Penny still up there?"

"Of course," Dave said. "She's sticking with the disgruntled teen act instead of helping us look for her sister. I want to go search outside again, but I don't want to leave the kids here alone. Or bring them out into a lightning storm, obviously."

"Is that boy still here?" I asked. "What was his name? Caleb?"

"I sent him away after I saw your text. He seemed a little...rough for her. And she didn't ask permission before bringing him up to her room, which is not permission I would have granted. So Caleb isn't allowed in our house for the time being. And Penny is grounded with no phone. Can the two of you watch Jason while I go look for Andra again?"

"Of course!" Stacey put an arm around Jason. "I like hanging out with talented artists."

"I think the chief will welcome your presence more than ours," I said. "We'll see what we can find inside the house."

"Are you okay with that, pal?" Dave asked Jason. "So I can search for your sister?"

"Okay." Jason leaned into Stacey's hug, putting his

arms around her.

"Good. I'll be as quick as I can."

Dave hurried outside, and the three of us went upstairs to check out Penny's room, the one from which Andra had disappeared.

I didn't want to say it aloud, not where Jason could hear, but Andra's quiet, unexplained disappearance from her bed late at night obviously mirrored the original Cabinet Jack murders decades ago. None of those children had ever been found, not until Jacob identified their burial place in the swamp the previous night. None had ever survived after being taken.

Stacey and I looked at each other over Jason's head as we hurried across the landing, and I could tell she felt as afraid as I did.

We continued to the hall of doors upstairs.

Chapter Thirty-Three

I knocked on Penny's door, and her greeting was an angry "What?"

"Hey, Penny," I said. "It's Ellie and Stacey. We just want to talk for a second."

"Why are you even here? I'm so tired of you two creeping around spying on everyone. Why don't you just leave?"

"Aren't you worried about your sister?" I asked the closed door.

"She's probably hiding in her stupid magic show room. Why don't you go down there instead?"

"Penny's…p-probably right," Jason said beside us, his voice trembling just above a whisper, like he was scared to speak at all. Stacey put an arm around his shoulders again, and this relaxed him a little. He spoke with slightly more confidence. "I think you should look downstairs, too. And maybe my basement idea."

"I definitely appreciate your input, Jason, but we

need to start where Andra was last seen." I repeated that last part louder, through the door, so Penny could hear me.

"She's not in here!" Penny shouted back.

"Can we just have a quick peek, and then we'll leave you alone?" I asked. "Or do we need to go get your dad?"

"Ugh." A long pause followed, and then, "Fine. But then leave me alone. Give me a minute."

It seemed to take more than a minute for her to get around to unlocking and opening the door. Penny looked more tired and drained than ever, her dark hair carelessly rumpled, her eyes dull.

She stepped back and swept her arm around her room, indicating the cluttered shelves and cabinets, the laundry pile on her bed. Andra's smaller bed, full of stuffed animals, was crammed into one corner. The room barely fit both beds and Penny's furniture. "As you can see," Penny said, "You can hardly even breathe in here. If there was another person with me, I'd know it."

"Thanks for letting us in." I crossed to Andra's bed and searched under it. I couldn't see much until I turned on my flashlight. With the power out, Penny was lighting her room with scented candles, a clashing mixture of spicy apple and lavender.

Beneath Andra's bed lay some of Penny's dirty laundry, nothing more. I nudged the laundry aside and rapped on the hardwood floor, searching for any sign of a trap door.

"What are you, expecting floor elves to come out?" Penny asked, her arms crossed. She again wore a thick, hooded sweatshirt over a pair of shorts, as if the upper and lower halves of her body existed in completely different climates.

"Are you absolutely sure you didn't see or hear anything strange?" I pulled the missing girl's bed out from the wall and checked the wainscoting behind it.

"Other than you two, right now?" She scowled when Stacey opened her closet and started rapping on the walls, searching for hollow spots.

"Even if you think you dreamed it," I said. "Even if you think it's not important. Anything at all?"

"Nothing." Penny fell silent as I knelt in front of her built-in bookshelves and opened a pair of cabinet doors. They revealed a single space large enough to crawl through on hands and knees. The inside held just a few large objects, including purple pom-poms and an acoustic megaphone featuring a stern purple Viking.

A cool, damp draft was palpable from within the cabinet.

I moved aside the spirit squad gear and pushed against the cabinet's back wall. It was already ajar and gave no resistance as I swung it open to reveal a dark space beyond.

"Ugh." Penny covered her face and lay down on her bed. "Why couldn't you have just gone downstairs?"

Jason sat down slowly in one corner, not looking at anyone.

"What's happening?" I looked between them. "What aren't you telling us? Penny? Jason?" I stared at the boy, who I expected to be less resistant than his older sister. "Jason?"

"Don't tell them anything," Penny said to her younger brother. "They won't understand."

"What won't we understand?" I asked, but they both refused to look at me.

I was torn between trying to pry information out of the kids and immediately crawling through the newly discovered hidden door in search of their lost sister. I couldn't decide which should take priority. Good thing I wasn't alone.

"Stacey, you stay here and figure out what they're talking about," I said. "I'll be right back."

I pulled the pom-poms and megaphone out of the cabinet and crawled into it on my belly, slithering along the floor, not exactly a good stance for defending against any attackers waiting ahead.

The rain on the rooftop echoed louder in the hidden passage between the walls. I could stand up in it, thankfully, and I quickly pointed my light in each direction, checking for dead things creeping up toward me across the bare studs and joists.

Nothing indicated which way Andra might have gone.

Something rustled ahead, though.

I followed, pointing my light along the irregular passage. It narrowed and lowered until I had to drop and crawl again.

He came at me from around a corner ahead, thudding toward me at almost inhuman speed, his form filling up the whole crawlspace.

"Stop!" I shined my light at him, and he recoiled, covering his eyes. He was shivering and panting. He was dressed as I'd seen him before—in soccer shorts, a thin gold-chain necklace, and a nose ring large enough to see from down the street. "Caleb?"

"What?" He looked back like someone was after

him. "Get out of the way!"

"What are you…" I began to ask, but then it clicked. "Penny had you up in her room. She sent you to hide in here. She must have known about her bookshelf—"

"Let me out!" Caleb shoved his way forward, crushing me against the side wall as he squeezed past. No chivalry in that guy. He continued on in the direction I'd just left.

I moved forward, going to see what he was running from, and less hopeful of finding Andra now that I knew it was him, not Andra, who'd left the hidden panel open in Penny's bookcase.

Beyond the corner, I could stand again, though I had to keep my head bowed, like I was praying. The passageway here was wide, with narrow branches off to either side. I couldn't imagine how it might fit, hidden, between the walls of the second floor, even in this labyrinthine house.

At the far end, a door stood open directly to the night outside, where the rain pounded the earth. Mud flowed in and across the wooden floor of the passageway, slowly flooding it.

This seemed surreal at first, then I realized it was impossible. I was on the second story of the house, not the first.

I approached the open door, passing crooked hallways of mismatched scrap wood leading to doors that were small and square, or strangely low or high, never a proper size or shape.

Lightning flashed outside, revealing the heap of dead trunks that marked Gabriel's grave, where he'd been buried alive in Jack's place.

The open door was the one carved long ago into the tree trunk, thick with moss and fungus on the outside, slimy with rotten black wood on the inside.

If I understood correctly, this doorway was unnatural, supernatural, and had enabled Jack to carry his victims directly from their homes to the swamp, slipping them out of their rooms at night and skipping all the miles of potential witnesses in between. *They gave me the power of doors and doorways, of coming and going.*

Muddy footprints led from the swamp door along the main passage where I walked, vanishing about where I stood, several paces in, where most of the mud had worn off.

I heard a wooden creak behind me and spun toward it, pointing my flashlight down one of the crooked side corridors. Its walls were mad jigsaw-like collections of broken balusters and spandrels that had been ornate in their day, like those adorning the front porches of the neighborhood, chaotically heaped together into high barriers.

I walked down the hall, following it around to a low open doorway.

Looking through, I saw that it connected to a once impressive foyer with a high ceiling and cobwebbed chandelier. I seemed to be peering out through a cupboard under some other house's front stairs.

The house had obviously been abandoned for some time. On the wall, someone had spraypainted a square door with a sideways stick figure jutting out of it. The stick figure wore a cap and held a sharp tool. Nearby was painted *close your cabinets tight or jack comes out tonight.*

Heavy footsteps descended the stairs above me,
above the cupboard. Soon he came around the spiral
newel at the base of the stairs.

He looked gaunt and dusty, almost mummified. He
wore his wide grin like an old habit, expressing no
feeling at all, like the skin and muscles of his face had
dried and contracted in that position over time, rigor
mortis rather than any joy or glee.

When he saw me, he approached, drawing a chisel
with a sharp beveled edge from his leather apron. The
apron was covered with dark stains, maybe blood from
his victims. At least he didn't have fresh blood on him,
and he appeared unsatisfied.

"Where is she?" He shuffled toward me, slowly
turning the blade in his hand.

"Who?" I asked.

"The little one." His pale eyes didn't blink as he
approached. "My new bunny."

"Your revenge is over, Jack," I said. "Her family
didn't harm you. Let it go. You need to let it all go and
move on—"

"Where is Andromeda? I heard she wants to play
with me." The sound of the little girl's name in his
mouth sickened me. I thought of Lonnie, calling for
Jack in order to scare his sister and brother.

Unseen others moved in the abandoned house,
scurrying wetly and whispering through walls. I could
only think of the dead children from the swamp.

I didn't know where Andra was, but I certainly
wasn't going to tell him that. If he thought I knew, then
he could waste his time and energy pursuing me instead
of finding her. I'd be the wild goose in this chase.

"I'll never tell you where I hid her," I said.

Then I slammed the door built into the back of the cupboard, and I turned and ran away down the passage.

Chapter Thirty-Four

The way back was not the same as the way in.

The passageways had shifted, growing longer and more winding. Their floors, walls, and ceiling were made of jumbles of wooden bric-a-brac, from wall paneling to hardwood tiles and roof shingles, dinnerware and bowls and cups that might have come from the old woodworking factory. There were broken chairs and children's toys—a rocking horse, a doll, toy soldiers.

All of this jutted up irregularly from the floor area. Sharp points of broken wood poked out from the walls of debris on either side. I kept tripping over piles of woodwork as I tried to run.

Hearing Jack's footsteps and the trailing chorus of wetly whispering voices, I turned down a side passage that looked wide and promising at first. It soon narrowed until I was crawling. Splinters of broken furniture above dragged like claws across my back as I wormed forward.

The crawlspace ended at a square red door decorated with a wreath that had long since shriveled to a brown husk. It was so low I would have to crawl through on my hands and knees; good thing I was already in that position.

I grabbed the green knob and pulled the door open.

Beyond lay the smells of freshly baked cinnamon bread and a crackling fireplace that lit the room. A modest fir stood in the corner, hung with a few homemade ornaments.

From the fireplace and woodwork, I recognized it as the front parlor of the boardinghouse, where the Browns kept their board games and television.

The television was gone, though, and the furniture was from a different era, heavier and handmade.

Cabinet Jack, looking more youthful and alive than the phantom I'd encountered, sat on the sofa near the fireplace, grinning wide and holding a couple of bulky, folded woolen stockings. On his lap sat Solange, and beside them her younger brother Raynard. I recognized the children from their photographs.

"Yes, the Christmas elves told me to deliver these personally," Jack told the children, waving the stockings around. "But only to the most special children in town."

"Pick me!" Solange said.

"Pick me, too!" Raynard echoed.

"Hmm…" Jack rubbed his chin, looking at Solange, who offered him a wide smile, as if trying to copy his expression. "Well, that certainly is a pretty smile."

"I have a pretty smile, too!" The boy pulled his lips

out wide in either direction, showing all his teeth.

"This one must be yours, then. The stocking for a special boy." Jack handed him one, and Raynard eagerly reached inside. He drew out a wooden locomotive. He gaped at it, then excitedly rolled it along the floor.

"Is the other one for a special girl?" Solange asked.

"Lucky for you, yes." He held it out to her, and she reached inside, giggling. Then she looked puzzled, until she drew out a wooden hairbrush with flowers and rabbits carved into the back.

"Oh, it's so pretty!" She immediately put it to use on her long golden hair. "I'll use it every day."

"Can you keep a secret?" Jack whispered, and the little girl nodded. "I made that brush, not the elves. But don't tell anyone."

"I won't," she whispered back.

"Do you promise?" he asked, and she nodded.

"Solange! Raynard! Why are you out of bed?" A woman's sharp, French-accented voice sounded from somewhere, though I didn't see anyone step into the room.

"Mister Jack gave us presents!" Solange replied.

"Surely they can stay up late on such a special night." Jack smiled a little wider.

"They cannot," the woman's disembodied voice replied. "To bed! Now!"

Looking glum, the children complied, taking their gifts and vanishing into the shadows.

Jack rose from the couch.

"Beautiful children," he said. "But of course, because they sprang from such a beautiful mother."

No reply came. The roaring blaze in the fireplace

withered and died, the Christmas tree vanished, and the room turned cold and dark.

Jack's gaze fell on me, as I watched from the hidden door in the cabinet.

He shifted into the version of himself that I'd known, the dried, mummified, half-dead thing that had just pursued me from the house. He drew a jackknife from his stiff, stained leather carpenter's apron and unfolded it as he stalked toward me. Its handle was antler horn, like the tools Jason had found.

"Where is she?" Jack demanded, his voice cracking and hoarse. "I need her."

Well, I wasn't about to get into a conversation with him. I slammed the back-of-the-cabinet door shut and pulled down the walls of broken wooden debris from the crazy passageway around me to block him inside.

Then I crawled backward through the tunnel of broken woodwork, because it was the only way I could go.

The Christmas-memory door rattled against the junk I'd brought down to block it. Then it slammed open an inch, nudging the shattered wood back. Another hard knock slammed it open wider, and his withered hand reached out, his moleskin shirt buttoned at the cuff.

The central passage was like a landfill now, loose pieces rolling under my feet, threatening to send me crashing onto sharp stakes of jagged wood. If these were the pathways and tunnels of Jack's mind, then nowhere was truly safe for me to run. I was a character caught in his crazed dreams, lost inside his madness.

Avoiding his approaching footsteps, I crawled down another twisting, slowly collapsing tunnel, ending at another miniature door, this one etched with butterflies and bunnies.

I wasn't surprised when it opened onto the small sleeping room with the window and the bunk, decorated with the butterfly and bunny motif.

Solange lay in the bunk, under a quilt. Jack leaned over her, a smiling shadow in the moonlight.

"Solange," he whispered.

She blinked at him sleepily. "Where did you come from?"

"From the land of secret doors," he whispered. "I'll show you. Let's go on an adventure."

"Mother says to stay away from you now."

"Soon you'll move away to a distant town and never see me again. This is our last chance to play together."

Solange seemed to think it over, then nodded and got out of bed.

Smiling, Jack turned toward me, because of course I was watching through the secret cabinet door through which he'd entered the little room, and through which he was preparing to kidnap Solange.

Jack must have seen me, because his big grin faded, which is an effect I've had on people before. He withered and mummified—I'm not taking the blame for that—and Solange and her blankets vanished. The room turned dark and cold.

"You." Jack approached, this time drawing his chisel and pointing it at my face. He had to kneel to approach the hidden door. "Show me the way to her."

"Never," I said, fairly confident in my response, considering I had no idea where she was.

Again, I slammed the door in his face, and this time

I pulled down double handfuls of woodworking junk, which seemed composed of stranger stuff than ever— arms and torsos of wooden mannequins, a wooden model of a head with a web of cryptic phrenology markings all over its surface.

Running, stumbling, pushing my way through, sending things crashing and tumbling behind me to litter the path, I finally reached another doorway, one that was wide, almost full height, and vaguely familiar, made of dark, heavy wood.

I turned the latch and opened it.

The interior of the armoire was roughly the same as I'd seen it before, but the clothes were different, mostly old-timey, high-necked dresses and housecoats that smelled like floral perfume. I moved them aside as quietly as I could, trying not to let the hanger hooks scrape the rod.

The armoire door was cracked slightly open. I stepped forward, past the clothes, and nudged it wider, hoping I'd found the way out of the maze of Jack's memories.

The bed was different, not Dave and Nicole's but one with a curved wooden headboard. The lacy ruffled curtains and pillows, the doilies on seemingly every surface, the religious paintings, and the cloying perfume smell in the air all pretty much screamed that this was an elderly woman's room.

The lady in the bed wasn't elderly, though. She wasn't Nicole, either. In the moonlight, I recognized Aurelie's haughty, pretty face from her photographs, her lips full and red, her golden hair splayed out in waves around her.

Beside her lay the shorter, lumpier frame of Charles

Collins, snoring softly through the gap in his teeth, his Coke-bottle glasses on the doily-draped nightstand beside him, under his late aunt's delicate hurricane lamp painted with songbirds.

"She gave herself to him," Jack whispered behind me, nearly freezing my left ear solid with the icy chill of his voice. "And how could he resist such temptation? No man could."

"So you murdered her children."

"Her rejection tormented me like fire. I needed her to suffer as I suffered. Then, I thought, she might understand me."

"You're beyond sick. And you really need to brush up on your understanding of consent in relationships." I pushed the mirrored door wide open and leaped out.

I landed on my feet and turned back toward him. I loosened a strap of my backpack and slung it around in front of me, then unzipped it and reached inside, ready to try my hopeful attempt at a secret weapon against him.

The closet lay dark and quiet, though the blue blazers inside swayed as if someone had just passed through.

The bed lay empty, and the master bedroom was restored to its modern condition, including our cameras set up to watch it by night.

Someone pounded on the door to the room and kept it trying to push it open, so I unlocked it.

The door flew open, and Stacey staggered into the room, visibly panicked. Neither Penny nor Jason was with her. The power was still out, and she swung her flashlight around the room until it landed on me.

"What are you doing here?" I asked, while she

asked the exact same question, effectively jinxing each other, though neither of us mentioned this out loud.

"It's…not going well," Stacey said, and she continued searching the room.

Chapter Thirty-Five

"Where are the kids?" I asked Stacey while she looked in the master bathroom and closet in a way that didn't really reassure me that she had any idea. "Uh, hello? Stacey?"

"They took off!" Stacey finally answered, nearly exploding in frustration. "Penny blew out the candles to make it dark, and the two of them just ran out of the room. She and Jason are in cahoots, I'm telling you!"

"In cahoots about what?"

"About ditching me, for one thing. They ran in here and locked the door. And now they're nowhere!"

I looked at the doors to the upstairs porch, but they were still latched from the inside.

"They must have left through the armoire." I pointed my light inside, revealing the back panel, which stood partially open.

"But wouldn't you have seen them?" Stacey asked. "Didn't you just come out of there?"

"I took a different path, though. It led through Jack's soul."

"Sounds twisted."

"Twisted, dark, and pointy." I slid Nicole's clothes aside and shone my light into the dusty passage beyond. "At least it looks normal again."

I took a deep breath, tried to ready myself mentally, and stepped once more into the mirrored armoire, and the hidden passage beyond it, which had reverted to its more natural form, instead of the nightmarish interior of Jack's mind.

"Penny! Jason!" Stacey called as she followed me into the narrow passage between walls.

"Andra!" I called.

"We are doing a terrible job of watching these kids," Stacey said. "I swear I was a better babysitter when I was sixteen."

"Caleb!" I added for good measure.

"Wait, the nose ring kid's back in play, too?"

"He's in here somewhere. Penny was hiding him in her room. Then, when we showed up, she put him into a secret passage that we didn't know about but she did."

"Ooh. Boy smuggling. Scandalous. And it explains why she stayed up in her room, even with the power out and her little sister missing."

We searched through the passageways. The door to the little windowless room where we'd found Penny with the mysterious carved jewelry was wide open, so we crawled out through that cabinet and looked around. The bedroom door was open, so we returned to the main upstairs hall, still calling uselessly for all the missing children.

"May as well check Jack's room," I said, rounding

the corner to the dark little hallway that led nowhere but the attic bedroom stairs.

The door was closed and locked from the inside. I pressed my ear against it and heard footsteps, then voices. Someone was up there.

I drew out my lock picks and worked as quickly as I could, while listening to their muffled voices through the door.

"Just lie there and let it happen," Penny was saying.

"Does your little brother have to be here, though?" That was Caleb, sounding nervous.

"He wants to see it."

"Uh, but—"

"Shh. Maybe close your eyes, okay?"

We'd found two or three of the missing kids, by the sound of it, depending on whether you wanted to count Caleb. I finished picking the lock and pushed open the long, rectangular trap door.

The attic was gloomy, lit only by a couple of candles. These weren't scented ones in glass jars, but tall white candles that might have been used in a formal dining setting, or maybe a church.

Every cabinet and closet door I could see in the thin, dancing red light was open, at least a little bit.

"Someone's coming." Jason's voice trembled with fear.

"I know," Penny said, sounding thrilled about it. "And he's almost here."

I rounded the bookshelves that had blocked most of my view of the bed.

Caleb lay on the bare wooden bed platform, eyes closed, looking like a human sacrifice waiting to happen.

Penny knelt beside him, her hand on his chest, as though she would be performing the sacrifice. She wore the beaded necklace, the carved ring with the jewel-like flower, and even the half-carved moon and stars bracelet that Jason's possessed hands had begun to make for her.

Jason occupied a chair in the corner, shivering, knees drawn up to his chin.

Penny scowled at Stacey and me as we arrived.

"Stop!" I yelled, running toward Penny and Caleb on the bed.

"Stop what?" Penny said. "We're just *sitting* here. Am I not allowed to *sit* in my own *house*? Who says? You? You don't even belong here, and you don't own me—"

Every door in the room, small or large, slammed open at once, as if a powerful gale blasted out of each one. The attic air grew as painfully cold as the swamp had been when Jack and his horde of dead children arrived.

On the bed, Caleb cried out in pain and arched up like he was being stabbed in the back. His eyes flew open.

Then he settled back, a wide grin splitting his face. His bright gaze landed on me.

Penny had been working on Jack's behalf, it seemed, bringing Caleb up here to be possessed.

And we'd arrived too late to stop it.

The possessed boy stood and stretched. There was a different look in his eye, a different set to his face and how he carried himself.

"Leave the boy," I said.

He smiled. "But I just got here. And it's so nice and

warm." He caressed the torso of the body he'd stolen. "You don't know how I've missed warmth. Death is cold."

"Only if you try to cling to life when it should be over. You have to let go and move on. Your time has passed. Everyone you cared about is gone. Even Aurelie."

"Aurelie?" He looked from me to Stacey.

"Yes. Aurelie moved on, lived her life, and passed away. You can do the same." The secret weapon in my backpack wasn't going to work here, after all. I had very little faith in the other one, but it was time to try it out. "Stacey, can you bring up Aurelie's letter on your tablet?"

"Sure." Stacey looked puzzled but pulled her tablet from her backpack.

"Can you read it to him?"

"Okay…" Stacey cleared her throat. She began to read in an extra-deep Southern accent, like it was a diary entry in a Civil War documentary. "My dearest Solange and Raynard…You are the twin lights of my life, the sun and moon in my sky—"

"She was French," I whispered.

"Oh, right." Stacey switched to a theatrical French accent. "All that I do is with the hope of making a better future for you. My deepest wish is that you both experience in your own lives the same wonder and happiness and meaning that you have brought into mine. My greatest fear is that the hardness of this world will overcome you, and that I will not have prepared you for all the challenges you will face as you grow. Adult life is a maze with few signposts—"

"Skip to the part about him," I said. The entity

inside the possessed boy appeared to be listening raptly at first, but he was starting to lose interest, to look around at the open cabinets and other dusty woodwork.

We'd had time to review the letter on the drive over. The part Stacey was skipping told the children about their fathers. Solange's father had been a cold, cruel, moderately rich man Aurelie had married when she was very young, under pressure from her parents. Aurelie had run away to America to escape him, though it meant throwing herself into poverty. In America, she'd begun calling herself a widow.

Raynard's father, whom she'd met in America, had been a traveling musician from Louisiana whose talent had impressed Aurelie so much it led to an affair, though Aurelie had not seen him in years at the time she'd written the letter.

"Both of you tell me how you wish I would marry Jack, the cabinet-maker," Stacey read aloud, still Frenching it up. "I know he seems kind to you. I can only say that Jack does not inspire the desire for marriage in me, and over time, I have grown more uneasy with him. Though he has yet to commit any sin or crime to my knowledge, in my heart I would not be surprised to learn he has evil in his past. Charles Collins is gentle and harmless, and I truly believe you will learn to grow more at ease with him, as I have—"

"Why are you reading this to me?" The possessed boy's voice seethed with fury. Penny, standing beside him, just gaped at him, while Jason shook harder in his chair, trying to draw himself into a tighter ball.

"To remind you," I said. "There is nothing left for you on the earthly plane. You've already had your revenge. Those who tried to kill you paid a terrible price, but they are all gone. All dead, all moved on. And your beloved Aurelie has died. We can read you her obituary." I gestured to Stacey, who hurriedly tapped at her tablet.

"I was never in love with Aurelie," he said. "I was in love with Solange."

"Oh, ew," Stacey said. "She was only twelve."

"I was thirteen," he said.

"You…wait." Stacey looked as perplexed as I felt. "What?"

"And revenge is why I'm here."

"What do you mean?" I asked.

He smiled and said, much louder, as if summoning a fiend from somewhere far below, "Come out and play, Jack."

Voices whispered from the small open doors all over the room.

The shadows inside them thickened.

The swamp children emerged from the doors, like muddy corpses crawling across the floor and ceiling, swarming over Stacey and me as if intending to finish what they'd started out at their burial spot in the swamp.

They grabbed our hands first—one dead girl with muddy red clumps of hair gripped my left firmly in her sharp little teeth—and knocked away our flashlights. My backpack, already barely clinging to one shoulder, was knocked to the floor, out of reach, while I was pushed hard against the wall.

Someone had learned from our last encounter. Ghosts are usually terrible at learning new things, being mostly obsessed with past traumas, but Jack wasn't exactly a ghost or a man, as far as I understood, but something in between. It might be easier for him to learn and instruct his minions accordingly.

Penny and Jason, not surprisingly, screamed bloody murder at the sight of the attic bedroom filling up with apparitions of reanimated child corpses. The dead children didn't attack the live ones, not yet, but focused on Stacey and me.

I struggled, kicked, and even tried bashing my head into that of the dead boy who pinned my right arm to the wall. As usual, physical violence was useless, because I was really fighting disembodied entities made of energy, and my moves passed right through them.

Jason covered his eyes.

Penny clung to her possessed boyfriend. "What's happening, Gabriel?" she whispered. "You didn't tell me about this part."

"He's coming," the boy said.

"You're Gabriel?" I asked the possessed boy, through teeth gritting in pain. The dead-kid club had restrained me uselessly against the wall, and done the same to Stacey, except she was pinned to the floor. "You were Jack's—"

"Apprentice." A different voice completed my sentence for me, one that had grown unpleasantly familiar.

Jack emerged from a small lower cabinet, headfirst, levitating just above the floor until he was all the way out. I recalled a drawing in Jason's room portraying a similar thing. He floated to a standing position, his eyes latching onto the possessed boy.

"I've continued to learn from you, in death as in life." The possessed boy disentangled from Penny and stepped away, leaving her to hug herself for comfort. He moved toward the tree-style headboard, with its cage-like arrangement of sculpted roots with hidden compartments.

"Where is the little one?" Jack looked more mummified than ever, like his skin would flake away from the dry bones beneath. He licked his lips and teeth with a cracked, gray tongue. Then he drew his chisel from his leather apron. "Are you hiding her, Gabriel?"

"I've been preparing for years." Gabriel climbed onto the bed and reached in among the sculpted roots that Jack had carved in life. "Watching you from my grave. Watching you bring them out, year by year, planting their bodies in the ground. Praying to the demonic thing you serve. I've learned how to destroy you. And it's time, at last, for you to die." He opened a compartment and reached inside.

And found nothing, because I'd taken the adze after it fell out and almost killed me. Apparently, his plan to defeat Jack hinged on drawing out the adze at a critical moment.

Oops.

The smile dropped from the possessed boy's face as his hand failed to locate the tool he'd wanted. He frantically opened the other little doors built into the bedframe, as if he'd simply forgotten the exact spot where the adze had been concealed. But he hadn't.

Jack, seeing his apprentice flail, advanced on the bed, his smile widening.

With one hand, he grabbed the possessed boy by the ankle and dragged him out to the foot of the bed.

With the other, he raised the chisel, preparing to strike Gabriel through the heart and murder the teenage boy he possessed.

Penny gasped. She'd retreated to stand by her younger brother, who remained in his balled-up position in the chair.

Stacey grunted, struggling to get free of the hideous yet pitiable entities who'd captured her and pinned her down. She probably wasn't feeling too much pity for them at the moment.

I tried again to pull free, but the entities attacking me clamped down, trapping me even more tightly against the wall.

I drew back one foot, imagined pouring every bit of strength and energy I had into it, and took a breath.

Then I kicked as hard as I could.

My boot passed harmlessly through the decayed boy-ghost in front of me, like the entity wasn't there at all.

It connected solidly with my backpack, though, and sent it sliding across the floor.

"Gabriel!" I shouted.

The possessed boy on the bed turned his head as the backpack thudded into the bedpost beside him. It was partially unzipped, and my secret weapon came sliding out.

The hand adze.

Gabriel/Caleb's eyes widened in surprise at the sight of it.

So did Jack's. His hand went to an empty loop on his apron, as if he'd just realized his adze was missing.

Gabriel grabbed the adze and swung it into Jack's chest, burying the hatchet-sized blade deep.

Jack staggered back from the edge of the bed, but Gabriel held firmly to the adze's handle, getting to his feet and walking with him.

"You can't," Jack said.

"I can do anything you can do," Gabriel said. "I was a good apprentice."

"You could be again. We could be together again, our lives restored. You were such a lovely boy. So eager to learn. Obedient, and compliant—"

Gabriel pulled the adze loose, gritting his teeth with the effort of ripping it free of Jack's innards. It was covered in black blood, as was Jack's entire chest.

Then Gabriel reached his hand into the gaping wound he'd just carved, as if he intended to squeeze Jack's heart in his fist.

Jack howled in pain.

Gabriel finally let Jack draw away. Jack wasn't dead, but he was swaying on his feet, his chisel dangling limply from his fingers like he'd forgotten how to use his arm.

"I watched you, and I learned." Gabriel walked past his former master, toward the closet door with the secret panel at the back. He closed the door and wrote on it with his fingertip, the one soaked in Jack's black-pitch blood. "I forged my own bargain with the dark things. They weren't truly from the swamp, you know. It was your evil that summoned them. Now they will claim you. I was sent to gather the harvest."

"What?" Jack breathed.

Gabriel finishing writing on the door.

He'd painted his own name in Jack's blood.

Jack, seeing Gabriel distracted, raised his chisel and ran at Gabriel, ready to stab his apprentice in the back. Not for the first time, I supposed.

"Gabriel!" I shouted, since apparently he was the

player I was supporting here. "Look out!"

Gabriel glanced back, then opened the closet door and stood aside.

Like the doorway I'd seen earlier, this one appeared to open directly onto the swamp where the children had been buried. I could pretty well recognize the place by smell at this point, its unique mixture of mud and rot.

This time, though, the door was filled top to bottom with thick, dark mud, which began to seep out across the attic floor.

Jack slipped and staggered in the mud. Gabriel grabbed him by the arm.

"You don't get to live forever," Gabriel said, leaning close to Jack's ear. In Caleb's body, he was as tall as his old master. "Now go where you belong."

As the mud drained onto the floor, it gradually revealed something hidden within it. A boy's skeleton, seemingly standing upright, as if Gabriel's door looked downward into his muddy grave. Gabriel had opened the door of the cabinet in which he was buried, the cabinet Jack had made.

"No," Jack whispered, horror on his face as Gabriel shoved him forward.

"Your final cabinet," Gabriel said, almost whispering. "It was meant to be you all along."

Then Gabriel shoved the bleeding, hunched, screaming form of Jack forward, into the mud-filled cabinet.

Gabriel's bones stirred. His skeletal arms reached out gently, almost sleepily, accepting Jack's howling, writing form like a gift, an offering to the dead. They wrapped around Jack and drew the murderer deep into the mud of the grave, silencing his screams.

Gabriel closed the closet door, then rubbed his name until it was an illegible smear.

Chapter Thirty-Six

"Okay," I said to Gabriel. I was breathing a little easier at the moment, now that the dead children had ceased their attack. They were still present, though faded, as if at a loss for purpose. "Great job, Gabriel. I'm sure now you'll be glad to stop possessing Caleb and move on to a serene afterlife—"

"I have already moved on," Gabriel said.

"That's what Jack said," I told him. "He was wrong. This isn't moving on."

"We must take life from others, or have our own taken," Gabriel said. "I deserved a life."

"Yes, you did," I said. "But you can't take someone else's."

Gabriel raised the blood-drenched adze, not like he was planning an attack—though I tensed up, in case he was—but more like a kind of trophy, like the head of a fallen enemy in medieval times.

The dim shadows of the children scurried like

spiders over the floor, ceiling, and walls, whispering, gathering in around him.

"Gabriel, don't," I said. "You don't want to become what he was."

"I've bargained with devils already," Gabriel said.

"You always have a choice." I actually wasn't that sure about it, but it seemed worth encouraging him to try. Anything other than following in Jack's footsteps.

Gabriel ignored me and looked at Penny instead. She shivered next to Jason, watching with horror. I started to ease closer to the siblings, in case I needed to protect them, but I didn't want to make any sudden moves. Not while Gabriel was staring at Penny with the adze in his blood-soaked hand.

"Come with me," he told her.

"You aren't what I thought," she finally whispered.

"I can give you what you always wanted. A doorway out of your life." Gabriel opened the closet door again. His swampy grave was gone, replaced by a polished wooden corridor with rosewood tiles, curving out of sight, gently lit by a soft golden glow from somewhere beyond. "The doors can lead us to other places...we just have to keep opening them, and we'll find a way."

She stepped closer to him, her eyes going from the possessed boy to the mysterious hallway, which seemed to tempt her deeply.

"Don't," I said. "Penny, don't go with him. He's not offering you anything good."

"Yeah, Penny," Jason said, just barely managing to get the words out. I hardly heard him at all. "He's bad."

"Let's go." Gabriel took Penny's hand.

"Seriously?" Stacey asked. "Penny, that guy has red

flags all over the place. For one, he's already dead. Doesn't even have his own body."

Penny appeared uncertain. Gabriel drew her closer, and they moved toward the door.

"Listen, Penny," Stacey said. "When you feel cold to the bone, and your wounded heart is reeling—"

Penny looked back. "Are you really singing—"

"And you're out on the range alone, feeling a range of feelings—"

"Please don't serenade me." Penny blushed.

"Is this anything like what you dreamed of?" Stacey asked. "Staying up late, imagining yourself with Delmar—"

"I like Branson."

"Right, I mean Branson. This guy is promising you some kind of living death. You don't want that. You want life. Surely. Right?"

Penny slowly pulled back from him. "The creepy paranormal investigator ladies are right."

"But this is what we talked about, all these nights," Gabriel said, fully inhabiting Caleb's form. "I have a body now. I'm alive again. We can be together."

"I changed my mind." Penny backed away farther. "I want to stay with my family."

"But they hate you." Gabriel held on to her, and I moved closer to them. Stacey was doing the same. We didn't have a clear plan, but if Gabriel attacked, we'd try to protect Penny. "You told me how they all hate you. So did my parents. Why else would they sell me to Jack?"

"We don't hate you, Penny." Jason could barely choke out the words.

"Quiet!" Gabriel snapped at him.

"I'm sorry, Gabriel. I was wrong. I don't love you."
Penny removed the wooden ring from her finger and
dropped it to the floor, where it landed with a clatter.
She removed and dropped the half-carved bracelet and
the beaded necklace, too. "I'm sorry."

Gabriel stared at her, aghast.

Then, slowly, a smile spread across his face,
spreading almost unnaturally wide, probably splitting
poor Caleb's lips at the corner. Gabriel's expression
looked much like Jack's, as if the apprentice had been
heavily shaped by him.

"You already chose," Gabriel said. "You can't go
back on your word. I won't let you lie to me."

The dozen ghostly children, who'd faded almost out
of sight, surged back with renewed visibility and
purpose. They surrounded Penny, rotten hands grabbing
her and hauling her toward the open door, and she
screamed.

"Let her go!" I grabbed onto Gabriel, wary of the
bloody adze he carried.

Stacey reached for Penny, only to have three dead
children climb onto her, clawing and scratching.

Two more of the awful child-phantoms grabbed
Jason, pulling him out of his chair so fast it toppled
over and banged into the floor. They dragged him,
kicking and screaming, toward Penny, who was getting
dragged toward the door.

"I need you both," Gabriel said. "I want both of my
friends back. Everything can be like it was."

"No!" Penny shrieked, but the entities that Gabriel
now controlled were dragging her ever closer to the
door. I gripped Gabriel's arm so he couldn't swing his
weapon, but he didn't try to fight me off, so maybe I

wasn't helping the situation that much.

"Gabriel Baylor!" I screamed. "Let them go!"

That didn't help. He grabbed me with his free hand, restraining me as I restrained him, all while dead things kept dragging Penny and Jason closer to that door. I didn't know what exactly would happen to them if they went inside and followed the hallway, but it sounded like they would become Gabriel's possessions, just like all the swamp children he'd apparently inherited from his bargain with the demonic entities.

"Stop!" a child's voice cried somewhere behind us.

Andra approached in the shadows, from the direction of the open trap door, and my heart sank at the sight of her. She was pale and soaking wet... looking exactly like one of the swamp children, though not decayed yet. Like a ghost.

"Oh, no," I whispered.

"Andromeda, get out of here!" Penny shouted.

"I...I'm not..." Andra stammered, advancing. "I'm not Andra."

"What do you mean?" Jason whispered. "Who are you?"

I had the same question, trying to figure out who might be possessing the little girl.

"I'm Grizalda, the Magic Witch!" Andra raised her rainbow-swirl plastic broom and pointed it at the teenager possessed by Gabriel. "And I'm here to..." She cocked her head as if listening to someone invisible. "To make the bad things disappear!"

"How will you do that, little witch?" Gabriel asked, his eyes gleaming at the sight of her, like he was considering taking a bonus child with him.

"With the help of my lovely assistants, Sunny and

Rainy!" Andra said, managing to deliver her often-repeated line despite her obvious fear.

I looked in the shadows, waiting for the ghosts of Solange and Raynard to emerge behind her.

"Who?" Gabriel's hold on me weakened—though mine on him didn't—as he craned his neck to try and see. He claimed to have loved Solange. It sounded like he'd been trying to replace Solange and Raynard with Penny and Jason. "Who did you say?"

Andra stepped aside and back, like she did not want to get too close to whatever happened next. That was probably wise of her. "Abraca-doozle," she whispered.

Sunny and Rainy didn't emerge as apparitions from the attic shadows, though.

They rose from the trapdoor, each draped in a bedsheet from the makeshift theater curtains in the playroom, like children in homemade costumes, the same form Rainy had taken when he'd approached me during the magic show.

The two sheet ghosts drifted across the attic, no taller than children, their hems dragging along the dusty floor.

"Solange," Gabriel said, and he wasn't gripping me at all anymore. "Raynard."

"Gabriel," a girl's voice said from the taller of the two sheet-draped forms, the sea green one printed with mermaids. I recognized the voice from my encounter with Solange in her old sleeping room, when she'd slithered up into the window curtain to speak to me. "We thought we heard our mother. Was she here?"

"We thought Mother was here to take us home," whispered a boy's voice from beneath the turtle-print sheet.

"Why are you here, Gabriel?" Solange asked.

"I…" The possessed boy looked confused and lost. "I was trying to fix it."

"You always thought you could fix anything," Solange said. Her sheet-draped hand reached out to touch his arm. "But some things have to stay broken."

"But I've finally taken everything from him," Gabriel said. "You don't understand what he did to me."

"The same as he did to all of us," Solange said. "Andromeda, don't look."

In the corner, Andra squeezed her eyelids shut and covered her face with both hands.

Solange and Raynard lifted the fronts of their sheets, letting Gabriel have a good look at what they'd concealed beneath.

They both looked freshly killed. The adze had torn long, deep gashes all over their bodies. Their faces were slashed beyond recognition, and blood soaked their clothes.

"I couldn't believe it," Gabriel said. "I couldn't believe he killed you. That's why I let him out."

"We all loved him, at first," Solange said. "It was a mistake."

"I've spent time preparing, laying plans…"

"So have we," Solange said. "During times when he grew lost, wandering in his own memories, we whispered and planned. It's finished."

"All I wanted was to be with you." Gabriel reached out a trembling hand toward Solange. He touched her cheek, smearing the streamlet of blood from her dark eye hole. He looked at the smaller form of Raynard. "All of us, together again."

"Then be with us," the dead girl whispered.

He dropped the adze to the floor and put his other hand on her other cheek.

I hurried to pick up that adze, since it had just been a critical weapon moments earlier, though I doubted I could use it for much now. I certainly wasn't going to hack up poor Caleb just because he'd had the misfortune to get possessed.

Gabriel leaned close to Solange.

She threw her sheet over him as he embraced her. Raynard moved closer, catching the edge of her sheet over his own.

They became a single mass, twisting and turning inside the sheet. A male voice grunted and cried out in surprise or pain.

The sheet-covered mass fell to the floor, continuing to writhe.

At the same time, one of the dead, mud-covered children crawled over to the closet door, with its open and inviting path to elsewhere. It looked like that ghost boy I'd kicked through at the railroad bridge, the pee-wee footballer.

With a wary glance at the collapsed sheets, he climbed through the door.

Inside, lit by the low golden glow, he rose a little straighter, no longer hunching and crawling like an animal.

He walked around the bend, into the light.

One by one, the dead children followed the first trailblazer into the golden hallway. They looked more whole as they left, less like the Daycare of the Dead.

The hallway within the closet grew dimmer with each one that passed through it.

Finally, the last one crawled, cricket-like, across the attic floor and into the closet. Inside it, she stood, her round face and long red hair gradually filling in as the fading golden light shone on her. She might have been the one who'd sunk her teeth into me at the swamp and again tonight.

Her eyes found me.

"Sorry for biting," she said. "He made me."

"Just don't do it again," I told her.

She pulled the closet shut behind her.

"Whoa." Stacey, her curiosity obvious, darted to the closet door and pulled it open again.

Inside were the same forgotten items we'd seen first time we opened it—dusty abandoned shirts, a comb, some toothpicks.

Stacey opened the secret door at the back but found only the plates and crockery inside the cabinet in the main attic.

Meanwhile, the lump of bedsheets continued to roll around on the floor, grunting and groaning. Not sure what to expect, I reached over and pulled back the nearest sheet.

Caleb continued rolling back and forth and kicking for a few seconds before realizing he was free. He sat up and looked around. There was no sign of any ghost in the room. His hands, chest, and soccer shorts were thick with Jack's congealed, nearly black blood.

"What happened?" He peered at my face. "Am I dead?"

"No," I said. "You just need a shower."

"Where's my girlfriend? Is my girlfriend okay?" He finally saw Penny and sighed in relief. "Oh, there you are, baby."

"Huh?" Penny blinked. It looked like she was entirely focused on checking the area around her for any lingering ghosts. "Oh. Caleb. I didn't really see us as a long-term...thing."

"What?" Caleb stood up, shaking off the sheet. "You know I'm only interested in serious, committed relationships, Penny. I need a girl supportive of my soccer *and* my music. I talked about that for a long time."

"Yes, you did," Penny said. "You really, really did. And right now, I'm just not that girl."

"Fine, then. You could have made it clearer before sneaking me into your room. Because I'm just not *that* guy." Caleb walked away but found himself looking into a closet. "Which way's out?"

"Over there." Stacey pointed with her recovered flashlight. "The trap door's open, so watch your step."

"Thanks." Caleb headed for the stairs, and we all silently watched him go.

Andra, stepping out of the back corner, smiled and waved cheerfully at him as he left, as if sending a guest home from a great success of a party, or taking applause from the audience at the end of a show. "Bye! Thanks for coming!"

Chapter Thirty-Seven

Dave returned soaked with rain after I texted him that we'd found Andra. Chief Tyler drove off without even a good-bye to Stacey and me, which surprised us not at all.

"But where were you, Andra?" Dave asked. He and Andra stood soaking wet in the kitchen, where we'd arranged flashlights and some of Penny's scented candles for lighting. Stacey was heating apple cider on the stove for Andra.

"Mr. Otis's house," Andra said, sniffing the rich, apple-filled air.

"Why?"

"Sunny and Rainy told me to. Jack was coming to take me tonight, and Otis's house is Jack-proofed."

"It actually is," I said.

"Did Mr. Otis know you were there?" Dave asked.

"No. They told me his back door was unlocked. It's a funny roll-up door. He didn't hear me because of the

storm, and I stayed in a back room. But then Sunny and
Rainy thought they heard their mom, so they came
here. I followed even though they said not to."

"It sounds like those two entities were trying to
protect Andra," I told Dave. "I think they even gave me
the adze…though they were clumsy about it…because,
like Gabriel, they knew it could be used against Jack.
They must have learned how to plot against Jack.
Maybe their bond as siblings helped them stay a little
more independent of his control, compared to his other
victims."

"But now Jack's gone, isn't he?" Dave asked.

"It seems that way. But let us know if you have any
more trouble."

"What about the more helpful ghosts?" he asked.

"They're gone, too." Andra spoke up, sounding
disappointed. "Sunny and Rainy had to help their friend
find his way home. I don't think they're coming back."

"And everyone else is fine?" Dave looked at Penny
and Jason, who sat sullenly at the table. They kept their
eyes down and said nothing.

"Gabriel, Jack's apprentice, was the one who
reached out to Penny and Jason," I said. "He taught
Jason to carve those gifts for Penny. I think, in
Gabriel's mind, he wanted them as substitutes for
Solange and Raynard, replacing the companions he had
in life. And he convinced them to help him possess that
boy, Caleb."

"That's…I'm not sure how to respond to that,"
Dave said, while Penny and Jason seemed to shrink
away, not saying a word. "Helping a ghost possess
another kid sounds like a grounding-worthy offense, at
least. Penny's definitely not getting the attic bedroom

for herself anytime soon."

"Not sure I want it anymore," the thirteen-year-old muttered, then put her head down on the table. "Maybe in a few weeks," she added.

"I think it was Gabriel, not Jack, who nudged the barbell onto Lonnie," I said. "To keep everyone busy while he took possession of Caleb."

"I didn't know he was going to do that," Penny said. "Hurt Lonnie, I mean."

"The local legend said that you could call for Jack, if you dared and he would come out of the woodwork," I told Dave. "Lonnie called him, you might remember, while teasing Andra. Otis said he did the same before Jack took his brother. Just to be safe, everyone should avoid doing that in the future."

Dave looked at a loss for how to deal with any of this. "Both of you wait here. Andra, let's get some dry clothes on." Dave and the younger girl left.

Stacey and I sat in an awkward silence with Jason and Penny.

"Gabriel said he was our friend," Jason said after a long moment. "I was going to be his apprentice when he came back to life."

"He was very confused," I said. "Gabriel suffered terrible things, and he was trying to deal with it as best he could. He was trying to piece his old life back together, but it was too late for that."

"So, was he evil?" Penny asked.

"Not like Jack was evil," I replied, after giving it a little thought. "I don't believe so. But sometimes good people fall under the influence of evil people. Or evil ideas. Or just fear and desperation."

"And then they become evil?" Jason asked.

"Sometimes," I said, because that seemed true enough to me. "But no matter what you've done in the past, you always have a choice, right now, to do what's right."

The kids just sort of blinked at my words.

"Aw," Stacey said, gazing at me. "You really would make a good mom, Ellie."

I didn't have a quick reply to that, certainly not one with the extremely high level of snark it deserved.

Dave and Andra returned in warm, dry clothes, and Stacey set mugs in front of them on the table. "Who else wants hot cider?" Stacey asked, but nobody did.

"This is so tasty," Andra whispered, breaking the silence, and then the lights came on.

Chapter Thirty-Eight

The Browns' troubles with the paranormal ended after that, but the case wasn't quite closed.

A couple of weeks later, I returned to Timbermill for their Independence Day celebration, along with Michael. We took his truck, since Chief Tyler probably wouldn't cotton to the sight of me back in town again.

We parked across the tracks, on the desolate side of town, where the parking was ample. We could hear the crowd in the distance, along with a local country band launching into "This Land is Your Land."

"It's dark out here," Michael said, looking among the closed shops and shuttered gas station. "That will help with tonight's grave robbery."

"We're not robbing a grave," I told him. "Now grab your tools and follow me into the cemetery. And make sure nobody sees you."

"Yeah, my mistake, this sounds completely legit." Michael climbed out after me. We shut the truck doors softly, though there didn't seem to be anyone around to hear us.

We entered the cemetery's main gate and approached the dividing wall. Small American flags had been placed out on certain graves, perhaps by Otis.

"Just be glad you never actually had to help me dig up a corpse in the swamp," I told Michael.

"Yeah, what happened with that?" Michael asked. "Not that I'm complaining about getting out of it."

"I know the brother of one of the children buried out there," I said. "His name's Otis. And he knows how to get in touch with family members of all the victims. So they were able to pressure the local government into exhuming the bodies. Some have already been buried here." I indicated a mound of fresh-turned earth, burial place of red-haired Angela Kilborne, who I believed had bitten me a time or two.

"And we're going to be disturbing their graves? Summoning up their souls? Something like that?"

"Nothing like that." I slowed as we reached the deep sag of the wall's most eroded area.

My flashlight found Solange's name.

"Here," I said. "We just need to break down this wall."

"The whole wall?" Michael looked from one end of the cemetery to the other. "That could take days. Or weeks. Plus you have to factor in the jail time that would probably follow."

"I think we just need to fracture the wall down to the ground. Enough for a breeze or a patch of fog to pass through."

"And why do we need to do that?"

"Because they deserve help. They earned my

gratitude. They don't like being separated, and that's something I can help with."

"Separated?"

I shined my light over the wall, showing him Raynard's grave.

"Brother and sister," I said. "Half-siblings, technically. They had to be buried on different sides of the wall." I explained about the segregated cemetery.

"Okay, then." Michael opened his toolbox. He'd brought hammers and chisels like I'd requested. "You'd better keep your flashlight off. I can see well enough by moonlight. Just for the record, this is still a pretty bizarre thing to get arrested for."

"You know how they say it's easier to ask for forgiveness than permission? I figure it's even easier to flee town and never take any responsibility."

"What could go wrong with a plan like that?" Michael began to hammer.

The dipped area between the siblings was particularly weakened by erosion, as we'd noticed before, and broke apart easily.

Michael worked at it until the gap extended all the way to the ground, essentially severing the wall in two. He left a fissure large enough to look through, to reach a few fingers through.

"Good enough?" he asked.

"I think so, yeah. We should probably get out of here before we end up in jail. You had a good point about that."

"You picked the right night to come. Everyone's busy with that festival and lighted drone show over there. Hey, want to go to that festival and lighted drone show over there? As long as we're in town for it."

"Okay, but be warned, the police chief isn't really a fan of my work. Hopefully, he'll be stuck in maximum Andy Griffith mode tonight and won't harass me in public. And we should probably park a little farther from the scene of the crime."

As I stood, I thought I spotted two small figures moving in the shade of the giant magnolia, where last time I'd glimpsed only one. They vanished when I turned my head to look at them.

"What are you looking at?" Michael asked.

"Just enjoying the sight of all those flowers," I replied. "Let's go downtown."

He stowed his tools in his truck, then drove us the long way around so we'd appear to enter town from the other side, and certainly not from the recently vandalized cemetery that we definitely knew nothing about.

Parking closer to downtown, we walked toward the crowd on the green. There were a lot of younger families with kids, residents of the recently built suburban neighborhoods, coming here on the Fourth of July in search of community in their new town, in search of each other.

A few street vendors added to the mini-festival atmosphere, including one selling organic ice pops. I bought a strawberry lemonade one for Michael to pay him for the night's manual labor. He bought me a key lime one, just to be nice.

I waved to Walt Lambert, who sold coffee from a tabletop urn in front of his shop, along with a cardboard box of vintage records that weren't moving at all, based on how full it was. He was deep in conversation with the hairdresser Doro, her hand casually on his arm, both of them seeming to enjoy each other's company. Doro held one of his raisin-pocked muffins and was easing it toward the nearby trash can.

"I like the salty chocolate ones," a small voice said somewhere near my elbow. I nearly jumped out of my skin, thinking one of Jack's minions was back for more.

It was just Andra, though, wearing a plastic Uncle Sam top hat, her lower face smeared brown and sticky, an empty wooden ice pop stick in her hand. She tossed it into a nearby public wastebasket.

"How are you, Andra?" I asked.

She shrugged and looked to the bandstand, where the band played "City of New Orleans" as the swarm of glowing drones rose into the air like giant fireflies against the night sky. "I like this song. It's about a talking train who says good morning to everyone."

"I did not realize that," I said.

Nicole and Dave appeared, wearing matching blazers. Nicole smiled and offered me a business card-sized refrigerator magnet with her and Dave's smiling faces on it. They looked ready to sell you a house and be cheerful about it. "How do you like the magnets? We ordered a box of five hundred. So now Dave *has* to pass the realtor exam." She elbowed him.

"They look great. How is…everything?" I doubted they wanted to get into specifics in public.

"Well, Lonnie's injuries didn't affect the organs, thankfully," Nicole said. "I think we're all getting into a better place. It's been hardest on Penny and Jason, with all that they saw." She glanced around the crowd, verifying that her middle children were still there. Penny and Jason stood together near the bandstand, watching the show at a distance from their parents.

Lonnie was much farther away, with his friends. He moved stiffly, like there was some kind of cast or support under his shirt, but otherwise looked okay.

"What do you think?" Michael asked when we walked away from them. He looked over their fridge magnet. "Are you considering buying a house out here?"

"If I had a burning desire to get half a million dollars in debt and live in a trendy suburban area, maybe." I watched the flashing drone array create spirals of color, then floral shapes, in the air above, to scattered applause from the crowd.

"And if you needed room for your four kids," Michael added.

"Um, no. For me personally, no, not four." I thought about the monstrous apparitions of children risen from their swampy graves, swarming over me, biting, grabbing, draining every drop of energy I had until I was ready to collapse. "I'm not sure I'll ever be able to handle kids."

"I don't think you have to handle them. I think, these days, you just give them a smartphone and you're pretty much done."

"See, maybe I'm not the only one who shouldn't be having kids."

"Then we'd both make terrible parents. It's nice to find little things we have in common like that."

"I didn't expect to see you here," said someone I wasn't expecting to see. Otis stepped out of the crowd, wearing a cap that identified him as an army veteran. His beard was neatly combed for once. "Is this your steady fella?"

"This is Michael, yes," I said, weirdly blushing at

the old-fashioned term, maybe because I'd never heard anyone phrase it quite like that before, in reference to the two of us. And probably never would again. "Michael, this is Otis, who helped us a lot around here."

"You helped me more," Otis said. "My poor brother's finally at rest next to our parents. Every one of those lost children, finally found and given a decent burial. Except for...did you hear they dug up the old cabinet in the swamp, where they buried Jack alive?"

"I did not," I said. "Chief Tyler and I aren't exactly bowling buddies. I'm completely out of the loop."

"I always wondered if that part about Jack getting buried in his own cabinet was true or just a local legend," Otis said. "Turns out, no, they really buried him alive. Or they buried someone, anyway."

"What do you mean?" I asked.

"There was no way of identifying the remains for certain. Old Jack Macgill didn't leave any dental records. But what they found was something nobody expected, not even an old-timer like me." He waggled his eyebrows, really stringing out the mystery.

"Which was...?"

"There were *two* bodies in that cabinet," Otis said, again raising his gray eyebrows a couple of times to emphasize how surprising this was. "One adult male, one adolescent boy. Who do you figure the boy was?"

"Gabriel," I replied. "Jack's apprentice who went missing."

"That's what I figure, too, but once again, there ain't no way to prove it. They're both buried in the town cemetery now. I can show you where."

"Okay." I reflected that we'd just technically

vandalized the cemetery a bit, even if it was for a good cause. "Maybe next time I'm back in town."

"You may not find me here," Otis said. "I talked to Mrs. Brown about finally selling my old family place. I could get me one of them RVs, tool around the countryside. My brother and I used to talk about that when we were boys. Of course, we figured we'd do it on motorcycles, but your priorities change. I can spend my last few years having a look around America, see what there is to see. Maybe even Canada."

"That sounds nice," I said.

"You take care, both of you. The years go faster than you think, and then they're gone." He looked from me to Michael, then he walked off into the crowd.

The smaller kids of the town cheered as the drones flashed, pulsing different colors as they formed the image of a bird in the air, then a few stars, all of its shapes clunky and simple, but clear enough to stir the imagination.

I spotted Andra gaping, pointing up at the dancing lights in the sky that kept changing shapes and colors, the horrors of the recent past momentarily forgotten in the happiness of the moment. Her parents stood behind her, watching over her, enjoying her simple joy.

Okay, maybe not all kids are terrible corpse-like swamp monsters who want to suck out your vital energy until you collapse. Some of them were definitely okay. Andra, with her imagination and courage and her ability to rebound from fear with enthusiasm, seemed like one of the okay ones.

And, if we're being completely honest, even that rotten-faced red-haired girl—the one who bit me a few times, but apologized for it once she got her freedom and her skin back—even that kid had her good points. Probably. One imagines.

But, no rush for me on the family and kids front. Not when the dead kept rising to threaten the living, and there weren't many people prepared to face that threat for them.

I tried to take a lesson from Andra and enjoy the dancing light show while it lasted, my hand in Michael's, the taste of cold lime and sugar on my lips. It mingled with lemon and strawberry when he kissed me. The crowd cheered and whistled as dozens of blazing, spinning starbursts formed above, a colorful, flashing grand tamale to the light show celebrating our independence.

The End

FROM THE AUTHOR

I hope you enjoyed this latest supernatural investigation with Ellie and Stacey. *Cabinet Jack* was a sort of oddball idea that pretty much insisted on being the next book in the series, though I didn't really know what it was about when I began writing it, just a lot of characters and weird situations. Hopefully it all fell together in the end. This book was definitely inspired by childhood legends like Bloody Mary, who supposedly can be summoned to a mirror by saying her name. I remember that scared me as a kid, the idea that the supernatural world was so close that you could summon evil spirits with just a short incantation.

The next Ellie Jordan book, which should be out in summer 2022, will be *Fallen Wishes*. As you'll probably guess from the title and cover art, this one deals with a haunted wishing well. I'm having fun working on this one already, and it's an idea I've been developing in the background for a couple of years. I hope you enjoy it!

Pre-order *Fallen Wishes* on Amazon at: https://www.amazon.com/gp/product/B09QGYW2Y6.

Subscribe to my newsletter to hear about new releases. And follow on Facebook for more frequent updates, ghost memes, etc.:

Newsletter (http://eepurl.com/mizJH)
Website (www.jlbryanbooks.com)
Facebook (J. L. Bryan's Books)

Also, if you're enjoying the series, I hope you'll consider taking time to recommend the books to someone who might like them, or to rate or review it at your favorite book retailer. Thanks so much!

Printed in Great Britain
by Amazon